Dan Tyte
The Offline Project

Dear Ryan.

Enjoy it. Dan

PS Remember, everything you put on the internet is there forever.

The Offline Project
Published in Great Britain in 2018
by Graffeg Limited

Written by Dan Tyte copyright © 2018.
Designed and produced by Graffeg Limited copyright
© 2018.

Graffeg Limited, 24 Stradey Park Business Centre,
Mwrwg Road, Llangennech, Llanelli,
Carmarthenshire SA14 8YP Wales UK
Tel 01554 824000 www.graffeg.com

ISBN 9781912213702

1 2 3 4 5 6 7 8 9

Dan Tyte
The Offline Project

GRAFFEG

Contents

Part 1: Online   6

Chapter 1	6	Chapter 11	87
Chapter 2	21	Chapter 12	95
Chapter 3	26	Chapter 13	105
Chapter 4	28	Chapter 14	115
Chapter 5	34	Chapter 15	130
Chapter 6	48	Chapter 16	137
Chapter 7	54	Chapter 17	145
Chapter 8	62	Chapter 18	151
Chapter 9	70	Chapter 19	159
Chapter 10	74		

Part 2: Offline   169

Chapter 20	169	Chapter 27	234
Chapter 21	177	Chapter 28	240
Chapter 22	185	Chapter 29	252
Chapter 23	193	Chapter 30	255
Chapter 24	199	Chapter 31	270
Chapter 25	209	Chapter 32	272
Chapter 26	226	Chapter 33	276

Part 1: Online

CHAPTER

1

The time on Gerard's iPhone said 14.02. The real time was 12.02, meaning he had to endure two more hours of Christmas Day with his family. Gerard's iPhone had set itself to Central European Time. The most central Gerard had been into Europe in the past twelve months was Disneyland Paris.

'Let's do selfies. Selfies are the way forward. I took selfies of me and Nanna Judy in the kitchen just then and she was trying to get the phone right after to see what the picture was like, like she wanted to vet it before she got tagged, like she was one of the girls on a night out,' said Stephanie. Stephanie was Gerard's twin sister. Gerard's umbilical cord had wrapped itself around Stephanie's seconds-old throat during childbirth. The midwife who skilfully untangled the box-fresh body parts was twenty-seven minutes into his first shift since a two-month leave of absence for a stress-related condition. His act was delivered with the dexterity and calm of a croupier in a busy Macau casino and earned him a one column story in the hospital's staff newsletter and box of mint flavoured Matchmakers from Gerard and Stephanie's father.

Even when I'm taking the picture, I always smile myself, thought Gerard. Gerard was sat in the living room of his mum's house on the three-seater leather sofa trying to read his Christmas book, but Nanna Judy kept saying stuff like, 'Some people don't even have electricity to cook dinner,' and, 'It's come around quick this year hasn't it?'

'Do you want toast or crackers with the smoked salmon?' said Maureen. Maureen was Gerard and Stephanie's mum. Nanna Judy was her mum. Gerard had given up reading *A Charlie Brown Christmas* and put it on the coffee table next to a twelve-inch plastic Santa. He was now talking to Del on WhatsApp. She didn't wake up until 11.09 when her mum knocked on her door and said, 'Come on, Delyth, the kids will be here soon. Christmas is for them, not for you.'

Del was Gerard's new girlfriend, although they were not yet Facebook official. Gerard thought that nothing was real until it had been verified online, although he used the thought selectively.

Today was only the third time Gerard had visited his mum's house since he'd returned to Cardiff from London. The first time was for an official welcome back meal (or 'croyso', as Stephanie had misspelled the Welsh for 'welcome' on a tissue paper banner). The second time had been to borrow some clean bedding from his mum. There had been a complaint about the freshness of the linen from an Austrian couple who had booked his attic room as a base for the Brecon Beacons but had been imprisoned in the house by some unseasonably seasonal wet weather and an inability to tie their shoelaces without entering into an existential argument.

Nanna Judy was sat in the living room on the two-seater wearing a white ruffle shirt, a gold chain and velvet trousers.

'I forgot I had them, the velvet trousers,' she said.

'Hold this, Nan,' said Gerard, handing her a gatefold LCD Soundsystem record. The title of the record was *American Dream*.

'What is it?' said Nanna Judy.

'It's the present you got me, Nan,' said Gerard.

'Oh yes,' said Nanna Judy. 'But what is it?'

'It's a record, Nan,' said Gerard, 'you know, like in the old days.' Nanna Judy looked like she didn't know.

'It's vinyl, Nan, a vinyl record.'

'Oh,' said Nanna Judy, more lucid now. 'I gave you my old record player, didn't I? See? I remember.'

Nanna Judy's old record player was under Gerard's bed in what was now the guest room, next to an old record player from Nanna Gwen. Nanna Gwen was dead.

'I have to put my snap up,' said Geoff. Despite the date, Geoff was working continental shifts. Yorkshireman Geoff was Gerard and Stephanie's stepdad but when they talked about him they said he was their mum's husband.

Gerard was lying on the three-seater writing Twitter statuses in his head for future significant life events. Favourable reviews for his short film, Xanadu, new cat (with girlfriend), new cat (without girlfriend). Nanna Judy broke his concentration.

'Do you remember a drink called Pony?'

'Oh, yeah, Pony,' Maureen shouted from the kitchen.

'I don't remember it, Nan,' said Stephanie, 'you're like ninety.'

'I remember me and my sister Audrey came home and sat on the worktop one Christmas Eve and drank a whole bottle. I think I poisoned myself. I was in the services then and the village squire had to keep asking my mother if I was well again.'

'A bottle of what, Nan?' said Stephanie.

'Port. A whole bottle.'

'Not Pony?'

'Pony?' said Nanna Judy.

'How old were you, Nan?' said Gerard. He had given up on life definition through 140 characters.

'Fourteen. Edith was seventeen.'

'How old was Audrey?' said Gerard.

'Audrey?' said Nanna Judy.

'Your sister Audrey,' said Gerard.

'Audrey is dead,' said Nanna Judy.

'Yes, Nan, but how old was she when you drank the port?' said Gerard.

'Audrey didn't like port. Edith liked port.'

'Right.'

'I didn't like port,' said Nanna Judy.

'Speaking of drinks, have another Sol, Gerard,' Geoff said. Gerard forgot he had a Sol on the coffee table next to the twelve-inch plastic Santa and A Charlie Brown Christmas. Gerard got up and followed Geoff into the kitchen. Geoff opened the garage door. A red Mazda MX sat there, glistening with condensation.

'Watch your head on this shelf,' Geoff said, touching the shelf as if to prove its existence.

'This shelf here has everything you need. Sol, Carling, everything you need. That shelf there, that's my shelf. Don't touch that shelf.'

'I won't,' said Gerard.

'Lime?' said Geoff.

'Sure. It is Christmas after all.'

*

In the two months since he started working at AlePunk, Gerard's taste buds jolted him back to bootcut jeans and fake ID every time he drank lager. He worked three shifts a week at the bar to supplement the loss of income he'd predicted and experienced from the seasonality of his Airbnb entrepreneurism.

Gerard had moved away from London for a number of reasons, most of which he'd forget or make up depending on the audience or the situation. His current favourite was that a city where people were unable to smile at strangers on public transport would struggle to put up a meaningful resistance to the imminent, in relative terms, extra-terrestrial invasion.

Maureen had caught Gerard one Sunday morning when, after two or three hours of fitful sleep, coming down and clothed in the bed of a girl who he liked but wasn't sure if the feeling was reciprocated, she had called. The offer hadn't been presented as an ultimatum, but it had felt as such. Grampy Joe's estate had finally been settled and the amount due to his mum and Geoff was neither wholly unexpected nor insignificant. They wanted him to come back home the following weekend for a family meeting to discuss the options. This was the first time Gerard had heard the phrase 'family meeting' from someone who wasn't a character on a television show.

Gerard had travelled back to Wales on the Friday night by Megabus Gold. He live-tweeted the journey back, resulting in three favourites and four unfollows. The family meeting had taken place the next morning at a Harvester Salad & Grill. Maureen had hurried Gerard along as he drank his tea and searched for WiFi signal in the conservatory so they would make the £4.99 unlimited breakfast deal. Over his second helping of black pudding, Geoff had cleared his throat and said, 'It's dead money is renting, son, especially at London prices. There was a mansion house for rent just up through the lanes the other week, looked like something out of Downton Abbey. The Mail said it cost the same per month as a two bed in Kensington.'

Gerard informed them that he didn't live in Kensington.

Geoff had picked up his coffee, slurped, and said again, 'Dead money, son.' Maureen had stepped in and said that what Geoff had meant was that it was about time now that Gerard had got a place to call his own, got his foot on the property ladder. He wasn't a student anymore. That the money from Grampy Joe could help with that, could help cover a deposit. He had no chance of this if he stayed in London. What was it he was doing there now anyway? And couldn't he do that from here, closer to his family, in a place he could call his own? She looked at him with the same green eyes he remembered from the primary school gates. And it was like that, in a chain eatery at II.II one Saturday morning six months ago over the smell of burning flesh, that Gerard acquiesced.

*

'I'm expecting Bronwen will phone soon, Nan,' called Maureen from the kitchen. Bronwen was Maureen's younger sister. Maureen was 8 years older than her and felt more like her mother at times. Maureen called Nan Nan even though Nan was her mum.

'Bronwen?'

'Yes, Bronwen.'

'She has a lot to cope with this Christmas,' said Maureen.

'She hasn't got a dining table, has she?' said Stephanie.

'Yes, I think she has,' said Maureen. Gerard didn't ask what else Bronwen had to deal with.

Phil Spector's Christmas album was playing. Geoff was singing 'Here Comes Santa Claus'. It sounded funny in a thick northern accent. Phil Spector was dead or in jail. Gerard couldn't remember which.

'Where's Pepsi?' said Maureen. Pepsi was the pet dog, a Lhasa Apso. 'This is the reason I didn't put anything really tidy on.' Maureen had spilt goose fat down her blouse checking on the roast potatoes.

'Sorry?' said Geoff. Decades of industrial work had affected his hearing.

'Hence the reason I didn't put anything really best on.'

'Sorry?' said Geoff.

'I don't know. Is she in the room, Pepsi?' said Maureen.

'Where is she?' said Stephanie.

'I don't know,' said Maureen.

'Is she asleep?' said Stephanie.

'I'm far from it,' said Nanna Judy.

Gerard took a photo of his new yellow and blue striped socks and posted it on Instagram. #thanksSanta #badboythisyear he typed. The 4.7-inch screen made Gerard's eyes ache, but his peripheral vision was above average. This meant he could see people before they saw him. When you've pissed on so many people's chips, this is useful, thought Gerard.

On Saturday, Gerard had been to a Peter Blake exhibition. Peter Blake had made hundreds of illustrations to the words of Dylan Thomas' Under Milk Wood. Gerard saw Angharad with another man in the adjoining room of the exhibition. The other man wore a silver suit that sparkled under the lights like a Panini shiny. Gerard assumed he was Angharad's new boyfriend as she had said she didn't enjoy the company of men she wasn't sexually involved with. Gerard thought about their relationship, how he was always the first to come and the last to fall asleep. He thought how the word cloud of their relationship would be borderline positive and include words like 'okay', 'farmer's market' and 'passive-aggressive' in thirty-two-point sans-serif.

CloudyLemonade likes this.

'How long 'til dinner, Mum?' said Stephanie. Stephanie turned Top of the Pops on. Maureen came into the living room.

'Does she want to bury that, Gerard?' said Nanna Judy. Pepsi was trying to hide a bone in between the cushions of the three-seater. Gerard looked at her with indifference.

'I said I'm living in a lost generation,' said Top of the Pops. A boy band entered the stage.

'Is it one of these who was—' said Nanna Judy.

'Gay?' said Gerard.

'—in the X factor judging?' said Nanna Judy.

'No, Nan,' said Stephanie.

'Nearly there, love. Just the Yorkshire puddings to go in and we're away,' said Maureen.

'Were you surprised who won the dancing?' said Nanna Judy.

'I don't watch the dancing,' said Stephanie.

'No, I don't either. Not usually,' said Nanna Judy.

'The girl loves sex,' said Top of the Pops.

'Oh, is this Top of the Pops?' said Maureen. 'I tell this story every Christmas when Top of the Pops is on. You'll all have heard this story, I'm sure.' Gerard knew which story she was going to tell.

'The Beatles were playing on Top of the Pops and I got a mint stuck right in the back of my throat. I choked and nearly died, remember?' Maureen said. Only Nanna Judy both knew Maureen and was alive at this time.

'A Murray mint?' said Nanna Judy.

'No, a mint thin. I nearly died, remember?'

'How old were you?' said Nanna Judy.

'Well, The Beatles were on, so figure it out,' said Maureen. 'I'll always remember what they singing.'

'How old were you?' said Nanna Judy.

'I Wanna Hold Your Hand,' said Maureen.

'Hello, yo, ho, ho,' said Geoff, answering the phone. It was his daughter, Jenny.

'The way you grab me. I just wanna get nasty,' said Top of the Pops.

'I didn't know they still showed Top of the Pops,' said Nanna Judy.

'Right, I'll go and check on the Yorkshires,' said Maureen.

'I just did a good thing for Mum,' said Stephanie. 'You know how when she's dishing up she always goes, "Oh, whose dinner is this?"'

'Vaguely,' said Gerard.

'So I arranged the plates chronologically in age. So Nan, Mum, Geoff, you, me. So now she won't forget whose plate is whose. It's good isn't it?'

'Revolutionary,' said Gerard.

'She can use it the whole time, not just at Christmas.' Stephanie had not helped with the preparation of the meal. Stephanie's idea of a cooked meal was a Pasta 'n' Sauce.

Gerard's phone pinged. It was a mention from @aledsavedlatin.

'That shirt is pure Prince. I love it. And that record is a blinder. Go on, nan.' Gerard had tweeted a picture of Nanna Judy holding the LCD Soundsystem record. @aledsavedlatin was the lead singer of a band called Kids in Glass Houses and had 27,926 followers.

'Nanna, 30,000 people who like emo have seen someone they idolise talk about your shirt,' said Gerard.

'Twitter doesn't work like that, they'd have to be following you too for it to pop up in their timeline,' said Stephanie.

'Nanna Judy isn't worried about the logistics of a social network, Stephanie. Nanna Judy is an internet phenomenon,' said Gerard.

*

'Right kids, get thee to the table,' said Geoff from the kitchen, his voice echoing against the plasterboard walls. Geoff could project his voice when he needed to.

'Yay. At last,' said Stephanie. Gerard finished his Sol. The lime hit his teeth.

'It's been a good year for music,' said Top of the Pops.

Gerard, Stephanie and Nanna Judy sat at the table. Geoff helped Maureen bring the plates through.

'I can't believe Pepsi's sat in the conservatory when we're eating. I don't think she's 110 per cent,' said Geoff.

'She's a dog,' said Gerard.

'Dogs get ill,' said Stephanie.

'Have we got lemon?' Gerard said, looking at his smoked salmon.

'No, love. I don't eat smoked salmon, so I don't know how it comes,' said Maureen. She looked sad.

'Is that bread okay? I toasted it.'

'Yes Mum,' said Gerard.

'Where's my tomato?' said Geoff.

'We don't eat tomatoes in this family,' said Maureen.

'We got married in 2001,' said Geoff, 'and I love tomatoes.' Gerard

Googled 'grey bits on salmon'. Yahoo Answers told him that 'bears that hunt salmon eat the grey fatty bit and chuck the rest as they're trying to put on weight before hibernating'. Gerard ate around the grey bits.

'Pull a cracker with me, Nan,' said Stephanie. Nanna Judy and Stephanie pulled a cracker. Geoff and Maureen pulled a cracker. Gerard waited for Stephanie and then pulled a cracker with her.

'You always win,' said Stephanie. Everyone put party hats on.

'Do you want a joke? I like it, which means it's terrible,' said Stephanie. 'What cough medicine does Dracula use? Think about it.' Everyone thought about it.

'Leechams,' said Gerard.

'No,' said Stephanie. 'Think about it.' Everyone thought about it.

'Coffin medicine,' said Stephanie. 'Actual LOL.'

Gerard went to the garage for a Sol.

'Another. Gerard, what do you call a man with a spade on his head?' Stephanie shouted out from the table.

'Doug,' shouted back Gerard.

'How the hell do you know that?' shouted Stephanie.

'I just do.'

'Okay, what do you call a man with a paper bag on his head?' said Maureen.

'Baghead,' said Stephanie.

Gerard sat back down and chugged his Sol.

'Geoff, you look like a drunk Santa with that hat on,' said Stephanie. Geoff had replaced his party hat for a Santa hat.

'I haven't got a hat, I've got a measuring tape,' said Nanna Judy.

'You have a hat on your head, Nan,' said Stephanie.

'I like the way you wear it on the back of your head, like a crown. Let's take photos of Pepsi with the Santa hat on.'

Stephanie and Gerard left the table, took Geoff's hat and went into the conservatory. Stephanie put the Santa hat on Pepsi's head and they both leant down to flank her for a photo.

'Mum, come and get this,' said Stephanie.

Maureen brought in the main course.

'Watch out loves, the plates have been warming in the oven.'

'Sit yourself down, love,' Geoff said to Maureen. 'You've worked hard enough.'

'Champagne anyone? Champagne, Mum?' said Geoff to Nanna Judy. Geoff called Nanna Judy Mum even though she was not his mum. Maureen didn't even call Nanna Judy Mum and she was her mum.

'Cranberry Sauce, anyone? It's Ocean Spray,' said Maureen.

'Go on, Stephanie, it'll be good for your cystitis,' said Gerard.

'Preventative not curative,' said Stephanie.

'Yes please,' said Nanna Judy.

Silence fell over the table. Everyone was eating. The cloth had a pair of miniature nail clippers and three dice on it. Maureen broke the silence.

'I drove past a people carrier yesterday, Christmas Eve. It was flying a UKIP flag from the driver side door. On Christmas Eve. There's no elections now, is there? I wondered if it was Nigel Farage.'

'Why would Nigel Farage be in Cardiff?' said Geoff.

'Cardiff is in the UK,' said Gerard, 'for now.'

'They celebrate Christmas in Australia, don't they Gerard?' said Nanna Judy.

'Yes, Nan.'

'I want to know the purpose of these dice,' said Geoff.

'I've never had champagne. It's quite nice,' said Nanna Judy.

'Champagne can be proper fine line, like,' said Stephanie.

'We'll be having lots of this next year. Nan will be ninety,' said Maureen. Maureen thought about how it felt to be the daughter of a ninety-year-old. She chewed on a sprout and thought about the 1970s.

'Do you feel ninety?' said Stephanie.

'No, I don't get it when people go on about age. Oh, I'm thirty, oh, I'm forty. I just carry on,' said Nanna Judy.

'Roll on with the good times, hey Nan'? said Stephanie. Nanna Judy looked at her blankly.

'Smile for a photo, Gerard,' said Maureen.

'I'll get in,' said Stephanie. 'It's lame to have one on your own when it's not taken at arm's length.'

'She's not well is that dog,' said Geoff. 'She's still got that cap on. She looks like bloody Tommy Cooper. She'll be saying "spoon jar, jar spoon" next.' Pepsi was still wearing the Santa hat she didn't know about. As far as YouTube had taught Gerard, Tommy Cooper wore a fez.

'If Pepsi's tail's down, it means she's down too,' said Maureen.

'She's emotionally drained,' said Geoff.

*

'After Eight?' said Maureen.

'Please,' said Geoff, 'and put the telly on.'

A weather reporter in a Christmas jumper from Primark came on screen.

'Some people have had it terrible,' said Nanna Judy. 'We're lucky here, not like Lincolnshire.'

'Yeah, Al and me were watching the news yesterday and it was saying there was gale force winds and floods and he was really worried for me driving home down the M4. Even Jess said I needed to be careful,' said Stephanie.

'Is Jess a weather lady?' said Gerard.

'No.'

'Well why did you say 'even Jess', like Jess was in charge of the weather?'

'Fuck off, Gerard,' said Stephanie's eyes.

'Did you have a nice time there, love?' said Nanna Judy. 'There' was where Stephanie's boyfriend Al lived in London, like Gerard did, once upon a time.

'It was lush. On Saturday we were walking down the street in Dalston and Al took my phone and me and Jess were in the street and Al went "picture?" and me and Jess did the same pout in a millisecond and Al was like, "oh my god," and then we made him and Dylan do it and they did.'

Gerard had not met Al yet, although Stephanie had floated the idea of a double date. He was unsure whether he was ready to introduce Del to a family member yet. He was unsure whether this was because he was trying to prolong the magical period at the beginning of a relationship when two relative strangers were lost in the lust of the blissfully ignorant or whether he was just not that sure about Del yet. He was three quarters certain it was the former. He sank a Sol.

'Look at this out here,' said Geoff. Geoff was pointing out of the front window. 'He's lost something up the tree.'

'What is it?' said Gerard. Gerard craned his neck from the three-seater to see.

'Might be a kite,' said Geoff.

'A kite?' said Gerard. 'On Christmas Day?'

'Oh, hang on...it's a remote control plane,' said Geoff. 'The kids look forlorn. They're taking pictures of it. They've gone for help.'

'Oh,' said Gerard.

'It might be a cat.'

'Sometimes you can tell how much you love someone by how many mutual friends you have,' said Stephanie.

Nanna Judy was asleep on the two-seater.

'I've not seen this. It's good. David said we should go as them when we did fancy dress in Benidorm but I said, "What's *Toy Story?*"' said Geoff.

'Woody is the cowboy,' said Stephanie.

'Is he a baddy, Buzz Lightyear?' said Geoff.

'It's ambiguous. At this juncture of *Toy Story 3* it's ambiguous,' said Gerard.

Nanna Judy began to snore aggressively.

'In work they had a competition for the best onesie. Get real. It was the day I was in London, thank Jesus,' said Stephanie.

'Why is Buzz Lightyear speaking in Spanish?' said Geoff.

Gerard was ringing his chrome-plated bicycle bell, a present from Maureen and Geoff. Pepsi was running after the sound.

'Ring it again,' said Nanna Judy, awake now.

'I think Pepsi tricked us into a false sense of insecurity,' said

Maureen.

'Oh, it's Tom Hanks is Woody,' said Geoff.

'I've gone back to Primark tights,' said Nanna Judy. 'I'd wear them once and they'd be in bits so I changed to a Boots three pack. I went off them too. Now I'm back on the Primark ones.' Gerard thought of Einstein's definition of madness.

'He's blacked his hair that Anton Du Beke,' said Geoff.

'That's Bruno,' said Maureen, 'Anton's old news.' Maureen won £13 in her office Strictly sweepstake. She thought that when Geoff had set up his new phone properly she was going to download the Twitter app, set up an account and tweet @OreOduba and say 'thanks xxx'.

'I bet they did all this before Christmas,' said Nanna Judy.

'You're right. This must have been filmed before last Saturday,' Maureen said, 'because they showed that judge on MailOnline with her hair cut up to here.' Maureen put her hand up to her ears.

Stephanie weighed herself in the downstairs bathroom. The digital display on the scales said '8'. She didn't know what '8' meant.

'Where's Scrabble?' said Gerard. Gerard wanted to play Scrabble tomorrow with Del. He thought about how a triple word score and an orgasm would make for the best twenty minutes of the festive season.

'My sister Mavis used to play Scrabble,' said Nanna Judy. 'She'd go every week to the village hall and play it with a group of friends. She was rather good at it. And quite pretty too.'

'Prettier than you, Nan?' said Stephanie. Nanna Judy didn't hear her, or decided to ignore her.

'Where she lived they used to grow lots of tulips. They called it Little Holland there. And they'd decorate these carriages with them, beautiful they were. And they named her the Tulip Queen. Yes, Mavis. She died when she was sixty-one.'

'That's a nice story, Nan,' said Stephanie, 'I think.'

'Have you heard of the butterfly farm? It's quite famous.'

'I don't think so, Nan,' said Stephanie.

'Well, Mavis' husband kept it. My brother Douglas had a farm called Old Leam Farm. His neighbour was Peter Scott, whose father sailed to the Antarctic. He lived where the wild things were on the marshes.' Maureen walked into the living room.

'Nanna Judy is telling us the family history,' said Gerard. Maureen sat down on the three-seater leather sofa next to Gerard.

'Geoff, love, come on in,' she shouted to the kitchen. Geoff was washing the plates before they went in the dishwasher.

'My dad died when he was fifty. The boys had gone to a football match and he wanted to plough the field. He couldn't leave things be, so he used the tractor which he wasn't used to. He was used to the horses. The dyke had filled up and the tractor fell into the water and he drowned. Douglas went to call him for his tea but he didn't answer.'

Geoff muted *Strictly Come Dancing*.

Gerard wondered about the unsettling mystery of a world where you couldn't check if someone was available just by looking at a mobile messaging service.

'I was pregnant with Albert so they didn't tell me. All I had was a photo of his grave. He didn't want to be a farmer so he went away on the boats and ended up in Australia. When the First World War broke out he joined the Australian army. A shell broke and they found him in a bunker. He had shellshock and it gave him a terrible stammer. He came back home and met his wife, my mother, in Manchester and they came back to Sutton Bridge. He never wanted to be a farmer. They used to call him Thomas Bowling because he always wore a bowler hat, one of the hard ones, you know?'

'I think so, Nan,' said Stephanie.

'Turn *Strictly* back on love, I can't hear what Tess is saying,' said Maureen.

Gerard had a notification: 'Paul Gomez invites Gerard to play My Singing Monsters.'

'Cup of tea anyone?' said Geoff. Everyone was asleep. 'Oh well, cheap round. Merry Christmas.'

CHAPTER

Gerard was self-aware enough to know that in the eyes of others he was classed as a hipster. He made lifestyle choices which both confirmed and railed against this fact, proving the perfect approach to its preservation. Gerard sneered at other hipsters, which seemed like a perfectly hipster thing to do, but behind the sneer was a fear that today was the day he was outed, the day he was unfollowed, the day that he was out of the in crowd and in with the out crowd.

Since Gerard was in lower sixth form, click and buy cool had led to an erosion of the outsider mentality needed for the formation of a proper youth culture. No punks, no mods, no goths, everyone in skinny jeans and just-so haircuts. The nots were hot, the barriers to entry easy, and an early thirty-something Gerard consistently unsure if being the highest bidder on an Ace of Base 1992 tour t-shirt was ironic or not and which was more favourable.

He'd figured leaving London would sooth this particular stress but the smaller provincial pool had made every decision vital, every mistake magnified. Complacency was the enemy, as was appearing to try too hard not to be complacent. Gerard told himself it was just another inconsequential thing to keep him up at night, the revenge of a mind blurred by amphetamines and a mobile device. In the morning, after two strong Nespressos, he felt sure the only thing that mattered was a strong online profile.

'Face to face is so niche,' he thought.

But he'd been drawn back to the bosom of his family. Had it been to fulfil his duty, to be relied upon, to play a pivotal role in the autumn/winter season of the lives of his blood relations? Or was it him who needed them, to be grounded in reality with people who knew him before the internet? He avoided reaching a conclusion.

Unlike many of his generation, Gerard was on the property ladder. The inability of his peer group to own bricks and mortar was much less to do with their leftfield inclinations and more the dirty rotten luck of coming of age post-boom, the warehouse rentals and ambiguous freelancing a side effect rather than a symptom. Gerard had been a little unsure if home ownership would prove the panacea that his parents' generation had promised. The setting down of roots back home in Wales seemed to signal the death knell for a nomadic vision of his imagined future self.

For once in his life, he'd said yes when his mother had pleaded. For once in his life he hadn't zoned out when Geoff had cleared his throat and assumed a paternal role, like a bargain hunter in a dead man's jacket.

Gerard was twelve years old when his father had died. The other kids at his school were used to dealing with divorced kids. It was weirder if the parents were still together. Those were the kids that got less stuff at Christmas or had their television watching rationed. But none of the other kids were dead-dad kids.

Two decades later it manifested itself in more modern ways.

He was connected to eleven profiles in the Family and Relationships section of Facebook: a sister, step-cousins, even Nanna Judy (a parody account set up by Stephanie, granted), but no father. Gerard knew he'd felt this broken-off branch of the Kane family tree, this empty space in the offline world. He was unsure if the sympathy he'd received as a child from strange adults had made him soft, weaker than normal people, emotionally reliant on others.

The chain of events which led to Gerard being the unexpected owner of 21 Sunrise Terrace was kick-started the day his dad dropped dead.

When people asked why he'd come home, if he was sick of the tube, the pace of life, he told them the real story. People always wanted the real story. He'd tell them, 'I came back to spend more time with my family. I love those guys.'

The fly in the ointment had been Stephanie. She had been on a city break in Berlin when Gerard had come home for the pitch, sitting awkwardly but attentively in Neukölln launderette bars while Al talked seriously about digital art with earnest, heavily-pierced Europeans he'd only previously met in an online forum. The pitch was the 'time to grow up' pitch, the 'new phase of life' pitch, the 'won't it be nice to be just around the corner' pitch. The twins had spoken on Messenger.

Gerard Kane: I'm bouncing on your bed

Stephanie Kane: Okay

Stephanie Kane: Really?

Stephanie Kane: Why?

Gerard Kane: Because I hate you...

Gerard Kane: Jokes

Stephanie Kane: Right

Gerard Kane: At Mum's I meant

Gerard Kane: The bouncing

Gerard Kane: Not Falseton

Stephanie Kane: Dalston

Gerard Kane: Yeah

Stephanie Kane: Oh, you're back for 'the talk'

Gerard Kane: Yeah

Gerard Kane: There's our twinny sixth sense in action again

Gerard Kane: The talk has been and has gone. Mum looked anxious.
Geoff looked prepared.

Gerard Kane: It seemed like they wanted it so much

Gerard Kane: So I agreed

Gerard Kane: I said yes

Gerard Kane: Ja

Gerard Kane: The return of the prodigal son

Gerard Kane: Steph...

Gerard Kane: Stepher?

Stephanie Kane: Hey! Soz. Patchy WiFi here.

Stephanie Kane: Taht's such good news

Gerard Kane: I figured digital artists would need a steady connection

Stephanie Kane: Such good news

Stephanie Kane: :)

Gerard Kane: This is not the time for emojis Steph

Stephanie Kane: ;)

Gerard Kane: Steph!

Stephanie Kane: Kidding. This is good.

Stephanie Kane: For them

Stephanie Kane: And for you

Stephanie Kane: Especially you

Stephanie Kane: And them

Stephanie Kane: You'll be there to replace me

Gerard Kane: What??

And that was how Gerard found out that while he was returning to Wales to be closer to his family, his twin sister, once separated by a placenta, would again be at the opposite end of 151 miles of motorway.

Facebook Messenger had become the main form of communication between the twins. They'd Skyped just the once, Stephanie freestyling with her iPad position *Blair Witch* style, an unsuspecting Nanna Judy stuck to the two-seater sofa with seasickness, muttering something about a choppy cruise around the fjords on a P&O ferry.

A life's work had meant Grampy Joe was able to leave his twin grandchildren a sum equivalent to a deposit for a small house in south Wales, the agency fee on a London flat and two Made.com furniture makeovers.

'Would Al be paying any rent?' Gerard wondered. 'Is digital art a lucrative career option?' and 'What is digital art?' Then, 'Did they know she was leaving when they made me come back?' and 'Did they make me come back?' before, 'Do the details matter anyway?'

CHAPTER

Hey, I'm Gerard!
Cardiff, Wales, United Kingdom. Member since 2016.

Hip guy tired of London, returned to the land of my fathers to work on generation-defining short film. My cottage is a cool and comfortable space perfect for exploring Europe's fastest-growing capital city. Close to cafe culture, park life, river walks, medieval castles, art pop-ups, traditional pubs, dive bars, mountains and lakes. Your space is a quirky attic room decked out completely in 1960s furniture. No children or buzz killers.

Reviews (12)

Stefan: Gerard (and his place) are so British. We were staying in Cardiff for a weekend to concert by our favourite band of Wales the Manic Street Preachers. My girlfriend (Laila) could not believe him when he said he KNEW JAMES DEAN BRADFIELD. He is big idol of ours. The room is nice and cosy even though I bang my head on ceiling going up stairs after concert. Gerard was really helpful with directions and he even called a taxi car for us. Danke!

June: After some confusion checking in, and a later problem with a leaky radiator, Gerard's cottage was ample as a base for the Welsh leg of the Three Peaks Challenge.

Response from Gerard: I'm glad we worked things out. Peace and love.

Halita: I had the best time staying at Gerards place. Cardiff wasn't on my list of must-see places in the world but thanks to Gerards hosting, we really got to live like a local. He drew us a map of all the best bars in town and even bought us tequila slammers when we bumped into him on the Saturday night. Forget New York and Berlin, Cardiff is the coolest!!!

Émilienne: Gérard était super sympa. Sa place était très rétro. Il y avait un petit problème avec la location de vélo, mais il a été tout réglé. Il est le bienvenu à Paris à tout moment.

+More reviews

Do you want to anonymously report this user?

If so, please choose one of the following reasons and our dedicated Trust and Safety team will look into it.

CHAPTER

It all started to go downhill the moment it became official.

Facebook official.

'Gerard Kane and Delyth Thomas are in a relationship.'

Gerard had let the notification sit there for a while, processing the digital domino effect of clicking accept. He had thought about the people who would pause as it appeared in their newsfeeds, taking in the information, sipping their morning coffee, formulating their line of commenting. He knew there would be notifications from Edwin, Lenka and Mac, his colleagues at the bar. From Robert, his teabag-economising former housemate. From Seren, the friend he'd always hoped would be more. But worst of all, his Auntie Bronwen. Gerard had only seen his Auntie Bronwen a handful of times since Grampy Joe's funeral but thanks to her online ubiquity was fully-briefed on her proficiency at herding livestock avatars. Since then, of course, there had been the incident.

Gerard hadn't been Facebook official for six years, since Angharad, in which time he had been offline official with Catrin Parker, Milly Zawistowicz and, briefly, Anna Day. He had made it a rule of thumb that by date three, generally at an unfussy eatery, often Lebanese, he'd tell them that he didn't do Facebook relationships as sophisticated online criminals were harvesting the personal information for a series of unexpected but inevitable attacks.

But it had been different with Del.

He had been different with Del.

He'd wanted news of their union to ride the waves of the World Wide Web like a lolcat meme. For the first time in his life, he was in love. Actual love. The real kind he'd read about. And all this with a girl he'd met on the internet. But one mid-January day when the globe in the top right of his newsfeed had pinged Stanley Kubrick red with the relationship request, he had scrolled and scrolled and scrolled down past blurred drunken Friday nights, motivational quotes and sponsored posts by online betting websites until the stabbing pain came into his frontal lobe again.

He hadn't felt that pain in a very long time.

*

The spring had brought change.

Gerard wondered if it actually had brought change or if his mind only worked in clichés. He definitely felt like the atmosphere between him and Del was different to how it had been three months before. He thought first about their sex life. He was aware this was a further tick in the cliché column and was certain he had been conditioned to think this way by the lifestyle media. In the early days of their relationship, Gerard had made Del come 99.9 per cent of the times they had intercourse. Today he felt like he was closer to a 66.7 or 33.3 per cent average. Gerard suffered from a mild form of number dyslexia.

Gerard would, after the one in three, or two in three, times he didn't make Del come, offer a scattergun of support, tea and compliments for the following hour, before breaking down in tears, repeatedly asking if she was okay and if her coldness was because of his deficiency. Del would tell him that she was okay and even if she wasn't, it wouldn't be down to his deficiency.

Last night, when this happened, she told him she wished she was a robot so she could switch off her hard drive at night and wouldn't have to put up with her thoughts keeping her anxious and awake. She'd downloaded a mindfulness app to help order her thoughts but was distracted by notifications from Instagram likes pinging through her Zen. Her anxiety had not helped Gerard. Gerard had a noise in his head when he went to sleep at nights. It sounded like space, like the sound you hear when you enter an empty room. The sound not of nothing, but of something very real, of particles colliding against each other.

Their social media situation had moved on since that relationship request. Every time Gerard appeared next to Del, on the sofa or at a kitchen worktop, she'd nimbly close down the application on her phone and he would see the Facebook blue fade into a screensaver of Del and her sister stood in front of the glass pyramid at the Louvre, wrapped in oversized scarves. Del's sister was looking to the left of the photographer. Gerard imagined a commotion among a group of

Korean art tourists. A quarrel with a street performer over a five Euro note. He pictured Del and her sister taking a break over a superfood salad in the cafe, Del's sister referencing the earlier incident and Del not following before agreeing and then, as they stared through *The Winged Victory of Samothrace,* saying that she hadn't known what her sister had been going on about in the cafe but had nodded anyway.

The post-Christmas months had led to an inevitable decline in tourists, so Gerard had supplemented his income by working extra shifts at the microbrewery. This had exacerbated the issues between him and Del. The working pattern of a bar captain did not correlate well with those of a junior creative. Gerard would arrive home late when Del had to work early. Del would wake early when Gerard wanted to sleep late. His nominal weekend of Sunday and Monday jarred with Del's more conventional rest period, his spontaneous Sunday nights out not the ideal preparation for a brand brainstorm at a Monday team scrum.

A few times over the past month, Gerard had sat in the staff room during his lunch hour, alone and without technology, to think about how and why things had changed. He found he could clear his mind by imagining himself in a lift going to the twenty-fourth floor, alone after a lady had got out at the second floor and the doors had closed behind her. It wasn't important for this exercise what the lady looked like. It was a mindfulness technique he'd learned from Del. He was able to reach few conclusions before reaching his destination.

Does she find me interesting anymore?

Am I interesting anymore?

Do I pay her enough compliments?

Do I pay her too many compliments?

Is it because of the blue cheese thing?

Or the sex?

Does she like sex?

Does she like boys?

Is it because of the blue cheese thing?

Gerard felt comfortable in the bar, among others who were young or relatively young, hip or relatively hip. The wall to the left of the bar hung illustrations of the employees, ninety per cent of whom had beards, tattoos or piercings, Gerard's angular jaw and upside down beauty spot stood solitary and timeless, preserved in sharp charcoal until the next round of redecoration or redundancy.

On his daily cycle through the park to work, he found himself staring with distaste at the office workers in their hurried haste. They appeared as a real-life record of his lot in London, seven long years of commutes and creased suits, the Northern line and a seamless decline into the zombie ant he swore he'd never become. Life was different now. He was an entrepreneur, an auteur, a bar captain, in that particular order. He was a family man.

His portfolio career didn't seem to have made a change to his effectiveness as a life partner, despite the early promise. He remembered the first time he'd noticed the change in their relationship. Del was procrastinating over what to wear to a launch party for a new seafood restaurant she had created the brand for.

'What's the weather like?' she had asked.

'Why don't you look out of the window?' Gerard had answered, perhaps rudely, although he was distracted by a broken-English request regarding towels from a potential Ukrainian house guest. (His house guest status was potential. He was most definitely Ukrainian.)

'I don't trust my own eyes, my own perception,' Del had answered.

This had been the end of the beginning.

The mid-season break finale.

This morning, Del had woken up angry and confused. Gerard reached his arm across the nylon sheets to find it batted away.

'Morning. What's up?'

'I'm confused.'

'It's Thursday.'

'I'm angry.'

'It's nearly your weekend.'

'I had a horrible dream...'

'Baby, you're awake now, it's okay.'

Gerard reached his arm over again but met the same response.

'I came home and found you fucking that Lenka or whatever her name is from work.'

'What?'

'I said I came home and found you fucking that Lenka or whatever her name is from work. It was horrible. I ran and ran and ran but the road outside had no end and it turned into the railway track from Auschwitz...'

'Oh baby, that is horrible...'

Gerard reached again. The same response, the push harder now.

'This is crazy, I can't be in trouble for cheating on you in a dream?'

'Your behaviour must have been projecting.'

Del rolled over, pulling the quilt from Gerard's bare bottom half.

Gerard went to the bathroom and realised he couldn't take a piss without taking his iPhone along and checking a social network with his spare hand. This impressed him and depressed him in equal measure, formerly because of the ingenuity it took to wire him into millions of other humans across the world from this small, damp room; latterly because even in this act that cried for solitude, he couldn't bear to be alone. He shook his dick dry, closed down Twitter and took a cotton bud out of the pot next to the mirror. He licked the end and inserted it into his right ear, spun it five rotations, disembarked and looked at his work. The cotton bud end was still white. Gerard doubted he was alive.

Later, while he was pouring a six per cent pale ale for a girl with green hair wearing a Los Pollos Hermanos t-shirt, Gerard felt a jab in his left ankle. He wondered if voodoo dolls would be digital now and just who would be hovering a cursor over the scar he'd got when he fell off his BMX aged eight, pressing Enter, Enter, Enter over and over and over.

He thought it could well be Del.

He hoped it wasn't Del.

Things had started so well.

CHAPTER 5

17 excellent moments in the brief but brilliant relationship of Gerard Kane and Delyth Thomas.

Excellent Moment #1: Thirty-five minutes and two cocktails into their first in-person meeting following four days of frequent, often manic messaging, which had begun on Tinder and quickly moved to WhatsApp, it became apparent that while neither Gerard or Del had dined at this particular Mexican cantina previously, both had evaluated its TripAdvisor presence. Their eyes met approvingly across the cork bench, as papier-mâché Day of the Dead skulls bobbed above, both knowing they were in the comfortable presence of another who entrusted the hive mind.

Excellent Moment #2: The twenty-four hours Gerard and Del had spent messaging on Tinder centred around a shared love of the long-running television series *Lost*. Gerard messaged that in the event of a bankrupt J.J. Abrams cashing in on a movie version, Kevin Spacey would have been the ideal candidate to play Ben, the leader of the Others, had it not been for the skeletons in his closet. Del replied, instantly, that when Ben had first appeared on-screen in SE 02 EP 14 she'd needed to Google who the actor was to check if he actually was Kevin Spacey. Gerard replied, 'No. Fucking. Way.' and felt a sharp butterfly in his lower abdomen.

Excellent moment #3: In the hours following the November night of their first date, Gerard had written four draft WhatsApps but deleted every one as they sounded either too breezy or not breezy enough. He wondered if the three-day rule popularised by the 1996 movie Swingers was still the accepted etiquette or if the availability of content from previous eras through Netflix had led to a blurring of moral codes across generations. 1.75 days later, Gerard sent Del a message containing just a URL link. When Del clicked the link she was taken to a Spotify playlist that started with The Waitresses – 'I Know What Boys Like', centred around Super Furry Animals – 'Play It Cool', and ended with

The Ramones – 'I Wanna Be Your Boyfriend'. Del had opened the message during a team huddle at her creative agency and postponed clicking the link until her bus journey home, part of her wondering if Gerard's profile had been hacked by cybercriminals. When she sat down on the number seventeen and decided to damn the consequences of a potential smartphone virus, she'd recognised the opening drum roll instantly and smiled her way through the remainder of the twenty-eight-minute journey. Joey Ramone's crooned request created first a jolt and then delight. She'd messaged back: 'Hey Ho, Let's Go!' The junior accountant sat opposite who watched her intently twice a day, ten times a week, wondered just what the look on her face had been all about and if it had anything to do with his new Chelsea boots.

Excellent Moment #4: The date that followed had been trailed in the playlist by the inclusion of a song by the Australian psychedelic-dance band Jagwar Ma. Del had held her work phone up to her headphones to use an app to identify the track, before realising that Spotify listed the tracks like a joyless if efficient version of the spidery handwriting on the mixtapes she'd pinched from her older brother's bedroom. The track was called 'Come Save Me'. Del had initially found the sentiment a little corny, before thinking that sometimes corny wasn't so bad.

In calculated synchronicity, the band were playing in Clwb Ifor Bach in Cardiff on the upcoming Friday night and Gerard had got them a pair of tickets. They stood towards the back of the 200-capacity room, far enough away from the small mosh pit which had formed at the front of the stage to hear each other's shouted reminiscences of more youthful nights. Del had made a point of avoiding Gerard's sideways gaze during the seven-minute live interpretation of the song. Gerard had shuffled nervously to the beat, wanting to touch Del with his body but not wanting to segue into school disco grind territory.

As the singer signalled the end of the performance by smashing his microphone repeatedly against the stage floor, Del turned to Gerard, mouthed the word 'deal' and forked her wet tongue into his mouth. As the crowd bayed for the band to come back on stage, a slow handclap reverberating off the sweaty walls, Gerard rested his pint against his waist and lifted up his right hand. Del did the same in reverse, her left clapping his right, two becoming one.

Excellent Moment #5: After this early elation, Gerard now felt comfortable enough to invite Del to an evening at the cinema. This predictable vehicle had been used by Gerard for each of the seven first dates he'd engineered.

Date	Film	Venue	Year	Repeat date?
Bethan Williams	Miss Congeniality	Cardiff Odeon	2000	N
Tiffany Price	Jurassic Park III	Cardiff Odeon	2001	N
Christina Chong	How To Lose A Guy in 10 Days	Cardiff Odeon	2003	N
Petra Müller	The Lives of Others	The Screen on the Green, Islington	2006	Y
Sadie Sedgefield	The Devil Wears Prada	Wandsworth Cineworld	2006	N
Eloise Kruger	Juno Cinema, Shoreditch	The Aubin	2007	N
Polly Davies	The Baader Meinhof Complex	BFI Southbank	2008	Y

*Gerard did not go on any first dates during Sept 2003-May 2006 as he was at university and the mechanism was not needed to attract a mate.

The 1983 David Cronenberg techfreak-horror Videodrome was showing at Chapter Arts Centre, a cavernous futuristic dentist waiting room space about ten minutes brisk walk from Gerard's cottage. Del met him at the bike racks, her early arrival meaning she watched as Gerard awkwardly strapped his cycle to the U-shaped metal. In the velvet crush seats of cinema 2, as an advert for a Scandinavian people carrier played, Gerard whispered that when he was younger, his mum had referred to their current experience as 'going to the pictures', which Gerard had thought uncool, favouring instead the Americanised 'movies'. The reverse was now true. Del told him everything was cyclical and, as Debbie Harry burnt a cigarette onto her bare breasts on-screen, put her hand on his knee.

Excellent Moment #6: The first time Gerard had made Del come had been at the third attempt in non-consecutive days. The first two attempts could most definitely not be characterised as excellent. Del had screamed with surprise and relief, her single housemate Meg responding to the noise from next door by plugging her earphones into her iPad mini and turning the volume on her movie right up, reaching for her phone and opening up a dating app.

Excellent Moment #7: Before they'd met face-to-face, Gerard had checked out Del's presence on all the major social networks, as well as a handful of more niche communities. He approved of her online persona. Naturally, Del had completed the same background checks on Gerard, reaching the same positive conclusion.

During a warm but directionless WhatsApp chat one day in late October, Gerard asked for Del's work email address in order to send her a link to an upcoming pop-up dude food festival taking place in a former textiles warehouse. Del had instantly complied, before later wondering why Gerard couldn't forward the information through the plethora of channels on which they were already connected.

Later still, she wondered if her colleague Emyr, previously an end of the night 'don't tell anyone at work' shag, would see the emails popping into her inbox, search Gerard's name online and start asking leading, if unwarranted, questions. Gerard didn't send an email until the next day, but felt a strange euphoria from the pleasing freedom that he could now contact Del in fourteen different ways, if he included knocking on her front door, which he hadn't when first doing the arithmetic.

Excellent Moment #8: On his first ever MySpace profile, Gerard had described himself as 'a lover not a fighter'. He'd also declared, in self-coded HTML, an ironic affinity for 'the lost art of letter writing'. Gerard had only ever written two letters in his life, both addressed to a girl called Jess or Joss from Coventry or Daventry who he'd met on the Costa Dorada while on a family holiday in 1999. Both were left unanswered.

On an icy evening in early December, Gerard had badly misjudged the meeting place for a date with Del, opting for a Latin American chain bar on a date favoured for Christmas parties by offices where the employees didn't like each other enough to spend quality time together close to the big day.

After waiting at the bar for over fifteen minutes, Gerard returned to Del to find two interchangeable young men, both in their early twenties and matching silver suits, sat opposite her. Gerard's route to the seat next to Del was blocked and the two Dark and Stormys he carried started to spill sticky liquid over his cold hands.

'Oh look, your brother's back,' one of them said. Del looked at Gerard, her pupils dilated in a way he hadn't seen in any of her 473 Instagram pictures.

'He's my boyfriend, shit for brains. Now get back to your organised fun before you miss Secret Santa.' This was the first time Del had referred to Gerard as such. The suits sloped off, sneering 'fucking hipsters' in their direction.

Excellent Moment #9: Gerard had waited for Del to ask him about his short film, hoping to appear to be treating its introduction into their conversation with an everydayness which she would find alluring. Xanadu naturally left a treasure trail across his online footprint which he was certain would be addressed in the early stages of their courtship.

By their fourth date, Del had discussed, in no particular order: Snapchat celebrities, the secret mechanics of food crazes, and her sixth form ballet teacher. There had been no mention of his impending auteurhood. Gerard felt enough was enough and had dropped it into the air, casually mentioning something about an ongoing location search. Del had listened intently, looking away only to say goodbye to a former colleague sat on a nearby sofa, while Gerard gave her his well-practiced elevator pitch.

He finished with his immodest expectation that some of the more boutique European festivals would very likely show interest in a director's cut. Del replied that if he needed a plus-one for Cannes, she was 'his girl'. Gerard reached his upper body over his hazelnut latte, cupped Del's chin with his left hand and said, 'It's a date,' kissing her on her right cheekbone. At this exact moment, Gerard remembered he'd felt almost complete for the first time since he'd moved home to Wales.

Excellent Moment #10: Gerard had woken up in the morning to find Del's long dark hair tousled over his bare chest, spilling onto his arm and covering up his tattoo so that all that showed was half a broken heart. Gerard inhaled her odour into his lungs and coughed slightly, although not enough to wake Del up from her dream, which Gerard didn't know was reaching its climax of a climax to a masked man who could have been but probably wasn't him. Gerard had felt good on this particular morning. It was the morning after the first time Del had stayed at his cottage without asking if she could stay at his cottage. Sleeping next to each other had now reached normalcy. There would be no looking back. Del stirred and the smile on her face convinced Gerard she had felt it too.

Excellent Moment #11: Del had been sat on the leather Chesterfield in Gerard's front room for two and a half hours. During that time, there had been less conversation than in the movie *The Artist*. This was not uncommon. Often the pair would sit silently, trying to listen the two floors up to the exchanges of foreign houseguests, stifling back laughter at their surprise that the castle didn't have any sheep and that there was a shopping centre where the mines should be.

But this particular night, it was different. There hadn't been a guest since the South African accountant who'd stayed for two nights to watch his native rugby team lose to Wales at the nearby stadium.

'Del, what's up? You don't seem yourself.'

'Oh, it's nothing.'

It was something.

'It's nothing, really.'

It was something.

Gerard worried it was him, them.

'Del, what's up? You can talk to me.'

Turns out it wasn't him or them. It was Del's housemate, Meg. There'd been a falling out that was sparked by a carton of unrefrigerated Alpro and had escalated quickly to full-blown character assassination. Gerard discovered that listening to Del unburden her problems was a relatively easy task, but then he started to think of the picture of a lone boat in stormy waters on the wall of Robin Williams' character in the film *Good Will Hunting* and he felt a tear moisten his left cheek.

Being this in touch with his emotions seemed to amplify his apparent ability for empathy. Del told him he was 'such a good listener' and, as she put her arms around him and he felt her medium-sized breasts push up against the buttons of his shirt, Gerard supposed that yes, he was.

Excellent Moment #12: Until this point, Gerard and Del's liaisons had been exclusive affairs, platforms for two new acquaintances to get to know each other outside and in.

One Friday night in early January, Del had unwittingly double-booked herself, agreeing to dinner with Gerard at a new sushi bar while her presence was also expected at the leaving party of her colleague, Ash. In a move motivated by guilt, Del messaged Gerard explaining the situation and saying they should meet up for drinks regardless.

He'd agreed. She'd instantly regretted this. The unwritten rule at her creative agency had been that nights out were partner-free, ever since a digital account manager had brought her fiancé to a cocktail making event and he'd spent the whole evening pitching 'the next Angry Birds' to Hiro, the firm's quietly maniacal CEO.

In preparation for the meeting, Gerard had drunk three cans of Tesco's own brand pre-mixed gin and tonic. Experience told him that three drinks was the optimum number to lose inhibition while maintaining coherence.

His arrival at the city centre bar was greeted by a cheer, catcalls and a sloppy kiss from an evidently tipsy Del. Grounded in the knowledge that her office often resembled a snake pit when talk turned to affairs of the heart, Del was concerned about introducing Gerard to her co-workers. But she was surprised at how proud she felt showing him off to the people she spent thirty-seven and a half hours a week with.

Gerard had worn a red checked shirt that Del liked on him and his hair was perfectly set in the new 1930s cut he'd had the day previous. He'd decided to affect an air of easy-going mystery, talking in affable cliff-hangers and laughing passionately at the group's observations. This approach had served to intrigue the females and frustrate the males, particularly Del's previous bedroom partner, Emyr, who'd shouted across an exchange between Gerard and the experiential marketer Carla to ask what it was that Gerard did, to which Gerard responded, 'That's a deep question,' before returning to his conversation on the merits of flossing daily.

Gerard found that he actually enjoyed himself, that in the main he liked Del's colleagues, and for an hour or two missed the camaraderie he'd experienced working in similar environments in London. Carla had told Gerard that she had 'Facebook stalked' him and emailed a cut and pasted picture of him to the other females in the office, receiving mostly positive feedback. As she told him Del was mentioning him with increasing frequency in seemingly non-related conversations, Gerard looked across the table to see Del locked in a chat with who he assumed from the 'We're Sad You're Leaving' badge was Ash, before she looked up to catch his eye. The couple – because that's what they now were – smiled at each other with, if not love, then no small amount of lust.

Excellent Moment #13: The following morning, Gerard had driven to an out of town retail park to stock up on toiletries for the impending arrival of a guest for a one month stay in the spare room. Del had stayed in bed, snoozing off her hangover in between responding to messages consisting only of a repeated thumbs-up emoji from the other members of a WhatsApp group entitled 'Work Bitches'. As he stood in aisle eighteen of a giant Home Bargains, wondering where the Italians stood on quilted toilet paper, Gerard's phone pinged with a notification. 'Delyth Thomas has mentioned you on Twitter'. This was a first.

'So @G_FK met the @weareisosceles crew last night. Verdict= thumbs up.'

Three weeks before, Gerard had mentioned Del in a status anticipating a night at a drive-in movie, receiving, within three minutes, a message saying, 'UNLIKE. I don't want the world to know what we're doing Gerard Kane.' But now Del was tweeting about him. Now her 2,892 followers knew that (a) @G_FK excels at meeting new people and (b) @G_FK was very likely someone special to her. Gerard slid down the aisle using the trolley as an impromptu skateboard, forgetting all about the toilet paper.

Excellent Moment #14: The month-long house guest was a Milanese cameraman called Federico who was shadowing the assistant director on the sci-fi family entertainment show *Dr. Who*, made by the BBC in the city and sold to seventy-two territories worldwide. Gerard felt confident this precedent would prove essential in the inevitable success of Xanadu.

Federico's broken English emails had flagged up a delay to his flight to Bristol Airport meaning his check-in time would be six hours later than anticipated, landing slap bang in the middle of Gerard's shift at AlePunk that night. Gerard assessed his options. His mum was nervous around strangers. On the sole occasion Geoff had been entrusted with the task, his thick Yorkshire accent had led to complications, an elderly French couple taking his broad vowels for brusqueness, leading to a lukewarm online review.

Stephanie was living out her new weekend routine in a warehouse somewhere in East London with Al. Gerard was too mistrusting of human beings to leave a key under a pot, and besides, he had no pots. His neighbours either side were still relative enigmas to him, his early attempts to introduce himself as the new guy in town leading to thirty seconds of nodding and smiling with a twelve-year-old girl holding a clarinet and an awkward explanation of Airbnb to a sixty-something man who periodically interrupted their conversation to shout up the stairs in Welsh to someone who Gerard assumed was his wife.

But what about Del? Del could do it. Del would do it, wouldn't she? Gerard had WhatsApped her to ask from behind the bar, ignoring AlePunk's policy that mobiles shouldn't be used on duty unless the bar captain was signed into an AlePunk social account. Gerard could see Del had read the message. Thirty-seven long minutes later she responded, 'sure', then, 'you owe me Gerard Kane'. They were a team. Gerard and Del were a team. Gerard celebrated by giving out free tasters without prejudice for the rest of the evening.

Excellent Moment #15: Gerard wanted Del to feel like he was the kind of person willing not only to attend, but to participate in, experiential theatre. He felt sure the best way to achieve this status was through drinking three pints of staff-discounted craft ale before the curtain raised, or whatever it did in experiential theatre.

The show had begun twenty-four hours before the date. An email from a relative in the Autonomous Republic of Cymru had informed Gerard and Del they were to arrive at Bristol Temple Meads train station and enter the code 1019 into locker number twenty-three. Therein would lie the first clues in the trail that would, God willing, lead to their illegal exit and eventual asylum from the TB-ridden Royal United Kingdom of New Britain and Northern Ireland (or NewK).

The hours that followed took in illicit document deals, edgy guards, and failed attempts at the UK Citizenship test. Gerard had been given, as a prop, a TB-free chest X-ray. He'd traded it for a blue Nokia 3310, remembering it as a memento of simpler times. When it had beeped with a text telling him to get off the train at Severn Tunnel Junction, Gerard's eyes first had to adjust to its lack of emojis before looking to see if Del had received the same instruction. Realising she hadn't and remembering his vow to participate, Gerard had exited the train without a word, following the instructions to meet a Mr Wong in the corner of the car park. Mr Wong turned out to be a Tai Chi-obsessed taxi driver. As Mr Wong drove, Gerard stared listlessly out of the passenger window into a smoking steelworks. He suffered a sudden and aggressive anxiety attack triggered by a fear his fellow asylum seeker Del might not make it over the border into utopian Cymru.

When he woke up some time later at the side of the road, Mr Wong, now completely out of character, encouraging him in a strong Newport accent to 'take it steady, spa,' Gerard had the absolute knowledge that Del was feeling the same way he was right now. A little bit scared, a little bit lonely, a lot glad they weren't real refugees.

Excellent Moment #16: Gerard's interactions with Del's housemate Meg had to this point been set against the backdrop of guilt on his part for Del's orgasmic screams and resent on her part for Del's orgasmic screams. Gerard had naturally checked her online profile and was intrigued by her Twitter bio, which read: 'Free-range human trying to break out of the cage. Don't work for change. Be the change. Also likes cats.' A cursory glance at her updates had positioned her as aspirational for a higher sense of purpose, albeit irritable in the extreme, generally about bus drivers, BT Infinity, or her housemate.

Despite their inauspicious start, Meg had invited Gerard to the inaugural Meegan Supper Club evening. Gerard was unsure what this was, but felt good that he and Del now got invited to events as a pair, even if the events took place in the house where Del lived.

Arriving at the house at 7 p.m. prompt, carrying a bottle of room temperature Pinot Noir in a wine bag originating from Stephanie's thoughtless birthday present from last year of a blended whisky he would never drink, Gerard found the front door ajar. The living room, which usually smelled of tzatziki and nail polish remover, was decorated with colourful bunting and people with beards and nose rings whom he had never met. An awkward chat with a cycle courier named Jose informed Gerard that the city council's transport policy was stuck in the dark ages and that tonight's menu was one hundred per cent vegan.

Gerard wondered how he hadn't worked this out and then why Del hadn't told him, before, 'Is Pinot Noir vegan?' He WhatsApped Del to find out where she was, hearing nothing until she entered the room carrying a starter of two-mushroom tapenade, winking at him suggestively like a waitress in a Carry On film he'd seen on YouTube.

Del continued the evening in a sexually aggressive manner that Gerard felt was at odds with the food on offer. Meg had given a nervous but well-rehearsed welcome and story of the provenance of her fledgling food experiment, encouraging the diners to share online content from the evening using the hashtag #MeeganFoods. She'd read on a popular self-help blog that the best way to work out if you could make a living out of something you loved was to run a trial using the safety net of friendship to catch you. Gerard's attempts to empathise, citing his own return from London and current portfolio career had been hampered by Del's insistence on stroking his penis through his tight jeans under the makeshift table. Halfway through a patchy tofu chocolate tart, Gerard came in a big splodge on his left thigh. Del patted his leg twice before messaging him 'me next'.

Gerard hadn't known a meat-free diet could be so invigorating.

Excellent Moment #17: 'Waking up in your queen-sized bed with far-reaching views through the large window across the Towy Valley, you'll feel as though you've died and gone to country house heaven...'

Gerard had found the email schmaltzy but had booked the room anyway. Earlier in the week he'd clicked on a blog from Radio 4 entitled 'Memory Experience', which had said that the most vivid memories held by people with dementia were around holidays. He was unsure if excessive internet usage would accelerate or decelerate this process, but figured it was best to err on the side of caution.

He asked Del to meet him at the cottage straight from work on the Friday and to bring an overnight bag, a onesie and a swimsuit. She'd messaged back an emoji of a happy man in a turban, before 'oops', and then one of Sherlock Holmes in a deerstalker holding a magnifying glass and three kisses. Gerard had felt first-crush mushy resisting Del's questions about a secret that centred around time spent alone together. He was Facebook-happy in real life. This had been a first.

Google Maps had told him the drive to the hotel was 58.4 miles and 1 hour and 8 minutes away. He prepared a ninety-minute playlist to allow for traffic.

Somewhere along the A40, violent rain attacking the windscreen as the vocoded voice of 'Mr Blue Sky' played from the iPad on Del's lap, smoke spewed from the bonnet of Gerard's hire car. Del later told Gerard that his face at that specific moment resembled Edvard Munch's *The Scream* more than the emoji of Edvard Munch's *The Scream*. As they waited to be rescued, snuggled up in the back of the car, her in a Moomins onesie and him as a minion from *Despicable Me*, Gerard whispered 'I love you' just as the lights from the Green Flag recovery vehicle woke Del from her sleep.

CHAPTER

'It was fascinating, Nan, I've never heard you talk like that before, about those things, I mean.' Gerard was in Nanna Judy's front room, a china cup of milky tea resting precariously on his knee, the armchair's plastic cover enabling his gamble.

'They say when they came back they never wanted to talk about the war. Just went into themselves,' she said.

'I don't mean about the war, Nan, I just meant about our family, about what you were telling us on Christmas Day—'

'Christmas Day? We had a satsuma between the household and were happy with that...apart from Edith, of course, she never did like satsumas.' Nanna Judy drank from her cup, the tea sluicing through her dentures. 'She said they gave her bile.'

Gerard hadn't been in this house for over a decade. It felt different but smelt the same. A potent combination of boiled vegetables and pear drops. Maybe it was him who felt different. On his last visit, Nanna Judy was the designated responsible adult. Now he felt the roles were reversed.

On a Thursday night one year ago, if he was lucky, Gerard would have been drinking with people he didn't like, their connection a job they didn't like and a shared cultural history they liked but pretended they didn't. Otherwise, he'd be surfing the web. He felt that term was disingenuous, 'surfing'. It implied a technique, a tactical approach, a training regime. Gerard's internet navigation was scattergun, an uneven web of chance click-throughs, fleeting thoughts enacted, time spent. It was chicken soup for his soul. He needed it. But now his family needed him.

'That's interesting, Nan, but tell me about how you met Grampy Joe.'

Gerard held his phone up to record Nanna Judy.

'Don't mind this, Nan, just keep talking.'

'What is it?'

'I'm just making a little film, Nan.'

'Is it a selfie? Like Stephanie showed us?'

Gerard paused and considered his answer.

'It sort of is, Nan. But it's more than that. The stories you told us at Christmas really meant something to me. I'd never really thought about how we got here, you know, our family, only really Mum and Dad, but never any further back than that. It feels important to me, particularly now I'm back here with you all, to know why I'm here, or how I'm here, or how I'm one of us.'

'Why are any of us here, Gerard love?' Nanna Judy said, her face sagging at the cheekbones, deadpan.

'Exactly, Nan.'

Gerard's battery was close to dead. He'd spent the morning watching motivational videos on how to make the most of your twenties. He'd reasoned that although digitising the memories of his forefathers wasn't quite directing his short film, it could, in time, prove to be an even more valuable pursuit.

'His laugh was the first thing I noticed,' Gerard urged her on with a raise of his eyes. 'He'd just appeared in the mess hall one day and I said to Bessie, "Adolf could have heard that cackle. We're done for."'

'Where were you, Nan? The army, wasn't it?' Gerard asked.

'No, not the army,' she looked away to the window, 'the WAAF. Bessie and I were having a wonderful summer, packing parachutes...'

'Nan...'

'...although she always had trouble fluffing her chute, "think of it like a pillow, Bess," I'd tell her.'

'That's fascinating,' Gerard said, really meaning it, 'who was Bessie—'

'—and when we weren't doing that we were on communication duties, codes and ciphers mainly, dot dot dot, dash dash dash...' She trailed off.

'And Grampy Joe?'

Nanna Judy looked back to the phone.

'Yes, Joe.'

'His laugh?' Gerard said.

'A cackle like a blinking hyena on gas.' She tried to imitate her husband but a coughing fit took over. Gerard shot up, discarding his phone to help.

'Nan, are you okay?'

'...some lemonade please, there's some in the kitchen next to the condensed milk.' Gerard went to the kitchen and opened a series of cupboard doors, revealing tins that looked like they'd come from another era. Sure enough, he found a bottle of lemonade next to two tins of condensed milk, just as Nanna Judy said.

Nanna Judy drank and composed herself. Gerard picked up the phone and reframed his grandmother. This would be useful for Xanadu, he thought.

'What was he laughing at, Nan? Did you make him laugh?'

'Not me, no, not usually. It was Helmut he was generally larking about with.'

'Helmut?'

'Bessie liked Helmut, though she didn't say so.'

'Who was he, Nan?'

'Bessie was my friend.'

'No, Helmut.'

'Helmut?' She'd turned to the window again.

'Yes, Nan. The one who made Grampy Joe laugh.'

'Oh, him. He was a handyman from Dusseldorf, a prisoner of war. He was always talking to Joe about the football. Of course, everyone was suspicious of him, being a Jerry after all, but anything happened that needed fixing, he was there in a flash, always with a smile, although he had these crooked black teeth.'

'That's nice, Nan, it's a really lovely story. I bet it made you wonder why you were fighting the Germans?' Gerard felt like this could be more than a family archive, that he might shoot enough for a feature-length documentary, that maybe through his direction he might uncover some beautiful truth about wartime which had remained hidden until now.

'We couldn't always understand him, but he meant well.'

'Was Grampy a pilot then, Nan?

'No, he was scared of flying, Joe was. Said, "It's unnatural for a human being to be that high up in a sardine can."'

'What was he doing there then, Nan?'

'Who?'

'Grampy Joe.'

'Joe. He was in the fire and rescue. They'd drafted in firemen from all over the country and stationed them at Sutton Bridge.'

'I didn't know Grampy Joe was a fireman.' Gerard had always been told his grandfather was a mechanic. His arm ached. He rested his phone against the mantelpiece behind him, readjusting Nanna Judy's seating position to keep her centre shot. The ache reminded him of how he'd felt after his one and only kettlebells class.

He'd spent twenty minutes constantly moving the weight around his body, passing it behind his back, lifting it to the air, curling it at his elbow. After an early wave of euphoria, his technique singled out for praise by the Eastern European instructor, he'd realised that to keep this up for the remaining eighteen minutes he was going to have to enter what athletes commonly referred to as 'the zone'. He was unsure he had the correct papers to enter. He survived by pretending he was someone else, namely Jean Claude Van Damme in a training montage from the movies *Kickboxer* or *Blood Sport*. He thought about how he should go to more kettlebells classes. He wondered if next time he could pretend he was Grampy Joe.

'Sorry Nan, go on. Tell me about the fireman thing...'

'Oh, Joe wasn't one for long, the war stopped him,' Nanna Judy said, 'and after that, the bombing he saw, he was put off fire for life. Your Uncle Derek wanted to be a fireman, when he was a little boy.' Her eyes took a wistful turn, just for a second. She mentioned her son's name so rarely that Gerard felt any such details must have been erased.

'Don't worry about Uncle Derek, Nan, it's Grampy we were talking about.' Gerard didn't want the can of worms his mother's brother represented to wriggle all over his recording.

'So, Nan, you were telling me about—'

'—I always thought he was more of a cat up a tree fireman anyway,' she interrupted, laughing a cackle of her own, coughing once, 'I'm fine, I'm fine.... Your Grampy Joe spent most of the time when he wasn't head in an engine on the sofa. He wasn't one for company, certainly not in his later years. I'd say, "Why don't you come to bingo with me Joe, meet some new people?" He'd say, "Why would I want to meet new people? I know enough of them already and they're a constant disappointment."'

Over the fifteen minutes that followed, Nanna Judy gave Gerard a potted history of her marriage, relocation, subsequent motherhood, widowhood. It felt reductive to condense a life into such a window, like a TV special for a dead presenter. He wondered about his and Del's narrative. He considered how they'd met. A love against the odds. Not thrown together in a world war but a blind date determined by an algorithm.

When he was her age, what memories would he be sharing with his grandkid? Would the data they salvaged from his hard drive feature Del in a starring role? If he was writing the script, he knew the answer.

CHAPTER

The online reaction had perhaps been the worst thing about the Uncle Derek ordeal, at least when judged through the prism of Gerard's perception. If bad news used to travel fast, in the internet age it fizzed like a Berocca in a wet pinball machine.

Gerard had reconciled himself with the reality that he was stuck with these core relations for the rest of his life. He was changing. He was trying to be a better person. It felt as if these people were important in that quest. He'd left one of the world's most happening cities to be closer to them.

Where he struggled was feeling affinity with the outer fringes of the family. The aunties he hadn't held a conversation with since puberty but still received birthday cards from, hand-written with ambiguous, well-meaning messages, delivered like clockwork, always two days after the event. The outlines of cousins with back stories that he mixed up with other cousins with other similar back stories, generally involving children, divorce and zero hours contracts.

And Uncle Derek.

Gerard felt he was connected to Derek by only the thinnest of blood, a pinprick in a melted ice cap, but the people of the internet wouldn't have cared about that. These were not genealogists. Blood was blood. Aside from the more obvious atrocities, sharing a surname with a paedophile would have made a huge dent in Gerard's online influence score. His followers would have plummeted. He'd have been blocked by users who'd previously been regular engagers. The online damage would have been difficult to recover from. He felt that perhaps the situation's only silver lining was that Uncle Derek was on his mum's side of the family.

There had been whispers for months. Offline whispers. Gerard had been in London so, unlike now, didn't have to tune out of conversations at the Sunday dinner table about the extended family. His mum's family update was the last hurrah of their weekly Skype conversations. Once the novelty of seeing each other on a 13.3-inch screen at opposite ends of the motorway had worn off, the notifications of their recent pasts ticked off in a brisk, business-like manner, they inevitably reached family matters. Gerard had grown accustomed to around six to seven minutes of births, deaths, marriages, loft conversions, redundancies, extra-marital affairs of people he barely knew, like a gossip magazine in a foreign country.

But this Sunday it had been clipped. Just like Maureen's tone. Gerard had known something was up. She still held firm to the traditional notion that bad news should only be delivered in person, but Gerard could always get her to talk. He was certain he'd maxed out all his emotional intelligence quota on his mother, his sixth sense for deciphering her coded idiosyncrasies leaving him at a loss to understand if the thoughts that festered behind the Mona Lisa smiles of Del or those who went before her were content or murderous.

The stand-off reminded him of the time he'd returned from a summer spent daydreaming behind a bar in southern France, pouring Pastis into dusty glasses and his young heart out to Carrefour checkout girls, Scandinavian *Seinfeld* fans and Le Grand Tour sorority sisters. The exchange took place a full seven years before Maureen had been coaxed into video conferencing, but the pattern had been the same. Despite minimal voice contact between the two for the preceding three months, Gerard's tips spent on Gauloises instead of long-distance calls, his mother's round-up of the lives and loves of the blood relations had been muted. Gerard's scrutiny was met with the resistance of a problem drinker at a free bar.

'Mum, what's up?'

'Nothing Gerard, everything's fine here.'

'Mum, what's up?'

'Nothing Gerard...it's so lovely to hear your voice. It really is.'

'Mum...

....

Mum...'

'Well, look, I really didn't want to tell you until you were back here...'

'Mum?'

'It's Goebbels.'

'What?'

'He's dead.'

Goebbels was the family gerbil, bought as a joint gift for the twins' fifteenth birthday by Nanna Judy. Stephanie had named him, inspired by her GSCE history syllabus, the name a nod to alliteration rather than admiration for the evil Minister of Propaganda.

The news of his demise, delivered through sound waves sent down the M4 to the early edition camera-phone he held in an east London flat, caused him to fall flat down on a mattress hidden under bags and boxes. It was the first day of Gerard's residency in a house-share in Hackney. The subsequent tears, which lasted in fits for three days, led his new housemates, a Greek actress named Andromeda and an Irish barman determined to be known as Tough, to whisper across the laminate of the shared kitchen that the outpouring of emotion may be a hint at much deeper emotional problems.

This time, the withheld information hadn't been a death. That may well have been preferable to all concerned. When Maureen had caved in to Gerard's well-practiced nudging, the initial details had been sketchy. She'd mumbled something about Uncle Derek and an investigation, that the police had seized his computer. She'd said she hadn't known exactly why, before clearing her throat and steaming up the camera, making the scene look like a stream from a suspect torrent. Gerard had completed the equation.

After the grand reveal, paedophiles always looked like they should never have been allowed in the company of children, but hindsight wasn't queuing up for laser eye surgery.

Derek was Maureen's brother, arriving to Nanna Judy and Grampy Joe three years after Bronwen.

Gerard was first aware of Derek's existence when his mum burst a tyre on the way back from Cardiff's first out-of-town retail park in the mid-nineties. He'd been waiting around in the entrance to his Portakabin classroom, a smell like old meat from a duffel coat which had hung on the hooks since its ten-year-old owner had moved schools last term adding to his creeping anxiety. Stephanie was at dance class but Maureen hadn't turned up to fetch him. This had never happened before. He'd only seen Miss Davies' there-there eyes directed at other kids. He was usually watching Nickelodeon by now, nibbling around the hot bits of a French bread pizza.

But on this night, Miss Davies (who Gerard recently saw in a discount German supermarket, a Mrs now and seemingly much smaller, creating in him a particular interest in the ingredients of a giant jar of gherkins in order to avoid a potentially awkward conversation) was next to Gerard, speaking in a too-happy tone that 'everything was just fine, Gerard,' and that 'your Uncle Derek has come to pick you up tonight because your mam's having car problems. He's just outside the door, there. You do know your Uncle Derek, don't you, Gerard?'

It had taken Gerard a full five minutes to match the balding man he could see shuffling through the glass with the shadowy figure whose roll-up smoke from the back of the kitchen had caused Maureen to judge the candles had been blown-out prematurely at Gerard's fifth birthday party, leading the assembled neighbours and relatives in a re-start of the song.

It was this new incarnation of Derek who had told Gerard he'd been stood outside a full five minutes and was freezing his arse off, pushing his skinny frame through the gates, calling him a 'squirt' in response to his nephew's protestation that the last time he saw him was nearly half his life ago and he had much longer hair in the small picture that hung at the top of Nanna Judy's landing.

Derek drove Gerard to a bedsit he rented just out of town in Riverside, next door to a Chinese supermarket, Gerard thinking the surrounding streets reminded him of a film he and Stephanie had watched on a VHS rented from Blockbuster. Gerard thought how these names, Blockbuster, Woolworths, HMV, used to be strong, how they used to be the saints of his childhood, but now all lived in his smartphone.

'Have you seen *Big Trouble in Little China*?'

'What?'

'I think that's what it's called. That's what Stephanie said.'

'Who?'

'Stephanie?'

'What?'

'My twin sister.'

'Oh, yeah, Stephanie. Shut it kid. Your mother'll be here in five minutes.'

Gerard remembered thinking he had definitely been colder in that bedsit than Derek had been outside the school, but he knew he shouldn't say this to him. Gerard's second memory of Derek was at the wedding of Auntie Bronwen's eldest daughter. Gerard was unsure if this was Karly or Katie and moved between them for ten seconds before Googling 'Auntie Bronwen daugheter older' and clicking through to a blog called 'My Front Porch' written by an Amish man named Jacob from Salt Lake City before remembering what he had set out to achieve when he took his phone out of his jean pocket.

A fairly representative puberty had passed over Gerard in the six years since the school incident, its scars being mild acne and major heartbreak, both on the way to repair by the time his cousin had accepted the proposal of a financially sound IT consultant from Ashby-de-la-Zouch who she'd met at a Mod Revival weekend at Minehead Butlins.

The teenage sticking plaster had been provided through the presence of Ellie Ferris, a rangey county tennis champion from the year below whose pleated skirts and tireless wrists made Gerard feel like a man. Gerard had invited her along to the day, partly to piss off Stephanie, who seemed to feel strangely threatened by her arrival, and partly because Gerard didn't really know any of these fringe family members he was apparently related to.

With Stephanie off experimenting with cigarettes and his mum and dad dancing with Bronwen and Uncle Eric to Sister Sledge, Gerard and Ellie had got a table in the corner to discuss the latest series of X-Files through whispers over a shared plate of beige buffet food. Derek pulled up a chair and said something Gerard always remembered.

'I don't know why they bothered going to all this fuss of getting married. Casual sex is so easy to come by these days, isn't it?'

Gerard had laughed before Ellie kicked his ankle and announced her dad would be expecting her at home now. Derek winked at Gerard as he led her out of the swing doors of the Rotary Club lounge, 'We Are Family' straining conspiratorially behind them.

Family crises brought out the best and the worst in the Kanes and the Davies'. Historically, their responses had ranged from Grampy's quiet resilience to Stephanie's forty-eight-hour hunger strike following the sudden death of her pet rabbit, Ikea. Responses to this new trough had been predictable only in their unpredictability.

Nanna Judy, from whose marbled loins future online paedophile Derek had sprung, now denied his existence, leaving his birthday off her page-to-month kitchen calendar, his headcount off showboating about offspring, a form of selective dementia reserved previously only for the names of Gerard's girlfriends and the All England Lawn Tennis Championships from 1982-2016 inclusive.

Stephanie, like a retrospective detective straight from the pages of a Phillip K. Dick novel, always knew Derek was an oddball ever since she claimed he had compared his twin niece and nephew to the Sweet Valley High sisters at their joint thirteenth birthday party.

Gerard had no recollection of the aforementioned joint party, remembering thirteen as an age just past the parental-driven convenience of two-for-one pre-teen celebrations and just before the peer pressure from hormonal friends to return to joint parties.

Auntie Bronwen, the closest to Derek in age, grieved for him as fans did in forums for The 27 Club, her Facebook profile sharing one part leather-jacketed reminiscence for every two parts Candy Crush.

Maureen blamed the internet because Geoff blamed the internet. At a family get-together, hastily arranged by Maureen for Gerard's first visit home since she broke the news over Skype, her aim to convince her son that the family was not wholly dysfunctional, Geoff had said that the internet was nothing but trouble and more than once he'd thought about cutting the wires at the exchange.

Geoff had a history of web-based dramas, his daughter Jenny having discovered her eldest son Stefan masturbating to a gay porn site in the home office. Gerard had responded that that was reactionary and that people were evil before the internet and would be evil after the internet, likely when it was replaced with a sentient supercomputer.

'Geoff, we shouldn't make excuses for Derek,' he'd said, before taking a knowing bite from a Scotch egg quarter. Gerard had looked around the conservatory and the assembled family members did the smile they did at funerals and nodded their heads slowly.

CHAPTER 8

Gerard had tried running. Runners had told him running was a key tactic in the quest for mental well-being. They'd told him the tarmac created thinking space. The capacity for clarity. Gerard tried to prepare the platform for progress through technology. He'd downloaded three apps from the iTunes store which would track his movements via GPS, delivering live information on his speed and the distance travelled direct to his earphones through the voice of an android.

Internet-based research had convinced him running shoes were perhaps the only purchase worth leaving the house for, that bespoke trainers would give his workout an extra ten or twenty per cent and minimise the risk of muscle trauma from the repetition of foot hitting pavement. A Romanian sales assistant who wore a bright yellow badge proudly announcing the name 'Steve' had measured Gerard's insole and informed him he had an 'awkward gait'. Gerard had paid the inflated price for the shoes, the equivalent of a weekend stay in the spare room, wondering if he would ever be able to master such a nuanced understanding of a foreign language.

On the four occasions Gerard had laced his running shoes, his thoughts, in the main, had been about stopping running, about giving up. He had tried once to think of the deeper issues he was hoping to address, about him and Del, to ruminate on the bigger picture of being an unmarried male into his thirties in a developed economy without a trade, but a beep from MapMyRun telling him he had passed two miles had broken his concentration.

'Are the free samples free?'

'Yes, the free samples are free.'

'What's the maximum number of free samples available per customer?'

'AlePunk leaves that to the bar captain's discretion.'

The man smiled at Gerard, showing off a pair of silvery fillings in yellowing lower molars.

'In that case, can I have a taste of the Bro Brew, the Happy Hops and the Black Death?' This man was the first person Gerard had seen in an hour.

'No, no, you cannot. Free samples are not available today.' This man looked like a talker. Gerard did not want the company. Unfortunately for him, he didn't have the luxury of solitude. The service industry had an annoying habit of involving other humans.

*

'God's honest, the first time I questioned, I mean really questioned, my new-found veganism was when the hashtag #steakandblowjobday was trending worldwide and I thought to myself, hey, Edwin, what the fuck are you going to do tonight?'

'Maybe just take the blowjob?'

'They come as a package, Gerard. Like fish 'n' chips or Google and data loss. The word vegan looks uneasy hashtagged in 140 characters next to a street reference for oral sex.'

'Touché. The vegan hashtag would be something more like #veganandchakraalignmentday,' said Gerard.

'Or #veganandtalkingaboutfeelingsday.'

'Ha, maybe #veganandsymbioticelationshipday.'

'Yeah, or #veganandsubtitledfilmday.'

Gerard stopped what he was doing, which was trying to back-pour a particularly gloopy craft ale into a bottle top and said, 'Meat-eaters can enjoy foreign cinema too, Edwin.'

The opening scene of Xanadu contained an exchange between futuristic super-robots, subtitled for ease of understanding by today's audiences, and Gerard was damned if the creative vision that first came to him through a troubled night's sleep during a fractious family holiday at Center Parks Sherwood Forest was attractive only to the niche segment of non-meat and dairy eaters.

The exchange between Gerard and Edwin was not untypical of their days spent together at AlePunk. Despite this abrupt end to the conversation, Gerard had ranked his fellow bar captains in order of 'ah, fuck' when he saw their name on the rota. Edwin was currently bottom but one of the list, which made him near the top of Gerard's most tolerated day companions. The bottom spot was reserved for Lenka, a Slovak girl in her early twenties. Somewhat vindicating Del's unconcious paranoia, Gerard had considered he would break his self-imposed rule of not having sex with people with tattoos on their face with Lenka, if indeed a petite anchor behind the ear counted as a tattooed face.

Since Gerard had returned home and started topping up his lodging income at the bar, Edwin had quickly become his de facto work companion. They both needed the money. Edwin joined a long line of necessity friendships forged through the indifference and ill-discipline of a series of jobs in which Gerard took varying degrees of interest. He remembered with mock fondness 18 months of nodding agreeably and then less agreeably, mirroring the facial contortions of his desk neighbour, Ahmed, as he endured another deconstruction of his arranged marriage leaning at the fußball table at their central London recruitment agency ('little sexual chemistry, but G-man, what daal!').

He found it hard to forget swallowing half ecstasy pills with fellow data analyst Sally, a stumpy goth in her early forties, as they sat down discussing the latent beauty of Excel spreadsheets in an old man's pub off Old Compton Street while non-judgemental near-retiree Terry took his Hush Puppies to and from the bar for a stream of unlimited pale ales.

On the face of it, Edwin fitted Gerard's hip criteria. His beard gave him the look of a summertime Santa, bush out and having a good time. His nose was home to a single silver stud. His left arm was moderately muscled, liberally tattooed. As was often the way, it was Facebook which fucked him. A frape by a disgruntled ex who took a punt on his lax password security had revealed the real Edwin to his 342 friends plus Gerard.

'Fuck you Eddie you fucking fraud', she'd posted alongside a picture of Edwin in bootcut jeans sporting a short back and sides. Gerard should have known his low friend count was a tell-tale sign of a new profile. Edwin had clicked the 'I don't like this post' button and hidden the evidence from his timeline. Gerard hadn't liked to ask. He tried wherever possible to steer clear of offline confrontation. Fortunately for Gerard's curiosity, Edwin needed little prodding.

'So, really I grew this beard because Maisie—'

'Maisie?'

'Maisie. Maisie from three months ago. Maisie who I told you about.' Gerard had only known Edwin for three and a half months.

'Ah, Maisie.' Gerard did not know a Maisie.

'Yeah, so Maisie had said in her OKCupid profile that she liked guys with beards. I was a guy without a beard.'

'And?'

'And then I was a guy with a beard. I felt a bit like when the scientist asks Arnie in Total Recall how he wants the titties of the girls in his vacation. She wanted a beard. I pressed a button and had a beard.'

'You pressed a button?' Gerard was half-listening, half-scrolling through AlePunk's Instagram feed.

'Well, not technically, Gerard, no. Nature pressed a button. The whole thing took about a month. I read a lot of blogs around that time on foods that aid hair growth. My pee stank so bad I had to stop going in public places.'

'And Maisie's profile was still active?'

'Maisie was about to get a whole lot more active.'

'You, Edwin Magellis, are quite fucking something.'

'From you, Gerard Kane, I take that as the highest of all the compliments.'

*

As he punched in an order for his twelfth halloumi burger of the shift, Gerard thought suddenly about the Twitter handle of a girl he'd been briefly infatuated with before he'd met Del. He remembered it as @ artbreak_her but was quite certain he'd self-edited history by making her profile pun funnier.

He remembered evenings spent on this girl's online presence, scrolling through images of beach holidays and marshmallow macchiatos, Googling the sources of the motivational quotes and empathising with long-gone commutes from hell. This had gone on for four or five days, Gerard peering through the window of her life without her ever knowing he was there. And just like that, it was over. He browsed elsewhere. Until now, he'd forgotten she had existed. He wasn't even sure what her first name was. He wondered how the internet had changed the nature of love, the surfeit of choice making everything more transient, more transactional. But without the internet, he'd never have met Del.

Gerard took his iPhone out of his tight jean pocket and checked WhatsApp. He'd disabled the alert function from all of his social networks. Using the logic of an addict, he'd reasoned internally that this had given his searches a purpose, his phone in-hand checking for important life-changing notifications, the hunt for recognition from relative strangers rather than aimless online meandering. In the seven minutes since he'd last monitored, he'd received:

–One ❤ for a lo-fi filtered picture of his new fixed gear bike leaning against a barrel of red ale in the AlePunk cellar,

–Two invitations to play Candy Crush from Auntie Bronwen and a Pedro Jones, who Gerard struggled to remember ever knowing offline,

–A new follower: @HitlerCats,

–A repin of a post of Jesse Owens at the 1936 Munich Olympics,

–And a GoodReads notification that Ben Elphick had completed sixty-five per cent of *Trout Fishing in America*.

But nothing from Del. Her WhatsApp status said 'Last seen at 12.47'. It was 14.19. Gerard wondered if she was okay or dead. He didn't need that baggage at this stage in his life. Gerard Kane: the guy with the dead girlfriend. He was already, potentially, if someone with only a rudimentary knowledge of the investigatory tools of the internet cared enough to piece it together, Gerard Kane: the guy with the paedophile uncle. He wasn't sure his online presence would recover from Del's death. For a start, he was fairly certain he lacked the patience to administrate a Facebook tribute page.

'Pint of Becks and a packet of Scampi Fries.' Gerard's train of thought was derailed.

'For the fifth time this week, you're barred.'

'Fuck off. Fuck the lot of you. You silly cunts.'

'Sir, I'm going to have to ask you to leave the premises.'

They got a lot of this. Regulars from the old pub previously on-site coming in and demanding a cooking lager, looking as out of place against the beards and brushed steel as an alien in *Happy Days*.

'Seriously, why can't they go and be with their own people?' said Edwin. 'Under a rock somewhere without WiFi, preferably.'

'True,' Gerard replied. The old man made a sound in his throat like a Spectrum 48K loading up and hacked a brown ball of phlegm past his gravestone teeth. It spun and spun, plunging through the temperature-controlled air with the poise and velocity of an overweight bungee jumper, landing splat on a Stars Wars limited edition of the board game Risk. Both Gerard and Edwin pretended this had not happened.

*

'But anyway, seeing as how you asked, I'm over Maisie anyway.'

'I think you'll find I did not ask.'

'A technicality Gerard, a technicality. We've got four hours left to eke out of this shift. So for the record, I'm over Maisie.'

Gerard knew he was right. Today was a Monday. Hipsters did not crave craft ale on a Monday. There were only so many times he could post life-affirming social statuses from the AlePunk accounts. Edwin's hyperbole would have to do.

'That's good to know, Eddie.'

'Edwin.'

'Sorry, Eddie.'

'Edwin...ah, whatever. Maisie's done. After all of the chasing, she just didn't live up to her social feeds.'

'That's the biggest problem of our generation,' Gerard said, 'forget the deficit or immigration, as the Brexiteers would have you believe—'

'Exactly, I mean the deficit hasn't affected AlePunk's core demographic. And the best art comes from hard times,' Edwin jumped in.

'And immigrants have so much to offer. No-one born around here knows shit about making Lebanese food,' Gerard added. 'But there are no – repeat no – positives to be had from offline people not fulfilling the promises of their online presence. It's our war.'

Edwin pulled the hairs of his beard taut, making a thinking face. The old man staggered past the floor to ceiling window and stared with the intensity of the displaced at the back of Gerard's head.

'Do you ever think we overcomplicate things, G?'

'Don't call me G.'

'Don't call me Eddie.'

'Fine.'

'Fine.'

'Really though,' Edwin started to spin his silver nose stud now, 'I mean, do you think cavemen had it this difficult?'

Gerard cleared his throat and fixed some beer mats at a right angle.

'What did you do before Wikipedia?'

'I, umm...'

'Exactly. You did nothing. You knew...nothing.'

'What did you do before Tinder?'

'I, umm...'

'You held your dick in your hand. Or you were attracted to someone in a bar purely for aesthetic reasons.'

'But Tinder is—'

'Not now, Edwin.'

'And what did you do before Uber?'

'I, umm...'

'You got wet in the rain waiting for a cab. And we both know that beards, especially beards like yours, do not wear well in the rain. Never forget that technology is here to streamline and simplify our lives. It's here to take the stress out of the little things so we can focus on the bigger picture.'

'What's the bigger picture, Gerard?'

'That, my fellow bar captain, is the bit we've yet to work out.'

CHAPTER

Xanadu
by Gerard F. Kane, @G_FK, gerardfkane@gmail.com

Ren has never shed a tear in his twenty-two years of life. He's never had to. The year is 2101 and the triggers of emotional anxiety have long become extinct, their drivers superseded by better ways of living. The notion of family became outdated a generation ago, the role previously played by parents and siblings in teaching their progeny the skills necessary to survive in the world replaced by web 4.0 youtorials and round-the-clock live chat.

In Xanadu, human-on-human sex is outlawed by High Commissioner+. New humans are hatched in battery farms, the semen secreted from men summoned for the role just once in their lifespan. The last known recorded incident of a tear falling was at the 2084 Olympic Games on the International Space Station II. The last known sexual partners, Steve A and Steve B, now co-host a thirty-six-hours-a-day motivational directive network streamed direct into the eyeballs of the population.

Ren works at the Department of Distraction, coding lolrobotcat gifs and poking strangers on Facebook. In the cloud space, his colleagues Lena and Gino often joke that all that would be left after the next nuclear holocaust is Candy Crush invites. Everyone trades smiley emojis. Life is good.

One day, Ren receives an email from a man claiming to be his 'father'. It says they have the same mole on their chin. Ren has never received an email before in his life. He does not know how he received this one, but he did. (GFK – Work on this bit? Coincidence worked for Dickens?) The network told him the word 'father' was from the old world, meaning the 'impregnator of the embryo'. A red-flag light flashes above his work station, alerting his colleagues to his search history. Words from the old world are outlawed. He loses twelve connections.

Ren just can't get the email out of his head. Tales about the old world had been passed down like ghost stories. He remembers a slogan he's seen painted on a bullet train. The network told him it was called 'graffiti'. Red flag. The graffiti said 'feeling is real'. When Ren looks for it the next day it has gone and he wonders if he imagined it. His work at the department starts to go only sub-viral. He can't concentrate on his social networking. Notifications are sent to his eyeball from High Commissioner+. His work must improve or his privileges will be curtailed. His unlimited access will be stopped.

Late one night in a chatroom, Ren meets a user called Joseph. He asks about Ren's mole. They move their chat to a private room usually reserved for mind pokes. Joseph knows about the email. He says he knows Ren wants to go to the old world. Ren says he wants to know about feelings.

Joseph warns him of the danger, but Ren says if he has to create another network meme he'll turn his switch off. Joseph tells him about a secret time travel programme which the High Commissioner+ had sanctioned to bring the vintage carbonated drink Tab Clear from the old world to 2101. The High Commissioner+ has a deep appreciation of Tab Clear. Joseph says Ren could get back to the old world where he could meet his father. But Ren would have to find a secret loop in the network to wire himself there (GFK – Thinking Tron vibes, but more futuristic).

As the status goes, the High Commissioner+ knows everything, so it doesn't take him long to catch on to Ren's plan. An elaborate entrapment rouse is constructed which deactivates Ren's red-flag so he is free to search content from the old world without alerting his colleagues and bosses.

Ren goes deeper into the dark old world web, learning about historic things like coffee mornings and Friends Reunited. When he reaches the secret loop to return to the old world, the High Commissioner+ is waiting for him.

The battle to end all battles ensues and Ren wins out by posting a picture on Instagram of the High Commissioner+ without a filter. His followers plummet in seconds and he's brought to his knees. Ren travels back to the old world and is met by his father, their identical moles sweating with the intensity of the moment. Ren's smartbeing beeps and welcomes him to the old world. The 2500G switches to 3G.

The closing shot focuses on a bead of moisture rolling down Ren's cheek, ambiguous in its origin.

CHAPTER 10

'Do you have any butter to go with the toast, Gerard?' The body the clipped Nordic voice came from was a waterproofed bratwurst sandwiched in the jaws of an oversized American-style fridge. Ice-blue eyes analysed the empty shelves while the head sat steady.

'We've got margarine,' said Gerard, the inflection in his tone rising as he scrolled through his phone, sat cross-legged on the kitchen bench.

'I do not eat anything that has been processed by machines. You should know this Gerard. I am very clear about it on my profile.' Del looked at Gerard in complicity. He missed or ignored her gaze.

'Stina, hey, I'm sorry,' Gerard said, leaving a tweet half-written.

'Of course I know that from your profile. We don't let just anyone stay here.' He laughed and looked to Del for support unsuccessfully. She'd returned to Instagram, her grey eyes scanning stage-managed images of celebrity vloggers and vegan cakes.

'There's a really, really cool deli just a short hop away and they make the best butter you'll ever have in your life. The salt's made by a colony of monks up on this mystical island called Ynys Môn. That's the Welsh for it anyway. It means the Isle of Magic. The monks haven't spoken a word to anyone since 1986 or something.' Stina looked at him with distrust. 'Apart from the odd thing about butter. Now, that stuff spread all over this artisan bread they have in the deli, with, like, polenta and pumpkin and all other things in it, is just the raddest.'

Gerard was unsure how bread could be rad but he had a guest review to think of and he'd determined the key to good hospitality was clean towels and contemporary hyperbole.

'There is a place in Denmark like that. A place where nobody uses the internet. And anyway, I already have the bread.' Stina had dislodged herself from the fridge and now faced towards Gerard. In her sturdy walking boots, she stood as tall as her five foot eleven host. Her taut body said more about her lifestyle than her age, which Gerard had hypothesised was older than thirty-five but younger than forty-five. Del had agreed, partly because she wasn't listening.

In the two weeks and four days since Del had confirmed her continuing existence, with a WhatsApp to Gerard, their relationship had experienced somewhat of a renaissance. Gerard had convinced himself that the by-product of his Excellent Moment internalisation had been the creation of a more positive environment in which their relationship could flourish.

In reality, the good vibes emanated from some rather more tactical happenings instigated by Del. Following his post-pub online connection with a number of Del's colleagues, Gerard had paid special attention to their various profiles in a vain attempt for some clue to Del's real intentions for their relationship, half expecting to spot a picture of her just a little too close to Emyr, leaning suggestively over an air hockey table or a sushi boat. He'd imagined Isosceles' research team using his behaviour as confirmation of an inherent consumer need for a gamification app for suspicious spouses.

He hated that sharing this creative idea with Del would give his game up and had instead half-completed the application form for Dragons' Den on BBC Two's website, but stalled on the question 'Do you have a business plan?'

What Gerard's snooping did find was that Carla's Instagram feed featured regular use of #experientialmarketer and #lovemyjob to hashtag a series of situations – from rollercoasters to red carpets – that three out of four times led to a 'Ur job rules' or equivalent comment, often from students in Beijing. Emyr seemed to post mainly about Formula One and the paleo diet, both of which Gerard felt were just the right side of non-threatening, at least for now. He was too nervous to follow Hiro.

Del had come to see Gerard at Alepunk an hour before the end of his shift the night he had wondered if she was offline or dead.

'You look surprised to see me?' she'd said.

'I am surprised to see you.'

'It's a nice surprise, I hope.'

'It's a surprise, which as the name suggests is surprising. Surprising but—' he paused, '—potentially nice.'

'Why is it surprising? I'm your girlfriend, doofus.' Girlfriend surprises had a history of meaning help me or heartbreak.

'We have instant messaging now, Del. People don't just drop in. It's not how our generation does things.' Del held onto the ale pumps, planted her Converse and let her body fall towards the floor, arching her back. She hadn't planned on this response but was determined to get to the real news.

'Well,' she said, bouncing back and forth on her heels, 'I thought I'd surprise you.'

'Mission accomplished,' Gerard said, turning his attention to a small bowl of pretzels.

'Don't be such a fun sponge, Gerard.'

'You are a fun sponge,' said Edwin, emerging from the servery, a giant beer-battered onion ring spinning on his thumb.

'Alright Banquo's ghost, you can fuck off,' Gerard said.

'Charming,' said Del, 'I'm here, if you were ever going to ask, to tell you I just got made,' she cleared her throat, 'Acting Head of Buzz Activation. Frank handed his notice in and Hiro did it right in front of the whole team. The whole team!' She had that happiness rarely seen in fully-grown adults.

'And I'm here, shitbreak,' said Edwin, 'to tell you the only remaining duty of your shift is to get the hell out of here and take your girl off to cel-e-brate.'

And since that moment, celebrate they had. Del's improving mood and pay packet had led to fringe benefits including but not exclusive of one south Indian street food thali, three bottles of Pinot Noir, a round of crazy golf, a pair of tickets to the Welsh National Opera's reimagining of *Hansel and Gretel*, two blowjobs and an upgrade to Spotify Premium.

But today, it was all on the rack again.

Del hated it when Gerard's hosting hit their couple time. It was one of her top five problems with their relationship, ranking just above Gerard's reluctance to introduce her to his family. He'd found a hack to change the settings of his proxy server to kid Netflix into thinking he was in North America so Del could watch *Together*, a film set in a commune on the outskirts of Stockholm. Gerard's attempt at propaganda had been moderately successful until a character said that doing the dishes was bourgeois and Del told him to turn the channel over. Gerard didn't think this was the appropriate moment to tell her that Netflix wasn't a channel, as such. When Gerard had probed as to why Del hadn't identified with the messages of the movie, she had replied that she was all for socialism until she stood on someone else's pubic hair in the shower.

Gerard's kitchen had the vibe of a real-life Roy Liechtenstein. The previous owner, a serious-faced spinster who did something administrative at the National Theatre Wales, had appointed the long, wide room with the staples of Americana. Del had hypothesised the red sheen of the cupboards would have been popular with the Wall Street set in 1986, complemented as they were by the black and white square tiles of the floor.

Gerard had turned the small breakfast bar into an information hub on the city region, piles of free maps, transport timetables and local entertainment guides he'd occasionally taken pictures for neatly stacked at right angles against the edge. In a reasonably successful attempt to recreate the feel of the diner from *Twin Peaks*, Gerard had installed a red leatherette booth and covered the Formica table top with old gig tickets and Polaroids of nearby castles, club nights and cool kids, the faded photo filter chosen not for likes but by technology's limits. He'd designed cards saying 'Gerard's Place' and created a hashtag so guests could share pictures of their experience. Stina didn't currently look like she'd be joining this particular online community.

'So if you're not going to hit the deli, what are your plans for today?' Gerard stopped himself attempting to shorten Stina to Steen, an affectation of the local dialect which he decided would not help the delicacy of the current situation.

'Oh, after I eat this dry bread, I'll probably go online and catch up on news back at home.' Gerard's face dropped. 'It is fine, Gerard. It is a joke. The dry bread is fine. You Wales people can be so serious.' Stina leaned against the breakfast bar and took a slurp from a mug of coffee. Gerard caught Del's eye and attempted to say that things weren't so bad and, also, help me out here.

'What's the hot news at home likely to be then?' Del asked. 'Probably something about your anorexic queen, the one who married her personal trainer, I'm guessing?' Del was well-versed on European royal families. Her knowledge had proved useful to Gerard in more than one pub quiz scenario. Its current application seemed unhelpful.

'You are nearly right, Del. The one you speak of is Princess Victoria of Sweden. Same same but different, as you say.' Stina paused and took a visceral bite from the bread, her right cheek filling up like a birthday balloon.

'Our queen is Margrethe II. She is a very accomplished painter but also a chain smoker. You cannot have it all, perhaps.'

'Beats the British queen,' said Gerard, 'I'm not sure she's accomplished at anything.'

'Oh, I believe she is,' said Stina.

'Like keeping a straight face at a funeral,' Del said, 'she's a boss at that.'

'That is a very important part of monarchy,' Stina said, snorting, before leaning back and shaking herself down.

'Our queen's paintings were actually used in the Danish edition of The Lord of the Rings books. She used to write letters back and forth with Tolkien.'

'Wow. Imagine that,' said Del. Gerard was unsure if her wonder was for the fact that people used to write letters. Either way, at least she was engaging positively. He stepped over to the booth, picked up his smartphone and sent Del a WhatsApp. Stina continued to chew her bread.

'Let's give her the tour?'

Del replied, instantly. A Mona Lisa emoji.

'Come on,' Gerard typed, 'potential brand advocate $$$?'

Del read the message, put her phone down and mouthed 'okay' through gritted teeth.

'Hey, Stina, once you've checked your profiles, how do you feel about coming on a city tour with us? We've compiled an insider guide to the area for our best guests. That's you, Stina. And today, we're offering a very special tour guide service too.'

'Gerard,' Stina said, tongueing some bread free from her front teeth, 'I would like that very, very much.'

Stina had booked Gerard's place for a fortnight, using the attic room as a HQ to follow in the footsteps of her great-grandfather, a ship's cook who had lost his sea legs in Cardiff after falling in love with the sixteen-year-old daughter of a Yemeni sailor.

'That's so Tiger Bay,' said Gerard.

'I don't know what you mean,' said Stina, sat on a motionless carriage at the central train station.

'Your story. It's so Tiger Bay. That's what they used to call the docks in Cardiff. They were like some kind of Futuretopia up until the middle of the last century. People of all colours and creeds coming together and making love not war way before racism was even a thing.'

'Racism's always been a thing, Gerard,' said Del. She was not a good traveller.

'Yeah, sure, of course, but there weren't any bad vibes about immigrants taking their jobs or anything. Everyone was an immigrant. Cardiff was an immigrant city.' Del rolled her eyes at Gerard's naivety as a teenage ticket collector asked the three of them for their fares.

'People settled their differences in the dancehall or over a dice game,' Gerard added.

'My research tells me that Tiger Bay was a very dangerous place,' said Stina.

'The history books are full of danger,' said Del, 'I shudder to think what they'll make of the start of the twenty-first century in the future.' The three of them made solemn faces, the kind of face you make when a hearse passes by but you can't quite read the message in the flowers.

'Space kids learning about shoe-bombers and Syria. When will we learn?' said Gerard.

'Space kids?' asked Stina.

'Space kids,' Gerard repeated. 'Stephen Hawking said the only future for mankind is to colonise other planets before we blow this one up. And he should know.' Gerard knew scrolling Buzzfeed when sat on the toilet was an appropriate use of time.

The train was still stationary.

'Okay, well the future will be what the future will be, but today I'm interested in learning about the past,' Stina said, smiling a little too hard. Del wondered if the next few hours would call for the emotional fortitude required during an episode of a celebrity genealogy show. More than once she'd found herself crying uncontrollably as a character actor best known for the Guy Ritchie movie no-one watched returned to the Scottish highlands to discover his great-great-great-grandmother had died during childbirth.

As the train finally started the short slide towards what had overwritten Tiger Bay, Gerard lost himself in the landscape. Kanes had lived in Cardiff for generations. Cities changed, but there were always remainders. Outside the glass he scrutinised the old, new and in between: wasteland where the real work used to happen, cubist university buildings where you could study video game design, high-rise student apartments with communal steam rooms, duplex blocks for online guests, 100 foot hotels for stag parties, office blocks filled with humans in headsets, a former munitions factory where Nanna Gwen had worked during the war, now a studio space for creatives; the manifold ways the city made its money in the year of 2000-and-something would have been space age to Gerard's forefathers, the towers of the brewery reaching to the sky for salvation among the only constants.

In light of this awareness he'd been spending more and more time with Nanna Judy, recording her stories. It hit him that the only other human being to share the same genetic make-up as him was Stephanie. Fifty per cent Kane, fifty per cent Davies. The rest of his relatives were variations on the theme. He calculated that even his mother and father were only half the same as him, a little uncertain on the maths.

He hadn't spoken to Stephanie since a Facebook exchange over a week ago, which had started with a query over the exact date of their mum and Geoff's anniversary but ended abruptly when Stephanie had chastised him for not knowing (it had been months previous, so why was Gerard asking now at II.I9 p.m. on a Friday, which also happened to be pay day party night for Stephanie).

His dad's brother, Uncle David, had spent considerable time, which he had, and considerable money, which he was infamous in the family for protesting he didn't, researching the Kane line. Gerard had half-listened before, but it now felt vital to his present, vital to his future.

When Geoff had got wind of the venture, in keeping with his hard-line view of the internet, he was convinced the whole thing was a pyramid scheme and that the stories had been fabricated, likely by the Chinese ('sinister people').

Gerard's great-great-great-great-great grandfather, Albert Kane, had been a blacksmith in a Cynon Valley town called Aberdare, his primary trade coming from making horseshoes sold in bulk for the ponies used in the nearby pit. Gerard thought of him like a historical Kwik Fit. It was good, honest work. He wondered what Albert would have made of Airbnb and craft ale.

Albert's son, Albert Junior, had moved the twenty miles into Cardiff, then a small town about to go through a Sim City-style boom. Gerard had imagined the uprooting was triggered through a falling out between the two over a suede waistcoat Albert Senior had been certain the residents of Aberdare just weren't ready for, but Albert Junior had worn on market day regardless. Despite his elevation to style martyr from the great-great-great grandson he never knew, the record of Albert Junior hinted at no such idiosyncrasies. His occupation was listed as shopkeeper. Gerard had since daydreamed about the shop, if it had been vintage and what vintage even meant back then.

Albert hadn't married until late in life, which Gerard had suspected both explained the suede waistcoat and solved a tactical staffing need at the boutique. His wife, Mair, had dropped two children, twins by the names of David and Angharad.

Angharad had been outlived by David, another shopkeeper who

had married an Irish girl by the name of Amelia Brady. Their son, David Junior, had continued the line of shopkeepers, as had his son, Daniel. Gerard had hypothesised he'd also been a bare-knuckle fighter, but not a very good one, because after Granddad Keith had a few pints, the story went that Daniel invariably had a broken nose or a black eye. His brother Tomos had moved back to the Valleys three or four generations after Albert Junior had left. He'd fallen in love with a sixteen-year-old girl from Mountain Ash, in the city for a Charleston night. Tomos had been politicised by the 1926 General Strike, and after surviving two hunger strikes had later died in the Spanish Civil War – the most hipster of all armed conflicts, Gerard had decided. Tomos Kane was by far the coolest Kane yet.

Daniel had sired Granddad Keith, who'd turned his back on his family's predilection for retail by getting his hands dirty in the steelworks. Like many Welshmen of his era, he was most comfortable when on a committee. Gerard remembered Granddad Keith as a man of many blazers. He'd been married before meeting Nanna Gwen. The report didn't say much about his first wife, other than that she had been killed in a road accident in Athens. Six months before he'd died of his third heart attack, after his fourth pint before midday one Good Friday in one of the blurry, non-descript early 2000s, Gerard had asked why she'd been in Greece when she died. He got an answer about the 3.15 at Cheltenham. Granddad Keith had been pretending not to hear him long before Del had made it her thing.

Montague Kane was born in 1968 in Cardiff. The story went that Granddad Keith had lost a bet to an Irish foreman by the name of O'Shaughnessy over a Five Nations rugby tie between their respective Celtic nations. When Gerard thought about this likely fabricated version of events, he pictured his grandfather as Richard Burton in *Where Eagles Dare* and he knew this was a leap of faith too far.

Granddad Keith was, if nothing else, a man of his word, and at the victor's behest his imminent son was called Montague, a name that sounded posh or English or both, which meant that it was a name that would get your ears boxed in Wales.

As he fled from another pack of bullies, Montague Kane worried what it said about the seriousness with which his father took his impending arrival that he couldn't have bet the Irishman a pint of beer or a pack of cigarettes like any other sane steelworker. If the young Montague came home with a cut lip or black eye, Keith would march him to the middle room, open the dresser and take out Johnny Cash at San Quentin. He'd make his son sit and listen to 'A Boy Named Sue' twice while staring at him intently straight in the darks of his eyes. The Kanes remained silent, still, not a flinch, even when Johnny screamed the finale.

Montague's existence after the needle stopped was satisfactory but short. He moved to London aged eighteen to study economics, his choice of course borne out of a desire to earn as much money as possible in order to get as far away from Granddad Keith as he could.

In what he later saw as an early precursor of globalisation, Montague's capitalist fire was soon distinguished by the realisation his Chinese classmates were textbooks ahead of him in their understanding of macro-economic theory. This was the first time he had been in the presence of minority ethnic people outside of a hospitality environment. A virgin at the time, Montague had spent a succession of early tutorials fantasising a romanticised future of impeccably mannered mixed-race children and Hong Kong holiday homes with any one of the prodigies sat in the front row of the lecture theatre.

His childhood had provided Montague with little of what his head of year at comprehensive school had described as 'gumption'. But what he did possess was an acute ability to pinpoint the exact moment when a battle was about to be lost, coupled with the wherewithal to hang on in there regardless. Gerard's mum Maureen had later crystallised this rather unfairly to a marriage counsellor as 'a total lack of self-respect'.

Perhaps if blessed with the abundance of knowledge accessible by his son's thumbs, Montague would have plucked up the courage to Google Translate a note and drop it on the desk of one of his female peers:

嗨，我真的很喜歡你的凱恩斯主義政策的看法。我真的很想過壽司和你談談這件事。此致，蒙塔古

Hi, I really like your view on Keynesian policy. I'd really like to talk to you about it over sushi. Yours, Montague.

But Montague was not that blessed. Instead, he spent most of his time outside of lectures struggling over Marxian economics in the university's library on Portugal Street or blending in seamlessly with the homeless people of Lincoln's Inn Fields. He'd met Maureen on Christmas Eve 1986 at a fundraising social for the people of Chernobyl. She'd taken his long silences as an unfortunate indication of his cool character.

Montague lost his virginity in the front seat of Granddad Keith's Vauxhall Viva. Seven months later, Nanna Gwen had answered the doorbell to Nanna Judy, then just Judy, and Maureen, bump just visible. Montague suspended his studies and moved home the next day.

He'd picked up enough in his time at university to secure a position as a junior bookkeeper at a cigar factory in the Grangetown area of the city. He worried in the early hours of the morning that he made a living counting the profits on products responsible for the deaths of millions.

Many of the significant global events of the 1980s – Live Aid, the 100-metre dash at the 1988 Seoul Olympic Games, the fall of the Berlin Wall – were hampered for Montague by a rabid tiredness brought on by a recurring dream where a cigar rolled in his factory sparked a military junta in a Latin American state he could never remember the name of when he woke up. At the age of thirty-one, fourteen minutes into a routine company medical, the doctor told Montague that he had contracted bowel cancer. He said it was 'the worry'. At the funeral, the priest had claimed it was a short disease, but those who knew Montague Kane knew it had begun the minute he was born.

And then there was Gerard. Thirty-one years old. Entrepreneur. Artist in the making, at least, if you counted a half-written screenplay saved in the cloud and a few hours spent filming family archives. He had no others significant enough to register on the record. Historians didn't account for Facebook official. Gerard was certain genealogists needed to modernise or die.

He had clicked a tweet that said 'The Internet Will Wipe Out History', which claimed that advances in technology would mean the entire digital record of the early part of the twenty-first century would be wiped out in the medium-term. Gazillions of gigabytes, the daily lives of living, breathing, neurotic millennials lost forever like an inconsequential dramady recorded on Betamax. Since that discovery, Gerard found it harder than ever to switch off and get to sleep at night.

The train screeched to a standstill at Cardiff's newest extent.

'We've made it.'

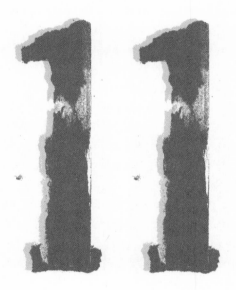

CHAPTER 11

Gerard and Del were sat either side of Stina on a wooden pew, looking through the window at a sailboat bobbing back and forth in the water outside. The hard back of the bench meant none of the three were comfortable, but Gerard had insisted they all face outwards to take the view in. A headland jutted out into the sea like a piece of Wales trying to reach out and greet the rest of the world. Del wondered if the people in the houses she could see were having a better day than she was.

'So, I have an Americano, a banana milkshake and a peppermint tea.' A middle-aged black man arrived at the table balancing a tray on his right hand. He didn't seem phased by the seating arrangement. Gerard was surprised, if only mildly, at the waiter. Baristas in this town were generally in their late teens to early twenties and Eastern European.

'And I've got some Welsh cakes here...'

'Now you're talking,' said Stina. She seemed to welcome the presence of the new person.

'Now that's not a Cardiff accent. Let me guess. Stockholm?'

'How dare you!' She grinned widely. 'I'm joking. It's fine. I'm from Copenhagen.'

'Ah, we have a great Dane in our midst,' said the man. His badge said his name was Tony. He lowered the tray and distributed the drinks according to the order.

'Well, my name is Tony and it's a pleasure to welcome you to the Norwegian Church. We haven't had a Dane in here for three weeks. Lovely people, you are. If you liked, I could tell you about the history of this place?' Tony took a cursory look around the quiet room and sat down before anyone could say otherwise, clearing his throat with a little rattle.

Gerard hypothesised he'd smoked roll-up cigarettes from the age of twelve until eighteen months ago, when he'd tried a work colleague's e-cigarette on a night out and hadn't looked back since. There was a mild smell of coconut vape juice in the air. It was not unpleasant. Stina poured hot water on her tea bag in readiness.

'Well, further back than even I can remember, Cardiff was the coal capital of the world. If we were sat where we are now 150 years ago, we'd have been submerged in the waters of one of the greatest sea ports anywhere on earth. Know what I mean? And where you had a sea port, what did you have?' Tony looked at the three strangers sat opposite him as if they were Dragons taking in the best pitch in eight seasons, as if Gerard was about to trade petty insults with Del for a seventeen per cent stake in the answer to his question. Del felt the tone made the question sound rhetorical but she didn't know the response. Stina played the good tourist, eager for knowledge she'd later forget or mix up with another dock like Liverpool or Boston.

'Scandinavians! That's what you had!' Everyone's expression said 'of course', apart from Del, who had taken to collecting milkshake in her straw, dripping it back into the glass like Jackson Pollock filling a grave.

'Great seafarers, your forefathers were. Now, Norwegian ships used to bring the Scandinavian timber over to be used as pit props in the mines, like. And on the return leg, they'd fill up with the old black gold.'

Tony paused and looked Stina right in the eyes. Gerard tried but failed to break his gaze.

'Now, this old place was a home from home for the sailors, full of newspapers from back home, friendly faces, letter writing facilities and what have you. They used to throw all kinds of dos here – socials, you know. Speak a bit of the old mother tongue if you know what I mean.' Tony motioned to pick up a glass but realised he was bringing the drinks, not drinking them.

'We was properly busy during the Second World War. Now the right-minded Norwegian fellas, well they didn't want to go back home with Adolf and his cronies in charge, so they used this place more than ever. Aye, like Piccadilly Circus it was here then.' Stina looked to Gerard. He mouthed the word 'busy' to her, while wondering how Tony, who looked to be in his fifties, had such a vivid recollection of all of this.

'And like that, it was all gone, the coal, the mines, the Scandinavians. Just like that.' Tony was staring past them now, into the middle distance. The rate at which things vanished or were replaced had only accelerated since, Gerard thought. A queue was forming at the till, Tony's colleague, a tall, thin, red-haired girl, struggling and seething at his lack of participation. She made up her mind that she would score him poorly in the teamwork section of his upcoming 360 degree appraisal. This hadn't been the first time.

*

Gerard, Del and Stina stood uncomfortably close in the lift to the ground floor of the Norwegian Church. Stina didn't do the thing British people did in such situations, the intense interest in the ceiling or the space beyond beings. She looked Gerard and Del back and forth in the eye, smiling encouragingly. A sea shanty played over tinny speakers.

'I like this,' she said.

Gerard took out his phone, brushing his wrist against the fabric of Del's dress. The dress's pattern was made up of hundreds and hundreds of cats playing miniature violins. It felt cold on Gerard's arm. He reached his phone up into one of the few pockets of air and pressed his finger on the screen. It was apparent what he was doing. A circle swept towards a whole as the device listened, its trademarked algorithm searching a database stored on a server 2,000 miles away from the cramped lift for a match in the time-frequency graph of the music. Anticipation filled the small space. The phone pinged.

'Sorry! We couldn't find a match, Shazam can not identify singing or humming,' Gerard said.

'Maybe the internet doesn't know everything,' Stina said.

The lift doors opened to reveal a Somalian man in a wheelchair crying uncontrollably.

The three walked along the manmade waterfront, the white wood of the Norwegian Church behind them. The air was crisp. The sun reflected off the water into Gerard's eyes but he couldn't make out the images in the ripples. He took his RayBans out of the inside pocket of his bomber jacket and hung the arms over his ears. Gerard's last visit to the Bay had been on a location hunt for Xanadu. He'd found a disused stone cottage on the side of the water which he thought would be ideal for Ren's first meeting with his father, a century rewound from life in the Department of Distraction. The building now had a sign saying: 'To Let – Retail/Cafe Unit.' Gerard told himself he really needed to finish his film treatment before even entertaining the idea of running a small plates informal dining experience.

'I don't think we'd have done it,' he said, 'the Welsh, I mean.'

'Done what?' said Del. The wind collected under the hem of her dress, blowing the cats and violins of its pattern skywards. She put them back in their place, carefully, expertly.

'Sailed all this way, like the Scandinavians did.' Gerard looked across the water and CGI-ed a thousand longboats on the horizon. Stina listened and tried not to knock over a group of excitable French school children, their backpacks bouncing energetically towards the Doctor Who Experience, a blue building like the back of a scorpion sitting on the water's edge just past the church dedicated to the TV show.

'Erm, what about Patagonia?' Del said.

'Patagonia?' asked Stina.

'Yes, Patagonia. Hundreds of Welsh people got so pissed off with the English that they got on a boat and sailed all the way to Argentina. They still speak Welsh there to this day.'

'I did not know this information,' said Stina.

'There's always an exception to the rule,' said Gerard, 'anyway, why did the Vikings leave home? Was it because there wasn't much to do in Scandinavia? I mean, I've seen *Wallander*. It's pretty basic.'

Stina was unsure if this was British humour.

'No, Gerard. This is a funny joke, I think. People don't just leave because home is boring. Leaving home can be more spiritual than just reacting to your surroundings, I think. I didn't leave because I was tired of my friends or the Danish landscape. I actually miss it a little bit, my home.'

'Hey, come on now. You're on holiday. You're staying at G's place.

Let the good times roll.'

'Vikings actually didn't rape and pillage. They've had a…how do you say? A bad press.' Stina did a belly laugh Gerard hadn't seen in non-emoji form for years.

'And anyway, the Norwegians who used that church weren't Vikings. Not every Scandi who gets on a boat has a beard and horned helmet.'

'Ah, I see,' said Gerard, elongating the vowel. 'The Vikings should hire Del to do a social media campaign to improve their image. She's the new acting head of buzz activation at one of the nation's most recommended digital agencies.'

'Yeah, the first tweet's always free,' said Del.

Stina either didn't understand or ignored this.

'My grandfather, for one example, he left home because he wanted to provide for his mother and father. His father had been injured in the leg when a crate of herrings fell on him from a great height. He had been a sailor himself but he was no use to the captain with one leg. And then my grandfather, he sailed here and he fell in love. I can see how. It is a very romantic place.' Del looked out to sea.

Gerard looked at her and tried to see beyond her eyes, to the parts that made her Del, to what he'd fallen in love with and what fell in love with him. He remembered when their being together created its own energy. Del looked back at him and smiled. Gerard sensed sympathy, but he didn't know who for. He was sick of the second guess.

'That's beautiful,' said Stina, walking away. Gerard hung back and tried to grab Del's hand with his, but she moved out of his reach. The slate steps and metal lines of the Welsh parliament building appeared on their right.

Stina stumbled over the inscription on the building. '*Cynulliad Cenedlaethol Cymru* – National Assembly for Wales. I feel like I am in the Lord of the Rings,' she said. 'Can you speak Welsh?'

'I'm a pretty fluent understander, but Del is the linguist in our relationship,' said Gerard. Del smiled sarcastically.

'*Diolch*, Gerard. That means thanks. *Tak*. Lesson two, same time tomorrow.'

'Diloch, Del,' said Stina, 'diloch very much.' Stina had told Gerard and Del that she worked as a producer on a Danish news programme called 'Bag om Borgen' for the DR1 station. Gerard had translated this, discovering it meant 'Behind the Castle'. He now realised that rather than listening to anything she'd said about her work, he'd instead gone into tour guide mode, explaining that there were three castles within twenty minutes of his cottage and she really should take the time to see them all in her fortnight.

On Stina's first morning, Gerard had been mild-to-medium hungover following an after-hours session at AlePunk. Stina had been sitting in the breakfast booth talking to a distracted looking puppy. A deep, nasal voice emanated from her Macbook speakers.

It was only later, following frantic Googling and a subsequent conversation with Stina, that Gerard confirmed that Danish dogs did not have the power of language and that the app had not yet been created which translated their barks and whimpers into speech. Instead, Stina's golden retriever, Jesper, was staying with a cousin. They'd Skyped three times in two days. Her cousin had recently undergone facial reconstruction surgery to correct a breathing difficulty and remained off-screen. Del had speculated that it'd be at least ten to twelve weeks before she could take a selfie again, unless she was a case study for an appropriately hashtagged awareness campaign.

'Look over there,' said Stina. 'Fairground horses. I haven't been on those since I was a very small child at Tivoli Gardens. Can we, Gerard?'

'Sure.'

'Del?'

'Sure.'

As the garish gold and pink manes of the plastic horses bobbed up and down, Gerard closed his eyes and visualised the waves of a chemically enhanced sea washing in and out on the shore of a dystopian planet. This was his muse for the Krishna consciousness. His whale music. His counting sheep. But as he span slowly around the waterfront, blocking out the bassy strains of a Europop tune playing nearby, the residue of his relationship with Del disrupted the calm of his special place. They were alone, together.

The ride clunked to a halt. Gerard's phone vibrated. It was a call. He couldn't remember his last. To his right, Del and Stina were laughing and hanging off their horses.

'Gerard, it's me....' Stephanie's voice struggled against the tinny dance music.

'...have you spoke to Mum? It's Nanna Judy...she's dead.'

CHAPTER

'Sandwich, love?'

'Del's a vegan, Mum.'

'Oh is she, love? Do they not do sandwiches?' Maureen smiled her way through the confusion. She was hearing the word vegan from the young people in the office with increasing frequency. She couldn't remember if vegans couldn't eat fish or couldn't eat dairy or if that was coeliacs or pescetarians or the gluten intolerant. Greg in her office was gluten intolerant. He had drunk vodka and soda at the Christmas meal and thrown up over her Secret Santa before the cheese board had arrived at the table.

Her office was the headquarters of a small charity called Go!Kids, which organised once-in-a-lifetime experiences for sick and dying children. She enjoyed the work. After two glasses of wine, she regularly told new acquaintances she felt like she was 'giving back'. After three glasses of wine, she regularly gave them a detailed picture of the tense turn of events following the birth of the twins, leaning in a little too close for most new people at the moment Gerard's umbilical cord was finally unwrapped from Stephanie's smurf-blue throat. Her line manager, Carl, had been very good about the death of her mother. She had been granted today off without having to cash in any hours from her flexi-time account.

'I'll stick to the crisps,' Del smiled back. She looked around the room. Around twenty-five people, most of whom Del calculated were at least forty-five or over, had congregated in small clusters around a mid-sized function room in the upstairs of a pub. Nanna Judy had never visited the pub. In fact, the only pub she had visited this millennium had been for the gathering after Grampy Joe's funeral. She had been disorientated by the post-smoking ban aroma of pork pies and flatulence.

Del noticed that no-one else in the room was smiling.

Today was the first time Del had met anyone in Gerard's family in the flesh, although she had frequently visited their Facebook profiles. She was friends with Auntie Bronwen and hadn't found this strange until she'd met her in person today and felt awkward when she'd mentioned listening repeatedly to a music video Del had posted last week. Del sometimes forgot that everyone she accepted as a friend could see the content she shared and not just the people she was trying to impress.

She had naturally wondered if the reason she hadn't met any of Gerard's family until circumstances conspired over the past week was because he'd been unsure about their relationship. When she'd hinted hard at this he'd said he 'just wanted to keep the honeymoon period alive'. She had been sure about their relationship. Had been sure.

Gerard had seemed so vital, though it had taken a time for Del to reach that level of dependency. She came to the conclusion that love at first sight only existed on Netflix or in the 1970s. Gerard's profile had passed her initial pre-requisites: his jaw sharp, his mousy hair both shaved and swept, as was the fashion. He was handsome enough, if a little hipster, although Del was aware it took one to know one. His likes included films and bands she'd never heard of, a cursory run by tastemaker websites confirming the choices as culturally sound.

Their messaging had been a welcome distraction from a difficult branding project at Isosceles. It soon became all-consuming. Del had wondered if in the future all the human soul would need was a perceptive robot with a passable profile picture. But a meeting had been inevitable. She'd delayed, a mix of cod-dating-psychology and ten bad experiences too many. She gave in after four days. ninety-six hours is a long time when the instant messaging app beeps non-stop.

Her internet dating history (Del and Gerard had discussed at length whether the internet prefix was still relevant. 'It's just dating now,' they'd agreed) had been mixed at best. At least ninety-five per cent of the messages she received were sexually aggressive, if not by the first engagement then most definitely by the third. The remainder were an online Star Wars bar of freaks, fantasists, time wasters and try-hards. In the moment, Gerard's schtick hadn't seemed pre-meditated, but he'd later admitted, after one AlePunk too many, that he'd picked up she was a fan of the TV series *Lost* from stalking her profile. His actual assessment, rather than the one he'd painted over those early messages, was that the show was 'pretty good, before the writers ran out of ideas'.

Del had given Gerard the silent treatment for the next forty-eight hours before accepting that this was the digital age and that she'd been guilty of the same technique more than twice.

Their first date had been at an internet-scouted Mexican cantina. She'd checked its reviews before agreeing to meet. Del couldn't cope with bad chemistry and average tacos, not after her recent romantic mistakes. Most recently there had been the French boy, Loic, who had seemed cooler and hotter and more interesting than he'd turned out to be, she'd later admitted, wholly because of his accent. Del had ended it after date four had climaxed in some culturally misaligned sex, his Gallic adventure and her Welsh unwillingness to accept a stubby thumb in the anus. It was 'for the best', her housemate Meg had said. 'Who wanted a daughter with hairy armpits anyway?' Del was unsure if Meg was joking. Meg had previous borderline racist form. She'd asked Del about Hiro, her boss at Isosceles, 'What kind of oriental is he?'

'He's Japanese, and oriental is not cool. He's not a rug,' she'd answered, before slamming her door. She'd figured her patience had the capacity for a maximum twelve more months of shared accommodation before she massacred Meg with a cannonball made of shared soya milk, tampon string and left-on energy-saving light bulbs.

Before Loic there had been Adam. Online he was a 'thinker/doer/ DJ', offline a complete and utter idiot. They'd 'hung out', not dated, for two months before Del decided that not every Sunday morning in bed should not start with a selfie.

And then there had been Alexander. Fucking Alexander. Del had deleted Alexander. Del had deleted Alexander's friends. Del had deleted the friends of Alexander's friends. Del did not talk about Alexander. Because of Gerard, Del did not think of Alexander. Meg had forbidden her. She had forbidden herself. Alexander was in a box with her bullying at girl scouts, the lesbian thoughts of her early twenties and her intense fear of pregnant women. The box was now creaking open.

The service had been nice, everyone had agreed. Del felt a strange sense of detachment she assumed was shared only by the priest, the undertakers, the altar boys – all the people who'd never met Judy when blood coursed through her veins. Today was Del's first experience of a Catholic church. She was disappointed; it was a lot less sexual than in the Scorsese films. She'd shared Gerard's car to the crematorium with Stephanie, her boyfriend Al and a great-uncle she didn't catch the name of. It was the first time she'd sat in the car's back seat. Conversation had been limited to logistical matters. Stephanie and Al had arrived the night before, their journey had been 'fine, yeah, fine' before they'd crashed out in Gerard's old room. It was bigger than Stephanie's and redecorated in a neutral tone. The great-uncle was bearing up after a hip operation, 'at his age, that was all anyone could ask for.' Everyone had laughed an easy, welcome, funeral laugh.

The journey to the pub had mainly concerned itself with Stephanie cursing Cardiff's 4G capability, Del becoming aware this morning had been the longest she'd gone without checking a social network while awake since around 2008.

Al had said little. His pencil-thin moustache did all the talking. From the way Geoff had play punched him on the shoulder and the uncomfortably long squeeze Maureen had put on his skin-tight shoulders, Del assessed that he was two or three levels ahead in the family assimilation. She was currently unsure if she wanted to join him on the journey. She remembered a feeling that her and Gerard had once got each other, really got each other, but now it was like they were playing Scrabble in different languages.

After the first date, Del had left Gerard outside the cantina with two lips on his cheek and a vague half-promise of a round two. Two days later she'd received a message. There was no text, just a URL link. She'd been reticent to click, fully expecting to be taken to an explicit site on the dark web. Dating in the modern age had left its scars, but bored fingers on the bus home from work damned the consequences.

Del had been pleasantly surprised to open a flirt-by-numbers playlist. Halfway home, she found herself day-dreaming of breakfast in an art nouveau house somewhere in southern California, brought to her bed by the shape of a man she hadn't recognised. She'd checked Gerard's profile immediately and had smiled when she'd seen his face, filtered as it was from the imperfections of reality. Caught up in the chords, Del sent Gerard a provocative message she'd soon realised was leading him somewhere she wasn't sure she'd wanted to go. That weekend, Gerard invited her to a gig of a band responsible for one of the only songs on the mix she'd found totally unlistenable.

Meg messaged her: 'what do you have to lose?'

Del replied: 'my virginity...'

Meg: 'ACTUAL lol'

Del replied: 'my dignity?'

Meg: ':) too late'

But was it, still?

*

'Del, this is Geoff.'

'Alright, love. Thanks for coming,' Geoff said, his Yorkshire accent much deeper than Gerard had mimicked.

'My pleasure,' Del replied, apologising with her cheekbones as the final diphthong escaped from her mouth.

'Don't worry, love. I know what you meant. Funerals are funerals. Life is life. Nice service, mind.' Del agreed.

'We'll have to see you again under more pleasant circumstances. Gerard's mum does a mean roast.'

'Del's a vegan, Geoff.'

'Oh, is she?' Geoff said, winking at Del as he moonwalked towards a trestle table of beige food.

'Geoff seems nice,' said Del.

'Yeah, Geoff's Geoff, you know?' said Gerard.

Del didn't really know. She agreed anyway.

After he'd taken the phone call on the carousel, Gerard had told Stina he had an urgent family matter to deal with. It was unfortunate, but he'd have to cut short the city tour. He'd pulled Del, confused but concerned, back towards the train station, not before insisting Stina tried the opera house tour at the Wales Millennium Centre and the teriyaki noodle salad at the new macrobiotic cafe across the road.

He'd broken the news to Del once they were far away enough for the carousel's sound system to drown out their conversation. Del later felt that Gerard had announced Nanna Judy's death as matter of factly as the time of day or the weather, though this may have been unfair. Grief affected different people in different ways. But unlike weather conditions, the facts in this instance would not change.

Nanna Judy, who Del had never met, was dead.

She'd looked back towards the water. The carousel bobbed and weaved regardless, oblivious of the news. Stina stood motionless, looking out at the horizon, half-expecting the tide to turn and blow her great-grandfather back into the docks.

Over the following week and a half, Del hadn't seen Gerard once. They'd messaged, of course, but not the open-ended messages she'd been used to. Gerard had managed to convey in just a few words that now wasn't a good time. It was hard to argue and she hadn't really wanted to. She hoped a rest would be as good as a change, before realising she sounded like a quote her sister would post online.

But she'd missed him more than she'd expected, or if not him, then someone. Before there was Gerard, there was the pursuit of a Gerard, and in the limbo of grandparental death, she had neither. She'd stayed longer at work each night, convincing herself she needed to prove herself to Hiro on this particular project, unable to admit that she was actually lost for other activities.

Across the week, she'd tried and failed to read a book, to make a mood board, to write a poem, before giving up each task and losing herself in the lifestyle porn of Instagram. This hadn't helped her sleep – she had beaches and bleached hair, red carpet pics and club sandwiches ingrained on her eyelids. After six days she discovered a welt on the back of her left hand and had no idea how it had got there.

At the funeral, she saw Gerard's sadness manifest itself through a busy efficiency. She remembered her sister Seren reacting like this when her pet chinchilla had choked to its violent, untimely death on a

Pokemon action figure. Seren was three years younger and four inches shorter than Del. Over the course of the next difficult fortnight, she had refused to acknowledge his name (Moo) and spent every morning and most evenings writing a radio play entitled 'The Little Voices', which to this day sits in a drawer in the study of their mother and father's house. Seren was seven years old at the time.

Their springtime trip to Paris was the first time Del and Seren had spent more than forty-eight hours straight together since Christmas. Before the train had entered the Channel Tunnel, Del had asked herself if they'd be friends if they weren't related. She asked herself who her friends actually were and counted them down in French. She needed the practice.

Un: Gerard (boyfriend)

Deux: Meg (housemate friend)

Trois, Quatre, Cinq: Carla, Annie, Carly (workmate friends)

Six: Emyr (workmate friend, ex-ish)

Sept, Huit: Smitha, Katie (uni friends)

Neuf: Philip (gay friend)

She'd looked out at the blackness of the tunnel, wondering how many of these were situation friends, millennial cell-mates. Seren had broken her thought pattern.

'Mam and Dad asked if they were ever going to meet Gerald.'

'It's Gerard.'

'Oh, touchy, Delyth. Ger-ard.'

Del reached over, instinctively punching Seren in the arm. Her high-pitched squeal turned the ticket inspector around to the passengers across the aisle before Del had the chance to shoot him a 'kid sisters' look.

Despite the age difference, Seren's sensible life choices (a junior doctor, an increasing sum in a cash ISA) earned her respect Del struggled to achieve from their parents. They'd responded to news of her promotion at work, delivered at the dining table of their semi-detached town house, with indifference. Del's father, David, had said through gritted teeth that this news was *gwych* (great). Del felt sick, then angry. She knew that when her father was positive, he said things were *ardderchog* (splendid). The only time he had used that word over the two-hour lunch was to describe some balsamic-glazed Chantenay carrots.

David's response hid a disappointment, not that their middle child had made Acting Head of Buzz Activation, more that she was happy with this. Along with his wife, Anwen, a childhood sweetheart five months his junior, David had tried to raise children with a moral compass, a sense of higher purpose. Boiled eggs were served not with soldiers, but *ffrindiau* (friends).

Their firstborn, Aled, showed an aptitude for benevolence from an early age. At Christmas, 1984, he wrote a letter to Siôn Corn (the Welsh Santa Claus) requesting that instead of delivering the BMX he'd previously coveted, a donation was made on his behalf to the Band Aid appeal. He was five years old. Aled was now a major player in the permaculture movement and the father to two ruddy-faced boys, born from the forgiving hips of a farmer's daughter from Mid Wales by the name of Gwenno. Del was unsure what the permaculture movement actually was, but she was aware it involved a lot of tweed.

To her parents, Del's job was crass, her purpose in life a prop to unnecessary capitalism. David was a sociology lecturer at a local Welsh-language sixth form college. Anwen was a non-executive director at a female empowerment organisation. They planned to spend their imminent retirement in Patagonia. David had familiarised the family with the town of Puerto Madryn via Google Street View on the sitting room's modest flat-screen, pointing out the exact street corner on which he believed his explorer forefather, David Thomas, had set up a barber shop. Del couldn't wait for them to go and spend her inheritance.

*

'So is London still full of cunts?'

Al's thinned-out eyebrows furrowed over his buffet plate.

'I'm joking. It was a joke. Gallows humour,' said Gerard. 'Yeah, I miss the place, kind of.'

'Ah, thanks,' said Del, getting in on the joke.

'The place. Not the people. My people are here,' Gerard said, looking first at Del and then around the room. His eye rested on the coffin, perched on a table next to the bar. This is why I'm back here, he thought. Mum. Geoff, kind of. Stephanie, who lives in London. Nanna Judy, who's dead. Family. Gerard felt hollow. The star of his film had quit the set, just as he was learning how to direct her. He changed the subject.

'Al's a digital artist.'

'Yeah, we met in the car,' Del said.

'We did,' said Al.

'Well, this is a weird first double-date,' said Stephanie. A Kirsty MacColl song overdubbed the scene. There were at least six people on the dance floor. Al's small eyes darted back and forth between their sways. He'd never seen people dance at a funeral.

'We could do better,' said Gerard, 'maybe come to my bar tomorrow? The pale ale's on me.'

'Ah...we'd love that—' said Stephanie

'—but we're heading back in the morning,' Al interrupted, his mind back in the game. 'Work.'

Gerard and Del shot each other a look.

'Al's been working on a big commission for a Russian—'

'—Ukrainian.'

'For a Ukrainian tech billionaire. He calls it 'OBVS M8'. It's going to be his shark in formaldehyde.' Stephanie stood back proudly, at least twenty per cent of this at her pronunciation. Al shuffled. The tassels on his brown loafers flopped through the thick air.

'And then after that, we need a nice, long, relaxing holiday.'

'Yes! That's it...' said Gerard. He thought it just might be.

'What?' said Stephanie.

'A holiday. We'll come!'

Gerard reached for Del's hand and smiled a big expectant smile. He looked at the others in the group. They smiled back. It was a funeral. Smiles of terror. It was his nan's funeral. Smiles of complicity. It was both of their nan's funeral. There was no way out.

CHAPTER 13

'I could tell you were a creative soul.'

'Yep, that's me,' Gerard replied uncomfortably. Del's colleague Carla was leaning on the AlePunk bar with both forearms turned up supporting her dimpled chin. Gerard couldn't decipher if she was flirting or just being nice. Either way, she was drunk. Gerard was able to diagnose that at least.

'So, tell me about your play. Del's always on about it.'

'It's a film,' Gerard corrected.

'Oh, a film?'

'Yeah, moving, talking pictures.'

'That's a shame.'

'Oh?'

'Yeah, a shame. They say Hiro anonymously funds a small independent theatre company.' Carla looked to her left for the drink she'd already finished.

'I'm sure Del could have hooked you up. Del and Hiro are tight,' she said, bumping her fists together aggressively and raising her over-plucked eyebrows in mock provocation.

'She could make en-eee-thing happen with Hiro.' Gerard was unsure if this was Carla's strategy or if she'd just spilled the juice on a hot office romance.

'Maybe next project,' said Gerard, cutting the conversation with a 'What can I get you?' to the middle-aged man in a blue linen jacket waiting next to Carla. As Gerard poured the three-quarter pint, he scanned the room for Del. She was in the middle of the bar, stood side on, laughing uncontrollably at something an unknown man was saying to her. This was happening a lot.

Isosceles had hired AlePunk for their summer party, a situation neither Del nor Gerard were best pleased with. In the weeks that followed Nanna Judy's funeral, AlePunk had become an escape from the procession of paying strangers the summer had brought to the door of the cottage.

Del's post-promotion glow had been replaced by a supportive girlfriend routine which had been replaced by what seemed to

Gerard to be extended pre-menstrual symptoms. The epicentre of her indifference revealed itself a fortnight ago. The Peruvian house guest, Che, had decided, under duress, to vacate the living room and sample a traditional Welsh pub for the evening. Gerard had marked stars on the map in his Lonely Planet book, arrows pointing to descriptions such as 'atmospherica auténtico' and 'cute chicas :)'.

Gerard and Del hadn't spent a 'cwtchy' (a Welsh word, meaning cosy/cuddly) night in since Meg had left a reunion for the call centre she'd worked in earlier than expected and caught Del lazily masturbating Gerard to an online porn channel dedicated to Asian girls. It was their period default. It felt a long time ago.

After starting and stopping three films on Netflix ('I told you we should have checked on IMDB first') and sharing a Vietnamese takeaway, Gerard decided they should spend the evening researching their imminent holiday to Egypt. Del went to half-groan but stopped herself, instead fake smiling and saying WiFi was playing up on her phone. Gerard got the message and said, 'Let's watch The Royal Tenenbaums instead?' Del cheered. It was a sure-fire Del pleaser. They'd already watched it three times together. On his way down from the toilet, Gerard had snuck back in the room and caught Del scrolling property porn on Rightmove.

'WiFi, hey?'

'Yeah, it's, erm, really patchy.'

'Seems it. What's up, Del?'

'Nothing.'

'Don't be a cliché.'

'Nothing.'

'Del...'

'It's just...'

'Yeah...'

'This holiday. We could really do with some time. Alone.'

Gerard's brow pinched north.

'It's not that I don't like Stephanie and Al, it's just that—'

'Stephanie is me. Practically. We're twins.'

'I know, babe.'

'And our nan's just died and she's moved away and we never see each other anymore and I want her to meet you, properly meet you.'

Del said 'sure', but Gerard thought her eyes were more like 'hmm'. Since then, Del's approach to the impending trip was one of conscientious non-objection. Gerard had created a WhatsApp group named LOLidays but Del had muted the notifications. She was resigned to her fate. An all-inclusive holiday to Sharm El Shiekh had been booked in her name. She would not be sharing this on her social networks.

This was their first ever flight-enabled holiday together. Del had never envisioned it would become such a social affair.

'It'll be real cruisey, babe, I promise. Just what we need. We can walk the Great Wall of China another time. Real cruisey.' Gerard had picked this word up from a blonde haired surfer dude from New South Wales, using his stay at the cottage to consummate cultural links with the females of the old country.

Del felt it was best not to clarify that his 'we' was Gerard and Stephanie. When Carla had asked her if she'd liked Stephanie, Del had replied that she had, she thought, but was a little scared of her.

'The big sister thing, right?' Carla had asked.

'Actually, Gerard is seven minutes older.'

Del had lost concentration, imagining Gwenno's friends asking similar questions about Del before she'd married her brother.

'Well, anyway, I saw her funeral selfie on Instagram, and I have to say: she is hot.'

'There was a funeral selfie?' Del almost choked on her Americano.

'There was a funeral selfie. Why miss an opportunity?' she said, 'I have to say I agree.'

'Hang on a minute, you've been checking her out online?'

'Del, get with the programme. Of course I have.' Del had too, of course, in the beginning at least, and was impressed by her choreographed combos of fashion crushes and fuck my life monologues.

'To be honest, Carla, I don't know why you care so much.'

'I don't care, Del, not in the slightest. This is the early twenty-first century. This is what people do.' Del had turned back to her Mac, finding it hard to disagree.

'Your chick looks like she's having a good time,' said Edwin, forty-two minutes late for his shift. Gerard shot him a scornful stare. He looked over to Del. She was laughing again. He tried to remember the last time he'd seen this.

'She works in a media agency. She's paid to look like she's having a good time. And hold up, did you just say 'chick'? And anyway, where the hell have you been?'

'You heard right,' Edwin replied, 'I'm bringing chick back.'

'Bringing chick back? I actually despair.' Edwin slurped an elderflower pressé through a straw. The bar had quietened down for a few minutes. The sixty or so guests, statement frames and slim cut denim, tailored waistcoats and on trend haircuts, were nodding positively to dub versions of Nirvana hits. Edwin sucked the last out of his soft drink.

'Seriously though, I totally dig what you and Del have.'

'Okay. And what's that, Edwin?' Gerard asked. He was waiting for the punch-line.

'A mutual respect.'

Gerard snorted.

'It's important, man. Just ask Aretha.'

'Ha. Funny.'

'Honestly, man. You guys obviously really dig each other, but you give each other the room to breathe. That's important.' Gerard looked at Edwin and across to Del. She was jiving with an unidentifiable middle-aged Asian woman.

'Thanks, man. From the bottom of my heart.'

'Anytime brother, anytime. I've had a bit of a personal epiphany on the lady front.'

'Maisie?'

'Keep up, Gerard. No, not Maisie. I've realised what I am.'

'And what's that?'

'I'm a Japanese puffer fish.'

'Of course you are.'

'I'm glad you agree.' Edwin smiled back proudly, his teeth recently overly whitened by a small cosmetic procedure.

'Is that it?'

'No, listen to me. The Japanese puffer fish is really plain, like totally normcore. It uber-camouflages itself against the backdrop of the sea and then, when they're least expecting it, he wins his woman through artistry.'

'Edwin, you have a handlebar moustache. You don't blend in anywhere.'

'Look around, G. Everyone's got a handlebar moustache. I'd shave it right off if it didn't complete my puffer fish vibe.'

Gerard raised an eyebrow.

'We think the AlePunk shifts are tough going. The puffer fish works twenty-four seven for seven whole days making this etch-a-sketch style pattern in the sea bed. The guy's a pure maths genius. It's total precision. It's absolute beauty. Then the chick's all his. She can't wait to lay her eggs all up in his design.' Edwin took a seat on a crate of All Day Session IPA. He looked sad.

'Edwin, have you been mainlining nature programmes on Netflix again?'

'I can confirm that I have.'

'Were you stoned, Edwin?'

'I can confirm that I was.'

'Oh, Edwin.' Gerard was self-aware that his response was worthy of the denouement of a sixties sitcom, both characters breaking the fourth wall, looking towards the audience with a happy exasperation. Was this what his life had become?

'There's a rub though. There always is. When the eggs fertilise, she does a runner. Leaves him to it, bringing up babies. My circles would be so hot I'd have a whole army of junior puffer fishes. We'd organise ourselves into peaceful protesters for a more egalitarian underwater world. But it could be worse. I could be an Australian jumping spider. They dance their arses off to win a chick and then she eats them alive. Imagine that.'

Del had been avoiding going to the bar all night. She was unsure if she felt embarrassed by Gerard, in this work situation. She'd told them he was an entrepreneur-creative. Hiro had nodded. Hiro's acceptance was important. She knew she felt a simmering anger at Gerard, mainly for the holiday, for blowing the one opportunity they had to get things back on track. Okay, maybe that was too strong, she thought, maybe making it more difficult was what she meant. Carla had chosen the venue just to fuck her off, she was sure of it. But then Carla didn't know Gerard's current approval rating, at least she didn't think she did.

'Going well?' Carla bumped into Del's hips.

'What? I can't hear you?'

A Spanish crooner now played over the sound system, a little too loud, a little too ironically.

'Going well?' Carla's voice raised now.

'No, still no. It's so noisy, I can't hear you, so yeah or no, whichever makes more—' Carla grabbed Del by the pouch of her dungarees and led her to the overturned oil drums masquerading as seats. Del's drink sloshed around the glass, saved from spilling by the gulps she'd taken to fill in the gaps in a conversation about fonts with a freelance designer who white-labelled his work during busy periods at Isosceles.

'I said,' Carla repeated, slowly for effect, 'going well?'

'What?' said Del.

'The party, the networking...'

'Oh, that, yeah, I'd, erm, give a tramp a blowjob if it meant I could be at home on the sofa with a vegetable jalfrezi and a box set right now.' Carla snorted. This was how they spoke to each other, Del and Carla, young, independent, creative career women, unafraid of a sexual quip, even when it was unnecessary. It made Del tired.

'Did you think I meant Gerard? How are things with Gerard?' Carla prodded. Carla was single. She was blocked from three out of the four major dating sites. This was her sport.

'Yeah, everything's...' Del said, looking to her right towards Gerard. He was balancing a stack of beer mats on his elbow, flicking them into the air and catching them on the descent. Edwin was approving via an imitation of a seal. '...fine, everything's fine.'

'He's a real catch,' Carla said, leaning in, 'he told me he really couldn't wait for your holiday.'

'He did?'

'Yeah, he's really excited, bless him. Who you sharing him with again?'

'His twin sister,' Del replied, turning her resting bitch face active, 'and her boyfriend, Al.'

'Oo, Al. Is he a hottie?'

'He's a digital artist.'

'He's a what?'

'A digital artist.'

'I don't know what that is,' the lines around Carla's eyes agitated, '...but is he a hottie?'

Del paused.

'Maybe he is, if you like pencil-thin moustaches.'

'Del, darling, beggars cannot be choosers.' Carla swirled the ice cubes around her tumbler.

'Drink?' said Del.

'Drink.'

'I'll go.'

Del weaved through the impromptu dance floor in its final twists and shouts of the night. Emyr was grinding next to a high-heeled digital ad sales girl from the local TV station. He caught Del's eye mid-bump and winked suggestively, drunkenly. Hiro was stood in the corner of the room, the cut-off collar of his impeccably cut Italian suit incongruous against the faux industrial wall. He was speaking quietly into the mouthpiece of his headphones, likely to his elegant life partner, Alicia, Del thought, the timing just right to catch her after the closing of her New York gallery.

She made it to the bar, resting her bony elbows on the brushed aluminum top.

'Busy night, boys?' Gerard and Edwin looked up, midway through a furious thumb war.

'Oh, hello you,' said Edwin.

'It's always the same at the free bars,' said Gerard, 'people load up early, make fools of themselves and stumble off.'

'I can only hope you're not referring to me, Gerard Kane.' Edwin busied himself with some limes at the other end of the bar.

'Well, you haven't stumbled off—'

'—yet,' Del cut in. 'Give me two more Ginger Collins for the road.'

'Ace. And then we can get out of here. I could really do with a hand tidying the cottage up. We've got this Dutch guy rolling in tomorrow for a month.'

'Oh, Gerard...'

'What?'

'I'm sorry. I can't go home after this drink. Work night out. Clients to look after. You know how it is. Apparently we've got a booth reserved at The Orange Room.'

'I hate that place.'

'Me too, but what can I do?'

'Come home with me. Edwin said he'd cover and close up. Edwin never offers to close up.' His ears pricked up at the end of the bar. He looked towards the couple and immediately back to his lime.

'Babe, I'm sorry. It's work.'

'Yeah, sure, fine,' Gerard sulked.

'Hiro said we could start at eleven tomorrow though, so I can come around and help in the morning.'

'What a hero.'

'Okay then, I won't.'

'Not you, Hiro. Don't worry about it. It's fine. Sleep off your hangover.'

'I won't have a hangover.'

'You will after this drink. Go sit down. I'll bring them over. I think

Carla's about to ingest that poor boy in the double denim. He looks petrified.' Del looked over her shoulder. Carla was sat astride Aaron, a pale-faced account executive, invisible lassoing to R Kelly's 'Ignition Remix'.

'Oh god. I'm sorry, babe. I'll make it up to you this weekend. I promise.'

Gerard shuffled to the back of the bar, picked up the cocktail shaker, unscrewed the top and drained out the residue.

He wondered if she'd keep that promise.

He wondered if he wanted her too.

CHAPTER

14

Dear Gerard!

Hi it is Lars.

I am in your house from 7 June until 5 July. I wanted to ask before I come. Is it possible to smoke in room? Airbnb was not clear. Is okay if no :-) Until soon, Lars.

Gerard spent the morning flitting between email admin, laundry and cleaning the house. In the early days of his hoteliership, he used the cleaning levy charged by Airbnb to pay Auntie Bronwen to blitz the place after guests had left. He'd recently taken to pocketing the extra cash and cleaning the place himself. Times were hard for entrepreneur-creatives. He'd initially assumed this was why she blanked him at Nanna Judy's funeral, before realising she was exhibiting all the social anxieties of an addict, Candy Crush as the opiate.

Gerard's forearms were tired from scrubbing a pre-wash solution into the sheets of last night's house guest, an exuberant Irishman by the name of Eamonn. His Airbnb reviews said nothing of his incontinence issues. On a rare occasion, the internet was no substitute for real life experience, he thought.

Gerard tried to use this manual labour as thinking time, like all the great auteurs had. He remembered reading something about Wim Wenders working summers in a builders' merchants. Or was it von Trier? And was it a scrap metal yard?

This week's Xanadu problem had been trying to work out if Ren should have an on-off love affair with his colleague, Lena. Gerard envisaged them as the space-age Ross and Rachel, but as he struggled with the stained sheets, he wondered if Gino would be the better lover, if bisexuality was more futuristic or if he should leave the romance out of the film at all costs and focus on the bigger themes that actually mattered. This thought made him feel blue.

He pictured himself at the Tribeca Film Festival in five years' time, the hand-painted signs that they'd made for him, that he had deserved, that his creative genius had moved them to make the night before, staying up into the early hours in their loft apartments, unsure

and then sure and then unsure that their third effort was the one
that would catch his eye and secure an autograph or retweet. He saw
himself introducing the lady on his left arm to De Niro, to the editor
of the *New Yorker*, to the rest of the prize committee. He couldn't make
out if the outline of her dress, if the shape of her body belonged to
Del or to somebody else. His phone pinged and derailed his train of
thought.

Stephanie Kane: Twinny!

Stephanie Kane: Two weeks today

Gerard Kane: What is?

Stephanie Kane: You're kidding>

Gerard Kane: Ahhhh. HOLIDAY!

Stephanie Kane: :)

Stephanie Kane: Excited?

Gerard Kane: Yeah, big time

Gerard Kane: Sorry, I was just cleaning up then. New guest today.

Stephanie Kane: S'cool. Soooo funny you run a B n B now

Gerard Kane: Thanks Stepher

Gerard Kane: FML

Stephanie Kane: Funny good I mean.

Gerard Kane: There isn't a funny good

Gerard Kane: haha

Gerard Kane: or peculiar

Stephanie Kane: Well there is now. Funny good. Helping you to live
your creative dream. Beats my job.

Gerard Kane: Yeah well the cleaning doesn't

Stephanie Kane: Thought Auntie Bronwen was doing it??

Gerard Kane: Sore point

Stephanie Kane: Oo. Sorry

Stephanie Kane: How's Del?

Gerard Kane: Hungover.

Stephanie Kane: Big night :)

Gerard Kane: For her.

Gerard Kane: I was working

Stephanie Kane: Ahh.

Stephanie Kane: Del seems nice

Gerard Kane: That seems loaded

Stephanie Kane: ??

Stephanie Kane: She does!

Stephanie Kane: I liked her

Gerard Kane: Your approval means so much

Gerard Kane: Let's see if you still say that after a week's holiday

Stephanie Kane: Why you say that?

Stephanie Kane: G?

Gerard Kane: No reason

Gerard Kane: I'm just tired

Gerard Kane: How's London anyway?

Gerard Kane: I can't believe it's me asking you that

Stephanie Kane: Times changed twinny

Gerard Kane: indeed they have

Stephanie Kane: It's cool. Work is schmirk but life is fun. Al's just finishing his installation for the Ukrainian dude. He needs a holiday

Stephanie Kane: Be nice to him? :)

Gerard Kane: DUH

Gerard Kane: course I will.

Gerard Kane: Is he being nice to you?

Stephanie Kane: He is

Gerard Kane: How's cohabitation?

Stephanie Kane: Yeah, it's different. It's good. He needs a lot of space when he's working

Gerard Kane: Isn't that what the studio is for?

Stephanie Kane: Yeah

Stephanie Kane: He stays there sometimes. Never know when the inspiration will come. Artists work funny hours

Gerard Kane: Funny good?

Stephanie Kane: Funny peculiar

Gerard Kane: Stepher the digital art muse

Gerard Kane: Like Princess in Mario...

Stephanie Kane: Fuck off

Gerard Kane: Actual LOL

Gerard Kane: Actually more like Mushroom with your new hair

Gerard Kane: Very London.

Stephanie Kane: OI

Stephanie Kane: When in Rome

Stephanie Kane: if you're not a hipster round here

Stephanie Kane: the other hipsters

Stephanie Kane: it's like racism

Stephanie Kane: ALMOST

Gerard Kane: Worth a mushroom head?

Stephanie Kane: Most def.

Stephanie Kane: Anyway...how's mum?

Gerard Kane: Good

Gerard Kane: I think.

Stephanie Kane: You think?

Gerard Kane: Yeah, I've not seen her since the funeral. I've been busy.

Gerard Kane: Two jobs

Gerard Kane: One movie

Stephanie Kane: Gerard!

Stephanie Kane: Go see her

Stephanie Kane: Her mum just died

Stephanie Kane: Isn't it why you're back?

Stephanie Kane: Family?

Gerard Kane: Fucking hell twin sister.

Gerard Kane: At least I'm here. Fine. I'll report back.

Stephanie Kane: Thank you

Stephanie Kane: Love you

Gerard Kane: Yeah, yeah.

Gerard loaded the washing machine, turned the dial to sixty degrees and hoped for the best. He was tired. Edwin had racked them up a pitcher of a new wheat beer after the doors had locked last night. Gerard had returned the favour. He'd cycled home in the middle of the road, a little drunk, his lights missing since a Korean guest had loaned the bike and carelessly left them attached to the handlebars outside the castle. He'd stayed up for an hour when he got in, checking his phone, determined not to message Del, but sure of his right to a 'good night' message back, at the very least. He fell asleep playing Snake on an online emulator. He'd woken at 10 a.m. from a dream where he'd become the serpent, trapped in a maze, hiding from his own appetite. In reality he had a headache, was fully clothed, his phone on two per cent battery. Del had checked her WhatsApp twenty-three minutes earlier.

Gerard had no new messages.

He crashed out on the Chesterfield sofa and rested his non-matching socks on the edge of the coffee table. His guest wasn't arriving for another hour. He reached for the remote control and starting flicking through the stations.

A cookery show. An antiques show. News. A cookery show. A daytime soap. Weather. As he surfed the stations he sank back further into the sofa, the act bringing on a nostalgia for teenage summers spent indoors, the on-screen flux soothing. The channel hop had been replaced by the scroll, the swipe. Gerard remembered fighting Stephanie for control of the remote, the divine right to stick or twist, the master of all media, Nanna Judy hushing them from the kitchen, bringing in fish finger sandwiches regardless.

He decided to call his mum.

'Good morning, Go!Kids: because you only get one chance to say goodbye. Maureen speaking. How can I help?'

'It's me.'

'Geoff? Are you bunged up?'

'Mum, it's me, Gerard.'

'Oh, God, is everything okay, love? Is it Stephanie?'

'What? No, yeah, everything's fine.'

'Oh, thank God...well...what do you want then?'

'Charming. To speak to my mother. Is that okay?'

'On the phone?'

'Yeah...'

'Right, okay love.'

'How you doing, Mum?'

'Oh, you know, fine, bearing up, as they say.'

'Yeah...that's good. That's good to hear.'

'Geoff said it never hit him 'til a full twelve months after his mother died.'

'Wasn't Geoff like seven though, Mum?'

'He was, love.'

'Well I think the circumstances here might be different.'

'You're right, love. It affects us all in very different ways.'

'Yeah...'

'So how are you?'

'Good, yeah.'

'Looking forward to your sunshine holiday?'

'Big time.'

'Bet you can't wait....I know Stephanie's looking forward to it.'

'Yeah...oh, I was going to ask actually, is Geoff still okay to check in those guests? On the Wednesday?'

'I think so, love...hang on...let me get my phone...he text me about it earlier.' Maureen's voice was replaced by an instrumental royalty-free version of Christina Aguilera's 'Beautiful'. Gerard recognised it right away, independent of software this time.

'Right, now he says as long as they didn't want to be in before twelve, it's no problem. He's on nights, see.'

'God, does he even text in Yorkshire?'

'You what, love?'

'Nothing.'

'How is Del, love?'

'Yeah. She's...fine.'

'We thought she seemed nice.'

'Thanks, Mum.'

'Greg in our office is a vegan, you know.'

'That's great, Mum.'

'Does Del know him I wonder? They're very close-knit, aren't they?'

'I'll ask her, Mum.'

'Anyway love, was that it?'

'That was it.'

'Come around for tea one night, you and Del.'

'We will do.'

'What will I cook a vegan?'

'Probably after the holiday now.'

'Okay love, I've got to finalise the details on a hot air balloon ride for a very sick kiddy by one, so I'd better get on.'

'Okay Mum, bye.'

'Love you.'

Gerard hung up. His screen showed a missed call when he'd been on the line to his mum. It was Del. She never called. He dialled right back. A picture of her mock Japanese tourist mode, her oversized RayBans and half-ironic horizontal peace sign filled the screen. As the tone rang and rang and rang, Gerard thought back to the day the picture had been taken.

It was a glorious morning, unusually so for February in Wales. Gerard had convinced Del to call into work sick. It was his first day off from AlePunk that coincided with an empty house for over a week. Del had cited an immoveable migraine, a symptom of women's problems. She'd coughed through the call, Gerard muffling laughter down at her non-symptomatic actions. The HR lady, Jan, a post-menopausal mother to three Maine Coons, had sympathised nostalgically.

He brought her breakfast in bed to celebrate, a plate of strawberry Pop Tarts and a cafetiere of Brazilian coffee, the beans a present from a patriotic guest. She ate around the non-vegan icing. They spent the morning lolling around in bed, watching episode after episode of *Frasier* on Netflix. Gerard did a mean Niles Crane. After the joke became tired, they drove to St Fagans, a Welsh folk life open-air museum. For weeks afterwards, the phrase #Folklife dominated their downtime, the call of trimmed beard, nice cardigan or banjo section evoking the same response, fingers criss-crossed into a hashtag.

They'd laughed.

So much.

The early sun had clouded over as they walked hand-in-hand through a row of cottages, recreated in the fashions of ascending decades. The almost resident coachload of Breton exchange students were nowhere to be seen, probably trying to order croissants in the pre-war bakery, Gerard had joked.

They reached the final building in the row, a cottage with a sign saying, 'Welcome to the 1980s'. Del crouched through the door and Gerard followed. Their hands untied and Gerard lost himself in the acrylic wallpaper, the concentric pattern taking him back to a faded photograph of the twins on Christmas Day, three years old, surrounded by wrapping paper on the brown carpet at Nanna Judy's house. Grampy Joe smoked absentmindedly in the corner of the shot, the twins responding, one with laughter, the other with tears. Gerard forgot which was which.

He felt a hand on his waist and turned around. It was Del. She arrowed her tongue into his mouth and jerked his body towards her, undoing his belt. Before he knew it, Gerard was open legged on a crushed velvet sofa, Del snaking on top, the feet of the sofa squeaking against the linoleum floor.

He put his hand over her mouth and held it tight until their bodies came to a rest. As they clung there for a moment, clenched against the breeze from outside, the air cold, Gerard's eyes fixed on the wood-panelled TV and VHS machine, the top loader open, invitingly. An elderly couple passed by the single glazed window, looking in and looking away again immediately.

This is it, he thought. This is love.

The phone rang out.

A knock on the door shifted Gerard's attention. A man stood in the doorway of the cottage with a familiar grin. Gerard thought it was sly, almost. He was tall, six foot four maybe, his thick body filling the frame. He seemed to be in his late-thirties. His face was tanned, robust.

'Gerard? It's me, Lars!'

Gerard led him through the living room into the kitchen area, offering to take his bags and bright waterproof jacket.

'Does it always rain in Wales? Haha.' He said the words rather than laughing, as if he'd learned them from a Facebook comment.

'Mostly, yeah. Actually, Cardiff has more hours of sunshine a year than Milan.' Gerard had learned this from repeated viewings of the city's Wikipedia page.

'Milan is a fucking shithole, man, haha.' Gerard shrugged, ushering Lars into the leatherette booth. He slid a welcome pack across the table while he prepared some tea. Lars flicked through the pages clumsily, interspersing his reading sporadically with grunts of approval. The kettle boiled and Gerard filled the pot. He reached for a tin on the worktop, lifted off the lid and took two Welsh cakes out of the packet. Two ladies, hand-drawn in traditional Welsh dress, looked at him encouragingly, their top hats and pinafores like a prediction of a forthcoming hipster fashion craze. Gerard lifted the tray and carried it over to the booth.

'*Croeso i Cymru*. Here's some traditional tea and cakes to welcome you to Wales.' Gerard had got the idea after a traumatic check-in experience at a Brooklyn booking. He'd arrived off the red-eye at 9 a.m., a blurry ring of the brownstone bell receiving no response. Hot and flustered, their rucksacks spread across the sidewalk, his then girlfriend Angharad had turned increasingly edgy at the people walking by watching their predicament. She was from a small village in Mid Wales and had been sheltered from multi-cultural society. They'd taken refuge in a nearby bagel emporium and argued for the next four hours.

On his eventual arrival, their host, a Belgian 'entrepreneur' by the name of Mathieu, apologised sincerely, slickly, an excuse about a crisis at the office and a crate of craft ale under his arm to say sorry. Since then, the welcome drink had become a cornerstone of Gerard's hosting experience. (The items on the welcome menu were non-negotiable.)

Gerard sat opposite Lars, the fibres on the knees of their jeans uncomfortably close for a millisecond, before repelling apart. Up close,

Lars smelt of CKOne and cigarettes. He took the welcome pack in his left hand and talked Lars through the contents, the hand-drawn map, the bus timetable, the best restaurants, bars and vintage shops, the beginner level Welsh words.

Lars chewed enthusiastically through the affable, robotic induction, Gerard's right finger highlighting historic sites of interest.

'Super good,' Lars nodded. A tour of the cottage followed, the new house guest seemingly already proficient in the mechanics of Yale locks, shower knobs and central heating. Gerard's phone beeped. Del. Finally. He eased it out of his pocket, a digital-age Jesse James. A yin and yang emoji appeared on screen. It was Edwin.

'Dude, I swapped shifts with Lenka tonight. Party on?' Lars was testing the pressure on the hot water tap.

'Lars, how do you fancy a beer?' He turned the tap anticlockwise. The water dried up.

'Gerard, my brother, I thought you'd never ask!'

Over a pint of local ale in the pub two minutes' walk from the cottage, Lars told Gerard his life story. He was born in Maastricht in the mid-1970s, the only son of a bank manager and schoolteacher. He'd left home aged fifteen, ending up in a squat in Rotterdam with a revolving door of artists and addicts. Lars had only ever been the former, he'd protested, 'haha'. And now he was an internationally-renowned photographer, one worthy of a retrospective in a foreign capital. His breakthrough had been a collection of hundreds of portraits of pilled up clubbers from the city's underground scene. *De Telegraaf* called him a 'sensatie'. He'd toured the world for the past twenty years, taking his camera on his shoulder.

'Only 35mm, you understand?' he said, swilling the remainder of his pint down.

He was in Cardiff for a show at the National Museum, under the curation of a fellow countryman on the board of the institution.

'I call it 'Life Through A Lens'. It's super good, yes?'

'Yeah...' Gerard said, sipping his pint and searching the back of his brain, '...it's also the name of a Robbie Williams album.'

'Oh, I do not know him.' Gerard felt ashamed he did, blaming noise pollution from Stephanie's room. Lars didn't seem to mind.

'Maybe I can take a photo of him. Maybe here in Cardiff. Yes. More beer?'

Over the next two pints Lars continued to talk, Gerard listening but thinking about Del. He thought about her promise to make it up to him, what she'd do, what she could do. The obvious currency in such situations seemed a hazy memory. He tried to remember when they last had sex and both of them had enjoyed it. Gerard and Del's relationship had become an action movie without the action. Two actors out of their depth, clunky dialogue delivered uncomfortably, both aware they were waiting for the explosion, both knowing it wouldn't come until the bigger budget sequel played out with a different cast.

The jukebox played a Smoky Robinson song, 'Tears Of A Clown'. Gerard hummed along without realising.

'This is not a very Saturday night song, Gerard. Not like the gabber clubs. Rotterdam techno ruled...before the neo-facists got involved, haha.'

'This, my Dutch friend, is a song for whenever.'

Gerard checked his phone. Still nothing from Del. He wasn't messaging her. No way. The yin and yang flashed up.

'Bro, town or what?'

'Drink up, Lars, let's go make party.'

'Super good.'

They hailed a taxi into town through Gerard's phone, joining Edwin, inevitably, in a craft ale bar. He greeted them with a two-arms-up cheer, his yellow hair untucking from behind his ears as he did so. He'd gone to the liberty of lining up three racks of taster glasses, the beers ascending in darkness and potency from left to right.

'Thanks for these, Ed.'

'No stress, man. I didn't pay for them.'

Edwin and Lars introduced themselves, Gerard's mind elsewhere. The next hours took in a bar crawl following the spots Gerard had highlighted on the hand-drawn map of the city.

'Dude, we should totally quit AlePunk and monetise this bar crawl business,' Edwin said. Stood next to them at the bar, the flames of a sambuca licking dangerously close to his chin, Lars seemed to be having a great time. His face had reddened. Everything was 'super good', particularly the ladies. On more than one occasion he mock followed one into the bathroom.

'He's Dutch,' Edwin shouted, hoping the explanation worked.

Over the loud indie disco at an Irish pub opposite the castle, Edwin said, 'I always tell Gerard he should only let hot chicks stay, but I'll make an exception for you, Lars,' repeating the compliment as the DJ played Talking Heads from an iPod.

'Psycho Killer, ba ba ba, ba ba ba ba ba ba ba ba ba ba,' Lars shouted, hands triumphant and threatening. He danced like a northern European.

'Let's get some food,' Gerard said, 'I'm starved.'

*

The three men sat at a table for four in a nearby tapas bar, Lars opposite Gerard and Edwin as if he was being interviewed for the part of exuberant foreign friend in a buddy comedy. The table was down five or six steps, their view a street-level window, feet passing by. Gerard slipped through a door signposted 'hombres' as Edwin ordered. The room smelt of sherry and urine. He'd recognised the waitress from her profile picture, shorter and squatter in person. She'd been a regular commentator every time the local newspaper website posted a story about Uncle Derek's trial. He didn't need that kind of recognition right now. A month's rent from Lars could depend on it.

He checked his phone. Still nothing from Del. She hadn't logged in since this morning. Should he be worried? Perhaps. He opened up Twitter. Nothing from Del for two days, since she'd posted a picture of a Nicoise salad (no tuna, no egg) with the hashtag #veganversion. Carla had been live-tweeting John Candy movies all day. Gerard scrolled down to find a picture of a gaunt dog in bed with the caption 'Drunk last night. When you wake up with no water next to the bed.'

Her previous tweet had been a group picture from 3.47 a.m. tagged #IsoscelesCrew. Del was stage left, one hand covering her eyes, the other draped across the shoulder of a conventionally handsome man in his mid-to-late-thirties wearing a roll neck sweater and a leather bomber jacket.

'It's June, douchebag,' Gerard said out loud, pinching the screen of his iPhone until the douchebag's face filled it. His eyes and mouth were pixelated but Gerard still sensed victory in them. He weighed up whether Del's arm had been on the man's shoulder just for this moment captured in time or for longer.

He decided to go and get drunk.

The table was busy with dishes and drinks. A cerveza frothed in front of him, spilling over onto a shorter, darker companion. Gerard lifted it to his nose, shuddered and drank. Lars handed him a plate of patatas bravas, grinning wildly, salsa on his chin. Above them, a television played music videos with the sound muted.

'It used to be one of my top-five life ambitions to play the romantic lead in a hit VH1 R'n'B music video,' Edwin said. There was no trace of irony in his voice.

'I hate to tell you this, but those guys are generally six foot six adonises and, in the main, black.' Gerard picked up the cerveza. 'And you, Edwin, are the whitest person I know.'

'Not true, brah,' Edwin said. Lars, his back to the television, was oblivious.

'Edwin, for a start, take your dancing last night. 100 per cent white guy.' Last night, Edwin had challenged some guy who Gerard was sure Del had a thing with pre-him – he hoped pre-him – to a dance off. They'd lasted thirty seconds of a Run DMC song before Gerard pressed shuffle, Edwin's dance move mimicking a card dealer.

'I do not. I got moves,' he said, straightening his back.

'The fact you said you got moves means you don't got moves.'

'Not true.'

'Why don't you go for soft rock? Be the floppy-haired guy lazing around in a Barcelona chair in a loft apartment with an acoustic guitar you've never played. Now that you could stretch to.'

'I once shot a music video,' said Lars. He was struggling with a piece of chilli squid, a rogue tentacle stuck in his teeth.

'You know the hip hop guys, they all fuck the big booty girls off set. One of them, she asked me to the trailer, but I said no, Lars is working, Lars is an artist. Super crazy times, haha.' Gerard lifted his short glass to his lips and sank the contents.

More drinks followed. They talked about Rotterdam, Cardiff, the diet of the road, a potential Teddy boy-style reboot, pubic hair trends, reincarnation, bushcraft skills, recognition.

'That's the problem with the general public. Collectively, they've got the power to make me famous but they're just clueless about what's good for them.'

It was unclear who had said this.

The drink had made Gerard queasy, the food sat on top of his stomach. He looked out of the window. Rain was splattering down on the pavement. Summer in Wales. A pair of feet walked into the frame. They wore Nike Air Max in gold and green. Gerard pushed past Edwin, ran up the stairs and forced his half-drunk body through the door. The heavy rain ran down the inside of the kerb.

'Del!'

'Oh! Gerard, hi...'

CHAPTER

15

It had all seemed plausible enough.

That was the residual feeling Gerard had when he awoke.

Plausability.

Del wasn't there, but the shape of Del and the smell of Del was. He was dreamy, hungover, unsure if the sex had been real or if he'd made it happen in his head. He remembered a warmth, a physical warmth he hadn't known for a while. That kind of thing soon gets taken for granted but when it's gone it leaves a gap that you can remember used to be plugged, but you just can't put your finger on what with.

On the sideboard, next to a novel he'd been struggling with and a day-old mug, was a new mug and a new plate. The new mug was plain, bright red and contained lukewarm tea, the new plate the same but with a bacon sandwich. Del never touched raw flesh. Ever.

She really must be trying to make up, he thought.

Gerard's body filled with a strange feeling. He welcomed it as an old friend, a prodigal emotion.

It was the balance of power.

He took a bite of his sandwich, cold now, stretched his arms and fell back on the pillow, confident that, at last, it had swung back his way.

He woke again, later, to a tingling sensation. The duvet cover was lumpy. He looked to the sideboard. A crust, teeth marks.

'This is going to be a good day.'

*

Del's excuse went a little like this:

After AlePunk, at the insistence of colleagues, she'd gone on to a tiki bar Gerard hated. Del hated it too, but, 'work was work'. It just so happened that her work that evening consisted of drinking rum-based cocktails from coconut shells and dancing to La Bamba with her suited clients, on the prowl for their third wife and company secretary for their organic tea empire. She'd awoke the next morning, disorientated and fully-clothed, to the unfamiliar sound of Meg ushering a second date down the stairs and out of the front door. She was so hungover even this didn't raise her from her grave. Gerard was aware Del would have walked over the molten shards of iPhone screens for gossip like that. She'd reached for her phone but it wasn't there. She'd stripped out of her clothes and turned back over.

The next thing she knew she was sat in a chair belonging to a street barber in what appeared to be the Vietnamese capital of Hanoi. Gerard nodded. Yes, he did remember she'd visited with her lefty father as an early teen. The barber shaved right down the middle of her dark hair, methodically going about his work, whistling an out-of-time interpretation of hair metal classic 'The Final Countdown'. As he swept through the final bang, a crowd appeared. Del knew, without looking, the way you just did in dreams, that they were all eunuchs. She saw they were wearing oversized heads of classic Disney characters and weeping uncontrollably. She'd woken in a sweat and was sure she could taste fish sauce on her bottom lip.

She'd reached for her phone with no joy again, dressed and climbed downstairs. The contents of her bag were arranged across the kitchen worktop in a design she claimed worthy of the Turner Prize. Her phone, upside down in a make-up bag, the piece de resistance. It was out of battery. She'd remembered her charger was at work. And Meg only used Samsung products, a choice allegedly influenced by finding Steve Jobs as played by Michael Fassbender creepy. Del had been walking to the Isosceles office when she bumped into Gerard. She was so glad she had. She'd wanted to see him all day.

The dream sequence accounted for eighty-five to ninety per cent of the time Del took on her explanation.

Gerard had switched off after that, his attention instead on searching dreamdictionary.com for 'head shaved in dream'.

'It means you're worried about losing power.' Del looked back at him blankly.

'And you have. To me. I'm in charge. Let's go bowling.'

'Yay!' Del responded, externalising all the enthusiasm she could muster.

Gerard hadn't wanted to push it too hard. He was all too aware they had a week's holiday to Egypt on the horizon. Del seemed to be anticipating it as positively as root canal surgery during a power cut. Gerard, on the other hand, was looking forward to the four-ball, to spending time with his womb buddy.

Stephanie hated it when he called her that. He'd sacrificed life in one of the world's most happening habitats to come home to his family and Stephanie had swiped it off him, like a Farley's Rusk, just when he was least expecting it.

And he could put the digital artist through the suitability test.

He'd instantly warmed to Stan, Stephanie's previous boyfriend, mainly, he later realised, for his wryly-observed, self-deprecating online presence. In person, Stan had been awkward, rude even, but his digital persona had bought his then potential brother-in-law's grace. Al had it all to do. His Instagram feed was too obtuse even for Gerard.

The trip also offered the chance to spend quality time with Del.

Over the past week, he'd run over the Excellent Moments again in his head, hoping to extend the franchise. But when he pressed his finger on the play button, all he got was buffer,

buffer,

buffer.

Del eased her foot out of her Nike Air Max, stood up straight and took them to the counter.

'Size five, please.'

The teenage girl in front of her had her hair shaved on one side of her head and a tattoo of a unicorn on the inside of her wrist. She looked earnest, like a good person who would do her best to be helpful, whatever the situation.

'Enjoy,' she said, handing Del a pair of red and blue bowling shoes.

Del faked a smile.

She sat back on the padded bench and undid the thick white laces. The air smelt of fried chicken and children's vomit. She looked over her left shoulder, down towards a football pitch-sized area filled with neon and noise. Gerard was otherwise engaged in a hostile shoot-out with one twelve-year-old boy and a thousand bloodthirsty zombies.

Del was relieved the make-up had gone to plan. She could only deal with short-term objectives right now. She wondered if her dream had been too elaborate. She was unsure where it came from. The details kept building up, the narrative taking her over. It was this flair for creativity which impressed Hiro. He'd never comment unnecessarily on the work of the rest of the team, but Del's ideas and execution drew praise. Mild but positive praise. It was the talk of numerous email chains at Isosceles.

Del knew she could be more than the Acting Head of Buzz Activation. With five to six more excellent campaigns and a mushy maternity leave brain from the colleague whose seat she was keeping warm, she could be Head of Buzz Activation by this time next year. And then what? And then anything. Her skills would strengthen any team. She could move to London, Berlin, Paris, New York, Sydney. She looked over her left shoulder again. Gerard was vocal in his encouragement for the twelve-year-old boy in a dance mat battle against a middle-aged woman.

Gerard.

His bar captaincy could travel. AlePunk was geared for global expansion. But his main source of income relied on bricks and mortar here in Wales. And was he ever going to start this film – what was it called? – that he kept going on about.

Where did Gerard fit into this life plan?

Did Gerard fit into this life plan?

Did she care either way?

She remembered an exercise her teacher had set the class in primary school. She still had the completed paper in a bedroom drawer at her mum and dad's house:

Pan fydda i'n tyfu lan dw'i eisiau bod.../ When I grow up I want to be...

yn ddylunydd ffasiwn / a fashion designer

yn geidwad Parc Jurassic / a ranger in Jurassic Park

yn whizz ar gyfrifiaduron / a computer whizz

yn entrepreneur moesegol / an ethical entrepreneur

yn fam / a mummy

*

'Let's bowl.'

Del was distracted as she typed their names into the bowling alley's computer system.

GER.

DEK.

She had pressed the enter key too early.

'Hey Dek, good to meet you, I'm Ger.' Gerard was knocked she hadn't logged him as GFK. On another day, he'd have brought it up. Today he'd decided to keep the conversation light and breezy, a carefully constructed combo of inconsequential gossip and in-game advice.

Del watched Gerard as he enthusiastically considered the brightly coloured balls, touching one, spinning it a little, rejecting it for the next. The bowling shoes anchoring his skinny jeans gave him the look of a hipster clown, something an east London parent would book for their child's jamboree. The flashing lights overhead brought out the bobbles in his sweater, a woollen US college motif on its front. It was an online auction purchase of which he was particularly proud. His hair was left long on top, brushed back in between two shaved sides, growing now. A disobedient tuft stuck up at the back. She thought how she hadn't shared a picture of him online for three months.

This was her man.

This time next week they'd be on holiday, stuck in foreign country with Stephanie and Al. This was what she'd signed up for, she figured. She remembered how she'd felt about their first trip away together. Gerard had been uncharacteristically mysterious, messaging to tell her to bring an overnight bag to his place after work. She'd barely been able to concentrate that afternoon, drifting off to the potential of the possibilities during a video conference on a new multivitamin chew they'd been briefed to 'viralize'.

The hire car had broken down in the back of beyond, smoke spewing out of the engine. She'd known he shouldn't have chosen the basic model. She'd woken up hours later in his arms, cold, her right arm dead. He'd told her he loved her. She'd pretended not to hear, but it felt okay.

'I love you.'

This was a long time ago.

'You're up. Last shot.'

Del walked to the rack, put her fingers in the closest ball and moved her feet to the centre of lane, five feet from the line. She lowered her right leg, swung her hand back and willed her fingers out of the hole. She watched the ball turn over and over, gaining ground, resigned to the fact she was powerless to alter its course now.

'Strike! Check the Dek! You get a bonus go now...'

Del stood impassively as the machine collected the pins, restoring order and setting them back into place again. She took a new ball in her right hand, swung back and closed her eyes.

CHAPTER 16

'Is that Jafar's Palace?'

'No, Stephanie, it's not Jafar's Palace. It's a mosque.'

It was Gerard who answered.

Stephanie had left twelve page impressions on the website of the fake Disneyland resort, lingering on the image of the waterslide which had been fashioned out of plastic to look like the palatial residence of Aladdin's nemesis. But when she had sent a link to the site in the WhatsApp group 'LOLidays', Gerard had sent her a direct message that said:

'Del is repulsed by Disney. Drop it.'

Del considered this their first holiday. And it was a double date.

Naturally, Al was also in the WhatsApp group. Stephanie and Al lived in a one-bedroom apartment five minutes and fourteen seconds from Dalston Kingsland overground station. Stephanie had timed it on her iPhone X. They had moved in four months ago. Al had phoned a man with a van to help. He'd been busy at the studio. Before Gerard and Del knew Al was a digital artist, they wondered what he did in the studio. During the ads before watching *Nocturnal Animals* at the same cinema they visited in Excellent Moment #5., they'd discussed that it likely wasn't dance and was more likely something with design software. They had decided that Al didn't look like he could manipulate a paint brush.

Al was sat in the front of an executive car that had picked them up from Sharm El Sheikh airport. Stephanie had pre-booked it online for the cost of £4.76 each. 'Call it a tenner a couple,' she'd said. She had felt superior in the knowledge that the internet had saved her from being charged an extra 50p by a tired taxi driver trying his best to provide for his eight children.

'Mosque, cool. There's a big one in Shacklewell Lane,' said Stephanie. Then, 'Has this cab got WiFi?' to the driver.

The driver pointed to the radio and turned the dial. As the taxi pulled up at the Lucky Star resort and hotel, Del looked out of the window and thought the outside looked like an Arabic Las Vegas.

'Sorry mate, we've not been to the cashpoint,' said Gerard, 'we'll tip on the way back.' The taxi driver said nothing and handed them their bags.

The call to prayer from the mosque woke Gerard the next morning. He looked at Del sleeping next to him. Here we are, he thought, holiday. She was lying on her front and her white bum rose and fell as she breathed in and out, making the tattoo of a butterfly on her left cheek seem like an effect in a 3D movie. This turned Gerard on. He wondered if he'd go to hell for having a hard on during the call to prayer, then thought, does Islam even have a hell?

Stephanie and Al were already lounging by the pool. Al was wearing a SXSW 2011 t-shirt. Al hadn't been to SXSW in 2011 or ever. The t-shirt had belonged to Stephanie's ex-boyfriend, Stan. Stan's mum was Chinese Mandarin. Stan had not been to SXSW 2011 either but when he wore it to the Turkish place on Church Street for Sunday brunch, Stephanie looked at the couples on the other tables to see if they were looking at Stan like he was in a band, or better, was an app developer. App development is the new rock 'n' roll, thought Stephanie. She looked at Al. He teamed the tee up with tortoiseshell clubmaster sunglasses. She still wondered what digital art was. She thought it definitely had transferable skills desirable in the app development world.

Stephanie was enjoying the cut and thrust of London. The haircuts and the underground. That's what she was telling herself. That's what she was telling Al.

She had worked in the restaurant on the fifty-fourth floor of The Shard, where it was always at least half of the restaurant's birthday. She wondered if being around people who were constantly celebrating sheltered her from the atrocities happening down below and quit before her constitution was irrevocably damaged, leaving her too happy and naive to deal with everydayisms such as itemised bills and grandparental death.

She'd created a content calendar to ensure she was sending regular positive updates from her new life back to her mum in Wales. Mondays were 'unpronounceable lunch picture' days. Wednesdays, 'safety reassurance' days. Fridays, 'tourist attractions you really must come and visit' days. She'd booked her mum and Geoff bus tickets to visit her on a weekend in her first month. The itinerary was packed. Al had made noises about having to work.

She'd sent him a link to an article on an aspirational lifestyle magazine site entitled 'London: It's over. It's not me. It's you'. In her five-year plan, they'd wrung enough out of the city by Q1 year 4 and could move to the east Kent coast to raise pugs and, maybe, babies. Al had responded instantly, 'I'll rot in this town.'

'Where are the others?' said Stephanie. Al thought that he didn't care.

You don't take a week off from a highly sought-after east London studio space to worry about the others. That'd be a cool name for a project, The Others, he thought, then, remembering the Nicole Kidman vehicle, drat, and then, still...maybe. The others rode by on a gondola. They were in 'Little Italy'. Al searched his mind for a memory of James Gandolfini in a gondola but nothing came. The name of the gondola driver was Mohammed. Gerard asked him how many times he went up and down the lazy river each day. Mohammed replied, 'Manchester United.'

Gerard said 'cool' and wondered if he should tell Mohammed that Jose Mourinho said the C-word in a press conference this morning but remembered Del was cranky with him for using data roaming on her iPhone so stopped himself. Del thought Mohammed looked like the man from the Gino Ginelli advert, Egyptian, but with the same amount of fat.

'Yes, y'all,' said Gerard as they approached the metal palm tree Stephanie and Al were lying under. No-one had asked a question.

'How are you this morning?' asked Del. It was 14.09.

Last night, Stephanie and Al had left Gerard and Del sat silently and apart, watching two young Russian couples and a middle-aged husband and wife from a Lancashire town they later couldn't remember the name of play 'Mr & Mrs'. The tie-break involved the older Russian couple and the English couple bursting balloons by hitting their bodies against each other as quickly as possible. The Russian man had the cocky assuredness of someone who had taken his girlfriend from behind in public before. The Lancashire couple's final balloon exploded water all over his Hackett polo shirt and her denim hot pants. Everyone laughed. They were crowned Mr & Mrs despite being two seconds behind on the clock. The mainly Russian crowd had cheered them to the public vote. Physical comedy knows no borders, thought Gerard.

Stephanie replied to Del that Al had been unwell.

'Thanks Stephanie,' said Al, his cheekbones rising with sarcasm.

'What's Delhi belly called in Egypt?' said Gerard.

'The Sharm El Shakes?' said Stephanie.

'Sounds like a dance,' said Gerard.

Before the Mr & Mrs competition, an early thirty-something Egyptian man, who had modelled his hair and body movements on the Brazilian footballer Neymar, had led approximately 175 small children, mums, nans and a pair of pot-bellied shaven-headed Russian homosexuals in a seven-minute group dance to the internet meme 'Harlem Shake'. They had looked like a flash mob unprepared for a walk-on role in a second world Olympics opening ceremony.

'The Cairo Pyro?' said Stephanie.

'That doesn't work unless fire shot out of your arse,' said Gerard.

'It did,' said Al. Al was bantering. It seemed this was what the twins did. In for a penny, he thought. 'Fire did shoot out of my arse. That's why Ras Mohammed blanked us at the salad bar at lunch. His pregnant teenage wife had to clear up the charcoaled porcelain remnants and now he thinks we're Western pigs.' Ras Mohammed was the name they had for the attentive and moustached high-waisted waiter who attended to them at meal times. Ras Mohammed was the name of an Egyptian national park.

'They're called the shits,' said Del. This wasn't the high level of conversation she was hoping for when she met Gerard. His dating profile had highlighted his passion for Italian cinema and West Coast psych bands, not these scatalogical tangents. A tote bag design ran through her mind: 'You were more interesting on the internet'.

A small Russian boy ran by. His t-shirt had seven cartoon birds in varying colours on its front. The slogan said: 'You Wouldn't Like Me When I'm Angry'. Ditto that, Del thought. She felt cheated out of a week of annual leave, but how could she disagree with a suggestion made at a funeral by grieving relatives?

Seeing each other three times a week worked, or had done, once. It was like administering medicine. Happy hour drinks, minority ethnic restaurant, sex, Netflix, takeaway pizza delivery, sex, brunch, broadsheets, sleep. But not this. This was too much. The call to prayer went out again and Gerard looked down at his shorts.

Gerard was reading a Miranda July book. He'd spent four minutes reading the first chapter and seven minutes lining it up perfectly against his sun lounger for a shot to share online.

'What are you doing? Does she even have Instagram?

'Miranda July created her own app, I'm sure she has an account on the world's second most popular social network.'

'Stop that talk. You'll upset Twitter,' said Del.

'Are Egypt and Italy friends?' asked Stephanie.

'Egypt has requested but Italy is thinking about it,' said Gerard.

'They're allies, Egypt and Italy,' said Del. She watched the Arab Spring unfold on the rolling news channel at Isosceles.

'Oh,' said Stephanie.

'Of course they're allies. Center Parcs doesn't have an Afghanistan Zone,' said Gerard.

'Oh,' said Stephanie.

Chill, thought Al. Al had eaten a quattro stagioni in the Italian-themed restaurant last night. That's what did it, he thought, his belly growling, ropey artichokes.

'Maybe it's because Italian culture is easier to photocopy and more favourably received than the Helmand Province.'

'A good point,' said Del, looking at Gerard.

Gerard raised his eyebrows, shouted 'CANNONBALL' and jumped into the pool. A Muscovite great-grandfather scorned him with his eyes. Gerard plunged his head into the water and pushed towards the ceramic floor with his forearms. As his hands touched the warm tiles his legs broke the surface and straightened up, pointing towards the sky. He counted...one, two, three...and wondered if it had been a good idea to come on holiday with Stephanie. Del seemed distant, even more so than recently. He thought about how Al wouldn't be a mate unless he was with Stephanie and how now Stan was gone he only had two ethnic friends, and one of those was Greek-Cypriot and he wasn't sure that counted.

..ten, eleven, twelve...

Gerard thought about the umbilical cord. He thought about their suicidal childhood cat. He thought about their dead dad. He thought about how mad Del had been when he turned up unannounced at her work night out at the Korean BBQ and wondered why. The chlorine stung his eyes even though they were closed...

...twenty-one, twenty-two, twenty-three...

...it was a good idea. A good idea. Gerard's hands slipped away and his head broke through the water. Through the rare silence came the slow hand-clap of the elderly Muscovite.

The water splashed Del and broke her concentration. She had been looking up at a disappearing jumbo jet, its white slipstream bubble-written against the blue sky. When she was seven, she'd asked her dad if the man in the moon had taken a jet plane. He had looked up from his crossword and said, 'If the man on the moon had taken a plane up there, don't you think Apollo II would have found it?' before looking back to his crossword. As she looked out at the horizon, past the plastic leaning tower, Del thought how that was the first thing she could ever remember. She looked left towards the mountains, then right to Stephanie and Al. She looked towards Gerard in the pool and closed her eyes.

Gerard woke up at 5 a.m. UTC. He wasn't feeling too good. The WiFi connection was patchy. He flicked through the channels of their non-flat screen TV, the sound muted to low. Del snored next to him. On Channel 20, an advert for cellulite cream played. The screen showed a before image, the skin mottled like the Egyptian landscape, before segueing into an after picture, the body toned and tan. Channel 21 played a football match. The camera work made it look like it was being played in the eighties, but Gerard could only count one white person on the pitch.

Channel 22 had an advert for the Daz doorstep challenge, but instead of Shane Ritchie a man dressed like Lawrence of Arabia was at the door of a lady who had spilt chocomilk all down her white robe. Channel 23 played an advert for the film *The Social Network*, showing at 7 p.m. that evening. Jesse Eisenberg and Andrew Garfield spoke in English but the subtitles on the screen reminded Gerard of the words painted on blankets waved by angry Arabs on the TV news on September 12, 2001.

Channel 24 was white noise.

Del groaned and rolled over.

Gerard turned the screen off and tried to taste the silence with his tongue.

CHAPTER

17

Can you get jet lag from a four-hour flight? Gerard asked himself. His body felt tired, achey. His brain moved at dial-up speed. He hoped the customers couldn't see the egg timer tumbling over and over on his forehead. Fortunately, the bar was quiet. A nearby street food festival had borrowed the city's hipster quota for the evening.

'Nice rest then, mate?' The inside of Edwin's right arm was covered in cling film.

'Oh yeah, real cruisey. I feel like I've had a week at the Betty Ford clinic.'

'Your rehab references are so old Hollywood.'

'They still prescribe passive-aggressive water park fun there, yeah?'

'If you have a note from a good doctor, I'm led to believe anything can be arranged. By the looks of you, one thing they didn't prescribe was a suntan.' Gerard's skin looked sallow, a chewing-gum white.

'Edwin, firstly, you sound like my mum's husband with that attempt at humour.' Gerard finished pulling a pint of cherry-infused stout and exchanged currency with the customer.

'And secondly, skin cancer is no laughing matter. Factor fifty for life.' Gerard had avoided the sun where possible on holiday, a combination of a morbid fear of the ageing process and Al's slightly superior physique. It was increasingly difficult for a squeezed entrepreneur-creative to fit a boot camp in between the split shifts, script rewrites and visitor maps.

'Anyway, what the fuck is that cling film on your arm?'

'Really? Did you leave your brain on a water slide?'

'What?'

'Repeat after me: tin foil is for smack addicts, cling film is for ink addicts.'

'Jesus, yeah. Maybe I'm still on Cairo time.' Gerard looked at himself in the back of a teaspoon. The warped reflection gave him no new information.

'So what did you get done this time?' Gerard's eyes were bleary under AlePunk's low-level lighting. He couldn't work out the design through the nappy rash cream and scabs.

'4REAL.'

'What?'

'The number four and the word real. Cool, isn't it?' Gerard grabbed Edwin's hand and took a closer look at the arm.

'Just what do you hope to achieve with this new tattoo?' Gerard asked.

'I don't know, a considerable boost in my social communities, an ice breaker with chicks...'

'I think you need to Google the origins of this phrase, Edwin.'

'I did. Kanye was pictured with it on a jacket a few years ago and the internet went wild.'

Gerard stopped what he was doing, which was turning bottles of ale so the open road hand-drawn on their label pointed towards the bar, and faced Edwin full on.

'Are you for real, Edwin?'

'Clearly, now I am. I suppose the real dream is that when you Google 4REAL in the future, the search results serve you up a picture of my tattooed arm.'

'You're a regular hero.'

'You're right, I do see the world in a unique way.' Edwin may or may not have been playing with Gerard now. Perhaps neither of them could really tell.

'They should name an Instagram filter after you,' Gerard snarked.

The holiday had passed without any major talking points. There were no shark bites. No superbugs. No Pharaoh resurrections. In fact, there wasn't much talking at all. Waiting for an omelette at the breakfast station on the second morning, Stephanie had warned Gerard that Al was more of a thinker than a talker.

'Go easy on him, I really like this one.' Del hadn't talked much at all. She'd spent most of her time eyes closed lying on an inflatable flamingo in a peanut-shaped pool, drifting aimlessly between lip-locked couples and hyperventilating children. On dry land, her phone took up ninety-five per cent of her attention, her chipped black fingernails swiping left and right, occasionally joining in conversations on cop movies or comedown stories when called upon.

Gerard had hoped that Del and Stephanie could become more than just Facebook friends. On the surface, they seemed to have shared interests. Online shopping, gossip sites, YouTube beauty tutorials, gender politics. But he'd come to realise his expectation was as shallow as expecting two men who liked football to develop an emotional connection based purely on that fact.

Stephanie and Del had got on well enough on the surface, teaming up for a game on a pub quiz app one night and trouncing Gerard and Al, a born lone wolf, in a capital cities of the world round. He'd imagined that without him they'd be the kind of friends to bump into each other offline and feel awkward and promise to meet for a drink but never do it. He realised this was almost everyone he knew.

Al was the enigma Edwin engineered his life to be. Stephanie seemed happy. She told him she was happy. She smiled as though she was. Gerard didn't possess the mystical sixth sense shared by twins. Three or four times a year he'd attribute a heart skip or a cold sweat to a terrible road accident or unspeakable terrorist atrocity, Stephanie caught up in the crossfire, her dying words, 'Tell Gerard I...'

His soothsaying hadn't been right yet. Stephanie half-joked she'd inherited the powers for the two of them. Gerard used to tell her she'd got lucky sensing a childhood wrist sprain and teenage pregnancy scare. Just good timing. But now he wasn't so sure.

'Take care, Gerard,' she said as Del helped the driver store the bags underneath a National Express coach at Heathrow Terminal Four.

'I'm here if you want to Facebook chat...about anything.'

*

'Did you watch telly last night?'

'Edwin, that is such a retro question.'

There were only six customers in the bar. Five of them had spent a highly-charged hour engaged in the board game Ticket to Ride. There was one hour to go until Sunday closing.

'I live an on-demand lifestyle. Content isn't king. I am.'

'Yeah, sure, alright man. I think the ink has poisoned your brain.'

The cling film on Edwin's arm had blistered. Gerard took his phone out of his pocket and tried to think of shareable content for AlePunk's social feeds.

'Anyway, I was round at Lenka's new house, she's not got WiFi yet and—'

'You were at Lenka's house?'

'Yeah, we've been...hanging out.' Edwin shuffled along the bar. He developed a sudden interest in a pump clip.

'Hanging out?'

'It kind of started when you were on holiday. We were on the rota together a lot...and, you know...'

'Edwin, I feel like you've cheated on me with my hypothetical work girlfriend.' Gerard's words were mock-joking. His tone wasn't.

'But you have a...thetical girlfriend.'

'That is not a word and that is not the point.'

'Two pints of Shapeshifter, please.' Gerard pulled the draught and wondered if he was only half-joking, what was the other half doing? Edwin disappeared for the next half hour. The rhythm of their working relationship meant Gerard knew he'd be in the cellar, filling the lift with bottles of craft beer with names like Psychedelic Surfer and Hip Hops. When the doors closed, Gerard popped the top off a pair of the former.

'I was just messing about Lenka you know, dude.' He took a sip, the undertone of caramel nowhere to be seen. 'It's awesome news.' He meant it.

'Thanks, man, we're just, you know, hanging out...'

'It's cool.'

'It is cool.'

A swarm of beards passed by the window.

'Anyway, what I was trying to say earlier, the telly comment—' Edwin was trying to change the subject.

'Oh.'

'So we watched this programme on the evolution of man. Lenka's into that kind of stuff.' Gerard raised an eyebrow, his face complicit.

'It was mind-blowing. It took us years and years to work out how to make a spear point and then BAM – 250,000 years later we're up in space.'

'And 250,050 years we've got Facebook,' Gerard said. He took a long swig of his beer. They sat for what felt like a long time, their mouths and their devices synced in silence. Gerard started laughing, loud uncontrollable belly laughs.

'Gerard, are you okay?'

'You know what, Edwin? I don't think I can answer that question right now.'

CHAPTER

18

'Thanks for coming,' Gerard whispered, 'it's just they keep asking and it's easier to say yes sometimes, you know?' Gerard looked Del in the eye, her pupils dilated. 'I'm sure you don't want to be here.'

'It's fine,' Del replied, forgetting to whisper.

They were sat on the two-seater in Maureen's front room. Maureen was in the kitchen, her stress level on red alert at the reality of hosting a real-life vegan in her own home. Greg at the office had printed her a recipe, but by step three of making the non-dairy chocolate brownies she'd realised she didn't know you could get milk from soya, let alone have any in her fridge. She'd closed her eyes, counted to five and added some double cream instead. She'd never tell, would she?

She'd texted Stephanie 'IS THIS 1 A KEEPER THEN?' She'd replied two days later: 'You'll have to ask your first-born'. Del chewed the brownie around her mouth.

'These are delicious.'

'Thanks, love. Up all night, I was.' Del wasn't sure if she was joking or not. 'Call me Maureen. I'd say call me Mo, but nobody else does.'

'That's my mum's attempt at a joke.'

'Oh.'

'Quiet, you.' Del looked back and forth between the two of them, like a cat watching Wimbledon. She thought she should laugh. She laughed. Nervously.

'We would have done a barbecue, but I wouldn't have known what to do for a—'

'Oh, these are more than enough.'

Cardiff was in the midst of a mini-heatwave. Gerard and Del wore denim shorts, unintentionally matching.

'Well, I can see you caught the sun more than my boy. You're a lovely colour.' Maureen was used to filling in the space in conversations. It was a key component of the training at Go!Kids, an essential tactic in owning potentially awkward exchanges with parents or donors. Her appraisals said she had a natural aptitude for the skill. Del lifted a china mug and drank some green tea. The cup squeaked as she put it back down on a saucer next to her phone on the coffee table. After a week at an all-inclusive buffet, her shorts were too tight for internet-enabled devices.

'I didn't know if you wanted the bag left in or out. So I thought leave it in, Maureen. She can always take it out.'

'This is lovely, honestly.' Del smiled. A splash of green tea dripped on her bottom lip, mixing with the dark lip-liner.

'So, did we miss much here then, Mum?' said Gerard. He wished she hadn't gone to all this effort, but he appreciated it all the same. After so long in London, he'd almost forgotten this rite of passage. Another thing for the 'con' column.

'Not much, love. We're all still plodding on.' This was the first time Gerard had seen his mum since the funeral. She seemed herself. When their dad died, he remembered she'd gone into overdrive. Helping with maths homework, signing the twins up for Beavers, Brownies, dance classes, piano lessons, fencing, volunteering every night of the week. Gerard's play-time had been severely depleted. He resented it at the time.

'Dad wouldn't make us do this.'

'Well, Dad's not here.'

Gerard was twelve years old. He hadn't really missed his dad. He'd spent most of the twins' life up to that point at the office. If he was at home, he'd be at the dining room table, his hunched, balding frame hidden behind stacks of lever arch files. He'd work away silently as the twins argued over the remote control or games console, Stephanie switching over Gerard's favourite show, Gerard pulling the power cord just as Stephanie was about to complete The Legend of Zelda.

When he died, the piles of files stayed on the dining room table for months afterwards. Gerard's mum hadn't known what to do with them at first. They'd continued eating their tea from trays in front of the television, chewing loudly, laughing occasionally, giving the phantom figure of their father and husband the space to non-exist.

One day, a man from the office came to the door. He was dressed in the same suit as their dad, but was taller, his hair thicker. He'd come for the files. Gerard hadn't recognised him from the funeral. Maureen offered him tea, cake, sandwiches, anything he'd like. He'd declined, politely, and mentioned the files again. They'd eaten at the table that night. Fish fingers, chips and beans. Gerard's favourite. Stephanie had asked Maureen why she was crying. They never ate at the table again.

Gerard wondered what his father would think of him now, if he'd be proud, if it mattered.

Gerard hadn't heard it spoken out loud since the man from the office came around. He looked at the mantelpiece. He looked at the walls. He couldn't see his picture. He reached out his index finger and brushed the top of his mum's hand.

'Anyway, tell us about your holiday, you two.'

Del wanted to tell her how she and Al had been dragged to the Middle East so her children could play out some recreation of their childhood, but she figured this was not the appropriate time. The woman's mother had just died. And she'd made her rather delicious brownies.

'It was lush, Mum. The weather was boiling.'

'Too hot, if anything,' Del chipped in.

'And we went on a load of water slides and drank a load of cocktails and ate a load of kebabs, well, I did, and generally had a load of fun hanging out,' Gerard said.

'That's nice, love.'

Maureen looked between the two of them, catching Del's eye for a little too long. Del knew she'd spoken to Stephanie. She doubted her approval rating had been five-star.

'Your Auntie Bronwen hasn't been well, love.'

'Oh...' Gerard tried his best to sound interested.

'She's been off work since your nanna died.' Maureen paused, swallowed.

'Stress.' Del nodded understandingly. Bronwen was hit hardest by every family crisis or tragedy. She didn't leave her bed for a month after the incident with Uncle Derek, Gerard's online game invitations reaching their peak during this period.

The living room door opened.

'Hello campers.'

It was Geoff. He was wearing a navy blue three-piece suit. His remaining hairs were slicked back over his scalp, mottled like a duck egg.

'Did you pair have a phar-aohld time in Egypt? Did you miss your mummy, Gerard?' Geoff leaned forward and poked Gerard in the ribs, winking at Del. She laughed.

'Mum, stop him,' Gerard said, twelve years old in an instant.

'Geoff, why are you dressed in your suit?' Gerard had seen Geoff in this suit twice in quick succession – Nanna Judy's funeral and now, today. The only previous time he'd seen him so smart was when he went on a speed awareness course for driving thirty-three in a thirty miles-per-hour zone.

The doorbell rang.

Pepsi barked.

'That'll be him, love,' Maureen said.

'Who?' Gerard asked.

'I'll get it,' said Geoff, skipping out of the room. Pepsi barked again, louder this time.

'Mum, what the hell is going on?' Gerard was agitated now. Del laughed.

'Hello Gerard!' It was Lars. He was wearing a red leather Harrington jacket and a denim kilt, just above the knee. His legs were shaved and sunburned.

'How was your holiday?' Geoff stood next to Lars, hands on hips. His face was beaming.

'It was...'

'Ah, I see you are confused about why I am here. ' Lars grinned. Gerard thought his mouth looked like Heath Ledger as The Joker. This made him sad, momentarily, before the confusion returned.

'You could say that.'

'Let me tell you—'

'He's here to take Geoff's portrait, love,' said Maureen.. Gerard choked on his tea. Del patted his back.

'Aye, Lars had a problem with the hot water. The boiler needed bleeding. Remember I wrote it on a bit of paper for you? Bleed boiler every June. Well, anyway. It's fixed now, as you know,' said Geoff.

'The showers are hotter than hell,' Lars laughed.

'We got talking, me and Lars, and three pints later...'

'Like a house on fire, as you say,' said Lars, his big meaty hand flopping on Geoff's shoulder. Geoff smiled, a little uncomfortably, Del thought.

Pepsi barked.

'Quiet, dog!'

'Geoff has the perfect face to picture. My portrait from my time in Wales,' said Lars.

'He's not even Welsh!' Gerard said.

'What is nation in the twenty-first century?' said Lars, 'Really? Make Wales great again, haha.'

'Can I get you a cup of tea or a coffee, Lars?' asked Maureen.

'Anything stronger?' Lars asked. 'It helps my art, haha.'

'Oo, yes,' said Maureen, nervously rushing to the cupboard filled with half-empty spirit bottles from holiday, 'I believe we do.'

'Get Lars a Sol,' Geoff shouted over his shoulder, 'they're on the shelf in the garage.'

'Lime, Lars?'

'Sure, why not?'

'He'll have a lime, love,' Geoff shouted again. Del buried her hands in Pepsi's curly fur. She tried to stifle a laugh. Her low expectations of a visit to Gerard's mum's house had been surpassed.

'Gerard, can you give me a hand with my equipment? It's in the car outside,' Lars said.

'You've got a car?'

'Lars has borrowed the Mazda, love. He's going to make a studio in the garage.'

'Of course he has,' said Gerard.

Geoff loved that car. Gerard had asked to borrow it last summer. He'd half planned a trip to the Gower coastline. He'd travelled all over the world but never visited these beaches, just one hour west of home. TripAdvisor had named Rhossili Bay one of the top-ten beaches in the world. He'd always come up with excuses when Grampy Joe had wanted to take him, but when the hive mind spoke he was interested. The request for the soft top had been as much about testing the boundaries; if a convertible was on tap at home, maybe moving to Wales wouldn't be so bad. Geoff had laughed. An unequivocal 'no', a bus timetable handed over.

Lars had already popped the boot of the immaculate red car by the time he and Gerard reached it. His kilt rippled in the breeze.

'He's a good man, your dad,' said Lars, handing Gerard a tripod.

'He's my mum's...' Gerard said, stopping himself, '...he's my stepdad.'

For the next hour, Maureen, Gerard and Del were employed as Lars' interns. Maureen, the eager-to-please runner, bringing refreshments, light snacks, frantically brushing Geoff's suit for crumbs. Geoff had tidied the garage beyond even its usual state. A variety of garden tools hung by the handles across the walls like an avant-garde installation. Masonry was arranged in small, neat, plastic boxes, increasing in millimetres from left to right. Lars loved the order of it all.

'The god of small things is the god of all things, ja!'

'Aye,' confirmed Geoff, slurping tea from his England mug.

'Why is Geoff in his suit, Lars?' asked Del.

'It propels the ordinary to the extraordinary, you see?' It was Geoff's turn to grin. Gerard had been stood on a tin of varnish, holding a flashlight for at least twenty minutes.

'Del, hold this, I'm busting.' He hopped off, nearly knocking Maureen and a plate of shortbread flying. He crossed through the kitchen, the living room and into the downstairs toilet. A small sign, a metal reproduction from an early twentieth-century building site saying 'No Erections Here' hung above the cistern.

Gerard peed.

He thought about how this was turning into a good day. He thought how he'd never have stumbled into this situation miles away down the motorway in London. He thought how Del seemed to be smiling at last. He walked back through the living room. Pepsi brushed his leg, depositing a rubber bone at his feet.

'Pepsi.'

She ran across the room and jumped onto the two-seater.

'Pepsi.'

Gerard picked up the bone and followed. She'd saved him a seat. He sank into the cushion and offered the rubber bone into her hungry, happy mouth. She panted. A noise came from the table. His phone. He'd not checked it for over an hour. He picked it up from the coffee table but his notifications were empty. Del's phone flashed back to dark. He pushed a finger on the bottom. The screen lit.

'Tinder notification: You have a new match.'

CHAPTER

19

You are cordially invited to Life Through A Lens:
A retrospective of the work of Lars Van Leeuwenhoek.
15th July 7pm
Refreshments and canapes served.
Dress code: Whatever makes you happy.

Gerard folded the invitation and put it back in his coat pocket. It was raining, in spite of the season. He was running late. He couldn't think of a reason why.

Maybe I want to make a dramatic entrance, he thought. He picked his pace up, walking past the castle on his left, side-stepping a group of Chinese tourists lost in the task of capturing the turrets against the sunset.

Gerard thought of all the pictures he'd taken, the minutes spent in getting the composition just right, the photo now filed next to thousands of other jpegs, never to be looked at again. Shooting for perfection for the sake of it.

His mum wouldn't be there tonight. This was for the best. Geoff was working nights. He'd had difficulty convincing his colleague Terry that his attendance at the launch of a photography exhibition by his new Dutch friend was a good enough reason to swap shifts. 'And I didn't bat an eyelid when the bugger wanted me to work his weekend so he could go to a Northern Soul weekender at Butlins. Short memory he's got, that lad.'

Del was stood outside the National Museum, her body fragile against the centuries-old Portland stone steps. Her open-toed shoes were proving inappropriate for the weather, rain drops collecting on her black painted toe nails. 'Four seasons in one hour in Wales,' her taid's (Welsh for grandfather) voice in her busy head. She'd not been in the museum since he'd taken her and Seren inside to shelter on an equally wet Welsh summer's day, the year 1994 or 1995. She'd cried when a prosthetic woolly mammoth had roared, the sound from a backing tape like an outtake from a Jurassic Park prequel.

'It's okay, *cariad*. It's not real. See, it's not real.'

Stood there waiting for Gerard to arrive, that day felt like ten lifetimes ago. Taid was dead for a start. Lung cancer. The curse of the coal mine. Maybe in the future we'd shrug in the same way when call centre workers contracted brain cancer from all the radiation, she thought. She took her phone out of her coat pocket. She needed something to cling to.

Gerard was also practicing diversion tactics. As he walked, he imagined himself as the thick-rimmed anti-star of a series of viral TED talks targeted at young creatives, the titles click-friendly. People are the Plot. Break and Make. Cleverlution. That was all he had so far. Their success would lead to a cover interview in a broadsheet weekend supplement, the now classic 'old meets new media' crossover collaboration. Lifestyle brands for solutions scratching itches humans hadn't even thought of yet would pay exorbitant sums to work their products into tenuously linked videos on his YouTube channel.

Gerard stepped on an uneven paving stone, water slopping up into his desert boot, soaking his sock. His concentration broke. There she was, Del. Her bright yellow raincoat zipped to the top, her face poking out of the hood like an elfin princess under a bridge.

'Hey.'

'Hey!' Del added the enthusiasm. 'So this should be cool?'

'Should be.'

'Well...shall we get in from the rain then?'

'Oh...yeah...good idea.'

They walked up the steps, close but not holding hands. Del reached out. Gerard sensed the movement, squeezed her fingers and moved for his pocket. Del got the message.

'7.32. We're late.'

'It's the fashion.'

'Anyway, how was your day?' Del asked.

'Ah, you know.' Gerard knew what he was doing. He was pushing for an argument. For once, he was certain he would win. Del hated ambiguity when she wanted detail. She'd told Gerard this on their date (Excellent Moment #8) when the incident with the creepy drunk guys meant his slacker mask dropped for a moment in blind terror that he might be called upon to prove his manhood in a way he'd rather not. After the scene had settled, he'd babbled to Del about his childhood, about Stephanie, about Geoff, Nanna Judy and his vision for a wholly successful, mainly creative future. Del had slurped the last of a two-for-one Tequila Sunrise and whispered something positive into his ear. Neither of them could remember what.

He's testing me. Don't bite. Breathe. Be Zen, Del told herself.

They reached the top of the stairs, Gerard a heartbeat before Del, and walked out of step through the double decker-high doors. The space in front of them was a glitzy rectangle of marble and light. Walkways ran across the top of solid stone pillars, the exhibits set behind them just out of sight. Gerard considered for a moment what it would be like to climb the rail and jump from the edge, glory and gristle, blood and vanity spilling over the postcard aisle of the gift shop. He wondered if it would be art.

'Welkom. Welcome. Croeso. Here for the launch?' The question came from a girl in a polo shirt. She'd dyed her hair grey. Gerard felt this was cute and, somehow, passive-aggressive. He couldn't tell if her face was attractive because he couldn't stop looking at her grey hair.

'Busted.' Gerard considered telling her Lars was his friend, but checked himself.

'If you hurry, you should catch the speeches.' She handed them a map. Gerard over-thanked her. He wondered if he was already flirting with the next Del. He wondered if this was all an act.

They crossed the floor in silence, Del busying herself by unfolding the matte-finished pamphlet. They passed a sculpture of a soldier boy from the nineteenth century sounding a battle cry on brass, his hair all curls and copper. Gerard ignored the sign and ran his finger across the mound of ground he was stood on. It felt warm to the touch, his finger clammy from the rain.

'My navigation skills have deduced it's upstairs,' Del said. She was holding the map upside down. Gerard nodded, the signal positive, his expression neutral. They climbed the stairs.

'Are you alright?'

'Me?'

'No, the statue, Gerard.'

'Yeah,' he said, 'I'm cool.'

The sound of small talk and pretension came from the glass double doors to their right. It drew them in. Gerard pushed the weight away from him and the noise got louder. The room was wide and long and adjoined to a series of other rooms through an open archway. It was filled with maybe twenty to twenty-five people. He didn't recognise anyone, apart from a lady with a short, severe bob, but he then thought he recognised her from television and then that he was just projecting. Some of the people were in suits, as if they'd come straight from an office job and hadn't had time to change into creased denims and an informal shirt in the shared toilet facilities of their workplace.

Others wore blazers with jeans and some wore no jacket at all. At first glance, the females seemed mainly to be wearing long, flowy dresses with long, flowy sleeves. Gerard was fairly sure this was boho chic. It was a common look at art events and at the backstage areas at festivals. One man wore a biker jacket with the words 'One Love' fading against black leather, the 'e' of 'One' almost completely wiped away.

Gerard thought that 'On Love' sounded like a collection of essays on the Romantic poets by an eminent Russell Group professor. He thought he'd say this to Del, but looked to his side and she was gone. He scanned the room and saw she was talking to an older mixed-race man in a velvet waistcoat who looked like he either was an artist or knew a lot about art or maybe was just a regular at exhibitions.

He needed a drink. He could see waiting staff were mingling between the crowd with trays of wine. It was always wine at these kinds of things. Wine or warm beer. He manouvered through the group and caught up with a teenage waiter.

'What is it?'

'It's red wine, sir, a cabernet sauvignon.'

A voice came over a microphone. It sounded nervous but happy that Lars had agreed to exhibit a retrospective of his work in Wales. Gerard thought it might have been the Dutchman on the board of the Museum, but his accent sounded more like he was from California. He looked around but couldn't see Lars. Some people on the outskirts of the room continued to whisper. Someone laughed.

Lars entered the room through the archway. It was clear he'd asked for entrance music but the Museum hadn't quite been able to fulfil his request. It sounded like Rotterdam house music was being played through a streaming service from one of the waiters' phones. Lars didn't seem to mind. He was wearing a kilt, leather this time, and a black t-shirt with the words 'Shoot Me' on the front in white capital letters. Gerard thought he seemed drunk.

His mind was elsewhere during Lars' speech, but his ears pricked up when he thought he heard him reference Geoff. The crowd clapped politely when he stopped speaking. Involuntarily, Gerard looked to his left to one-hand clap with Del, but she wasn't there. He tapped his chest with his right hand, the wine in his left. The sound was negligible.

The heat from the other bodies made Gerard want to take his coat off. Everyone else had clearly got the message about the cloakroom. He saw Del. She wasn't wearing her yellow raincoat. He grabbed another red wine. The people dispersed around the edges of the room, moving in an identifiable pattern around the photographs mounted on the off-white walls.

Gerard began moving clockwise around the space, stopping and starting for a few paces to the next exhibit at irregular intervals. His standard gallery practice was to approach the piece, attempt to guess the artist, look to the accompanying sign for confirmation. He'd generally guess wrong, before reading the interpretation, then looking properly at the artwork, assuring himself he'd sensed the emotions or motifs or bad childhood or war angst he'd just read about. On this occasion he was even more unfocused, standing to contemplate for a minute, sometimes for three, but mainly he looked at his phone.

It beeped.

Del: Where are you?

Gerard: In front of the pregnant lady in the barber shop chair

Del: I loved that one

Gerard: I like her belly

Del: Her belly was gross but I loved that one

Gerard: The chair is the real star

Del: I'd like it as my throne

He didn't ask Del where she was. The woman with the short bob walked in front of him. He looked up at her, her hair stationary as the rest of her body moved slowly, surely to the next photograph.

Del: Have you seen the pig farmer?

Gerard: Er no

Del: It made me sick

Gerard: Okay

Del: Physically :(

Gerard: I'm looking at the portrait of the maths teacher

Del: oH not seen that one

Gerard: She has a knitted Pie jumper

Gerard: Haha

Gerard: Pi

Gerard: 3.14

Del: Haha

Gerard: I wonder if she was Lars' maths teacher

The background music turned into the default iPhone ringtone, Marimba. Everyone in the room reached for their pocket or their bag, relieved of the distraction from the art and the reach of another human being through the prism of technology. A young waiter dropped his tray and ran towards a small cupboard, his remaining glasses dropping to the floor but not smashing. Regardless, the thwump of glass on wood diverted the attention of the room to where he just was. The music returned, the beats of the tinny track resuming. Everyone turned back to the art.

Gerard felt a twinge in his stomach. He thought he was either hungry or it was just because. He ran his tongue over the inside of his teeth. A grain of rice worked its way loose. He remembered he'd had supermarket sushi two hours ago. It wasn't hunger. He moved to the next picture.

Del: Haha. That was funny.

Gerard: What?

Del: The music thing

Del: I thought it was house music for a second

Gerard: Yeah

Gerard: Where are you?

Del: At a picture

Del: It's quite dark

Del: It's this old lady with a tattooed face

Gerard: I don't trust people with tattoos on their face

Del: Me neither

Gerard: I don't trust people who....

Del: ...put sugar in their tea

Gerard: No

Del: ...have tepid bathwater

Gerard: No

Del: ...are sound sleepers

Gerard: No

Gerard: I don't trust you Del

Gerard looked for the waiter with the wine but couldn't see him, then headed towards the doors. Lars called his name, his kilt flapping as he shouted, but Gerard didn't hear. He followed the stairs down, past the statue of the soldier, past the place where the girl with grey hair greeted them and outside, into the night.

'Gerard! Wait up...'

He turned around halfway down the stone steps. Del stood in front of him, the rain soaking through her checked shirt, her yellow raincoat forgotten at the cloakroom. Her eyes were smudged black.

Gerard walked up the stairs, reached out and held Del close to him. He could feel a thousand statuses crackling through her slender body; the first Instagram post he saw of hers, a healthy snack box on her cluttered desk, the first time she tagged him in a tweet after their night out with Isosceles, the bored hashtags when they were on holiday. He wondered if this was all their collective memory amounted to, stream of consciousness posturing archived by a monolithic conglomerate.

These details, the building blocks of personality, would become inconsequential, forgotten in time, leaving the outline of a person. There would be nothing hidden away in a shoebox to jog the memory, the photos deleted, the megabytes released for something else.

Del wanted to ask him where he was going now.

But she didn't ask.

He didn't have to answer.

*

As Gerard walked back to the cottage the city passed him by oblivious, taxi drivers, dog walkers, teenagers talking and laughing, uncaring of his fate. His head felt empty, heavy, like when he'd finished his A-level English Literature exam and he'd made decisions based on books he'd never read.

He took his phone out of his pocket instinctively. Safety in technology. He remembered something Stina had told him that day in the Bay. He swiped his finger on the screen, trying to unlock the safety net with his print. He'd done the same one hundred times today.

Fingerprint not recognised.

Enter back-up password.

'Am I alive?' he said out loud, looking at the moon through the no-battery black sky.

*

The doors of the museum had been closed for hours, the last of the guests leaving pleased they'd accomplished the task they set out to achieve; for some, the opportunity to tell the colleague they were sexually interested in that they'd been to an art show last night, leaving them to visualise the life-enriching midweek activities they could share together in an alternative universe; for others it was just hanging around long enough to share a status of their attendance and subsequent opinion on social media.

The grey-haired girl had been in bed for forty-five minutes, one eye open as she searched the hashtag for the event, trying to see if Gerard had tweeted about his evening and if she could stalk him and eventually send him a direct message and have a series of dates which would lead to a short-term strained relationship culminating in a city break in a former Yugoslavian state and/or an unplanned pregnancy scare.

A man named Mariusz glided across the wooden floor of the museum on a cleaning machine. Its efficiency meant Mariusz only earned two hours of pay three evenings a week instead of the six hours he really needed to live even his low expectation lifestyle. Mariusz had studied at the Warsaw School of Photography & Design, but now only took photos on his phone to send suggestively to girls he met on the internet.

He stopped his machine in front of a photograph that caught his eye. He admired the composition, the way the man stood tall, his face red and proud, the subtle geometric pattern of his suit complementing the right angles of the tools hanging from hooks all around him.

Mariusz's phone beeped as he drove his machine away.

Part 2: Offline

CHAPTER

20

Dear Stephanie,

I talked about it in my first ever internet profile, that other lifetime ago. We've all felt embarrassed at a Facebook Memory (is there any other kind? I'm kidding. Half-kidding), but that one reminder seems truer than anything I ever said online. It was in the HTML for the 'hobbies' section:

The lost art of letter writing.

Yeah, I know what you'll say, I was showing off, trying to impress someone. Probably that girl from Coventry we met in Spain that year, the dusty blonde with the braces (Caren? Carol?), the one Nanna Judy said had 'sturdy hips', making a mocktail squirt out of your nose.

So here it is, the lost art revived. Just for you. But you is essentially me, isn't it (give or take a chromosome)? I figured you'd understand.

It's so un-London here, you'd hate it. (How is London? I'm asking more out of a sense of good letter writing etiquette. There's no right of reply here.)

So...me. Most mornings follow the same routine. I wake up around six or six-thirty from the sunlight breaking through the small window in my bedroom. I don't think I've slept in a room without curtains before. You'll remember the Thomas the Tank Engine ones I had as a kid. 'The best part Ringo ever played,' Dad used to say. Waking up this way felt, I don't know, not right at first, like a piece of the room was missing or like a pervert could watch me undress, but I don't think there are any perverts here. If there are, they hide it pretty well. It's a pretty pre-paedo kind of place. The point is, I've got used to the no curtain thing pretty quickly.

There's something about being woken up by the sunlight instead of a computer-generated musical instrument breaking into your dream and saying 'time for work, fucko', or whatever it is you needed to get up for, that puts you in a much better mood. My moods have been better. It just feels more natural. Like you would have woken up this way thousands of years ago, when we lived in caves and windows didn't even exist. I like that feeling, that connection to the other humans, the generations before us. We can learn a lot from them, that's what I'm learning.

For the first few weeks my body would involuntarily reach down the side of the bed for my phone, pre-conditioned to scroll through my social feeds while still horizontal. Sometimes I'd be stuck there for an hour: scroll, click, comment. That's seven hours a week. Yoko says that I could take that time and do something useful with it, that I could learn Danish in six months. It seems a stretch, but she should know, she's done it.

But for now, I just ease myself into the day. I warm a pan of water on the fire and add a squeeze of a handful of berries from the garden. It's the new macchiato. (I bet I've not spelled that right.) Anyway. I tell myself it's nature's caffeine. I've been wondering if caffeine is natural anyway, but now the speculation just sits there, like it used to. Remember that? When we didn't have the answer to EVERYTHING at our fingertips. That was what our brains were for. For remembering and forgetting and remembering again.

Just this week I have remembered that Bonn was the capital of East Germany and that eggs float in water when they're bad and that to get the number of miles from the number of kilometres you have to half it and add a quarter. At least I think these things are true. I'm content with the probable.

When I'm drinking my drink, some days back in bed, other days on the porch, looking out over the straw grass and tall trees that surround the hut, I just sit and let my thoughts go where they want. Sometimes I try and play a little mind game, making my thoughts be about something specific, like, I don't know, umm, peaceful protest or Auntie Bronwen (actually, never Auntie Bronwen, but say hi).

The brain doesn't really like being told what to do though. It makes me think of when we were kids and I'd creep into your room when you were asleep and whisper 'Gerard is the king' into your ear in the hope I could influence your dreams. That never worked, or at least if it did, you were a staunch republican. We use dreams a lot here. They can tell you all kinds of things. Tap you into things you didn't know you were ever a part of.

The brain just does what it wants.

Mainly I end up thinking about Xanadu. One day last week I wondered if that's where I was.

(Xanadu is my film by the way, but I'm going to pretend you already know that. I'm just providing clarity here for the future academics poring over these letters, wondering if you were the inspiration. NB: Stephanie is not the inspiration. Stephanie is an inspiration. You don't share a placenta and leave a brother unblemished.)

My route stays mainly the same. I cut through the grass, into the forest and through the trees, their thin trunks like basketball players made of branches reaching for a slam dunk in the big blue skies. The colours are the kind I'd only ever really paid attention to online shopping for sweaters, ochre and ombre and acorn, and I crunch the leaves under my feet and it feels like the only sound for miles around. I'm living in the moment and I'm loving it.

One morning last week I walked this way and found myself thinking of Dad. I think I'd actively tried not to think of Dad for the past fifteen years. He was such a big character in the early series of our lives that when he was gone, it kind of felt like when a protagonist dies early on in a box set and you're open mouthed on the sofa, udon noodle clinging to your chin. He didn't even have a big character, but he somehow still bagged the role. Must have nailed the screen test I guess, Mum the casting director. Actual LOL at that image.

Did Dad get too big for the Gerard and Stephanie show? (We need to work on the name.) But where else did he have to be? I don't think I've ever believed in the afterlife. I guess I just needed to believe in life first.

The picture I had in my head that day was Dad sat at the dining room table, but it wasn't in our old house; the off-white wallpaper was replaced by Perspex and I couldn't quite make out what was on the other side. At one point it seemed to be the inside of an underground tunnel, the flashes of tiles and lights that catch your eye as the tube flashes by at 100 miles an hour. That feeling of movement through the unknown, the uncertainty, the un-Google mapped. The dining table was mahogany. It didn't have the scratches from the time we made the papier-mâché human brain and you glued the frontal lobe to the top and scraped it off with a spoon. A pile of lever arch files stood on the table, alphabetised and at right angles, perpendicular to the grain. To the left of the files there was an executive toy, I don't know the name or if it even has a name, but it's the one where the ball bearing drops from a height, plummeting towards zero until it hits an identical ball bearing, sending it straight as an arrow in the opposite direction.

The ball bearings are held by some kind of wire string, like two pirate ships on a predetermined collision course for the rest of time at a Kafkaesque theme park. Dad's face looked like da Vinci drew him in biro because the Mona Lisa wasn't ambiguous enough. I believe the look was contentment. I'm not sure he ever looked that way in real life.

Do you remember when Mum was really ill when we were nine or ten and we overheard Dad on the phone to Nanna Judy and we thought we heard Dad say 'cancer' and you told me what it was, that it was like a really bad cold without the sniffles that killed you and that you knew because Daisy Taylor's stepdad had it and I cried myself to sleep and you just laid there? And then the following day, Dad asked us what we would like to do most in the world and we said, 'Go to Oakwood' at the same time and Dad laughed and said he didn't think theme parks were open in October but he would look and he did and it was and Dad drove there for two and a half hours in the rain listening to The Beatles' Red Album twice over and we sang the wrong words to 'She Loves You' and Dad tutted and then cried? And when we got there, the only people in the whole park were us, a handful of half-asleep attendants and an enthusiastic German couple on a theme park tour of western Europe for their honeymoon, their dress sense borrowed from the staff at the Hard Rock Café.

We'd all agreed that the worst thing about theme parks were the queues, but without them we felt like Michael Jackson when they used to close down toy stores to the public so he could shop at his leisure without having to sign autographs or do moonwalks for snotty

-nosed kids and Dad said we could go on the rollercoaster one last time but that we absolutely, positively were not getting a monkey for a pet? Have you still got the photograph from that day? You begged Dad to let us have it.

He joked he was going to haggle over the price because it was the only one they'd sell all day, but you told him that wasn't true because the German couple would definitely buy one and he handed over a fiver and told the boy to keep the change even though there wasn't any?

Over the past few years, I must have taken tens of thousands of pictures on an ever-evolving succession of smartphones and I don't remember any of them as clearly as I do the one from that day. You're on the left of the bright red carriage, your hair like a speech bubble on the side of your head, your hands in the air. I like to think they're celebrating life. I'm on the right, my head on the safety bar, the hood of my green cagoule caught by the camera mid-dance with the wind and velocity. Dad is sat in the middle of us, his expression a man in a passport photo who already knows the plane is going down.

A couple of months later, we asked if he'd take us again. He said no. He didn't even check if the park was open. But Mum was better then, or at least if she wasn't better, she didn't have the thing that Daisy Taylor's stepdad had that made me cry that night.

As I thought about Dad and Mum and you and us, my feet kept moving, the crunch of the leaves a little bit like the ticking clock in a hypnotist's office. I had no idea how long I'd been walking for. My brain is only just getting used to timing events outside of relation to how long it is since they've been posted online. The tops of the trees seemed to be curving inwards, but I didn't feel claustrophobic, more like a living, breathing fisheye lens.

My body started telling me it was time I ate something. And not just chips and dips or edamame or Wasabi peas. A metropolitan snack wasn't going to cut it. My body needed sustenance. Energy. I remembered an op-ed piece I'd read on inner-city foraging. I tried to remember what I learned, which brambles were filled with essential nutrients, which berries made you sick. I couldn't remember anything. I thought harder. The hunger hurt. I couldn't remember if I'd actually read the piece or scrolled past it. Which was it? Is this what I'd done for the past few years, glanced at bookshelves and assumed I'd read the pages inside?

Well, I'll tell you something, Stepher, that broad brush content curation approach does not help you out when you're stuck in the middle of a forest miles from home and you're hungry and it's dark and you're wondering what the fuck you can eat that isn't in a Pret wrapper and won't poison you to death.

I don't know how what happened next happened. A lot of the things we do here have opened my mind in ways I didn't think was possible. When I looked down, I was on a giant trampoline and when I say giant, I mean I'm talking festival-site big, maybe even small-city big. On the way down, I had this horrible, heinous fear that by the time I reached the canvas it would have lost its bounce and I'd break both my legs and I'd be stuck there, on this conurbation-sized thing forever, the bones in my legs piercing through the skin that first grew next to you inside of Mum, poking out like the trunk of a Christmas tree through the boot of a hatchback.

But that didn't happen.

I bounced.

And on the way up I soared through the sky and the air wasn't made from molecules but from memories. They didn't seem like my memories, but I was in them and you were in them and so were the others. There was one which seemed to be in a general goods store in Germany or Austria or in a German or Austrian community in America. The year was around 1919 or 1920, post-Great War. Don't ask me how I knew that, I just did. I was stood at the counter but I couldn't see over the top and the ink on the note I had from someone who felt like my mother (but wasn't our mother, actually it felt more like Del) had ran so much in the rain that I couldn't make out what it was that I was supposed to buy and I could feel the tears and smell the sweat on my face.

And in the next one I was on a plane, but I wasn't sat in economy premium watching a rom-com and eating peanuts, I was flying it and the goggles sat on my nose and even though the engines were intense I could hear the chat about sweethearts and baseball from Edwin and Geoff in the back and I could taste the gum in my mouth and see the rice fields below and feel the hard-on in my pants.

And then I was sat in a press conference at the top table and the reporters were smoking and swearing and staring and waiting for the answer to the question you asked me in French and it was 1961 and my brain was searching for an answer but I couldn't find it and Mum had a camera as big as a Smart car on her shoulder and Nanna Judy was laughing uncontrollably, drunkenly, except that Nanna Judy was half her age, and overweight and underpaid and on her last warning and I knew all of this without having ever spoken to them.

And then it woke me up. And I shit you not, shit for brains, this is true, every single word. I woke up with a deer licking my hand. It pressed its head against my body and I flinched, but it didn't want to hurt me.

I reached out and stroked its side, its skin like a suede jacket I bought on eBay and wore just once (on a second date with a Chinese girl I met online) before watching a what's hot and what's not-style vlog and discovering they were not. Its face brushed me again, its nose sniffing me out. I could smell myself. I was not deodorised. But it didn't run. Its eye looked right into mine and I looked right back. I searched its black pupil and in the darkness, I swear I could see your face.

I haven't been this close to nature since Mum and Dad took us to Penscynor Wildlife Park and I put the 10p in the vending machine and ate the llama food for myself.

I don't feel hungry anymore.

Yours, Gerard.

CHAPTER

21

Dear Lars,

It'd be inappropriate for me to start this any other way. This isn't a 'wish you were here' note. The purpose of this letter is to say sorry and to say thank you. You probably saved my life back there. Okay, that might sound a bit dramatic, but what do you expect? I grew up with the internet. Really though, things were looking touch and go there for a little while. And I'm here, not here specifically, but here on this mortal coil, in part down to you.

I appreciate this isn't what you bargained for when you decided to rent someone's spare room on the internet. I'd even understand if you left me a rotten review, a worse than an uncomfortable pillow, a worse than a dirty hand towel review. One time a Nigerian student nurse in town for ComicCon left me a review (two out of five), claiming her inability to connect to the WiFi meant she missed a photo opportunity with Lando Calrissian's nephew, who now did personal appearances for Lando Calrissian on account of his ill-health.

I'm confident I salvaged the situation, responding publicly that the connection issues had been city-wide and that Lando Calrissian's Wikipedia page said the actor who played him was still alive and active. I think my steady bookings since prove who won that argument. For all I know, you may have already left me a zero. But I doubt it. Through your actions you've treated our relationship not as a click and collect but a covenant, a bond that transcended the bandwidth and became human.

The doctors told me afterwards that it was one of the worst cases of nervous exhaustion they'd ever seen, which seems funny really – I didn't realise I was nervous or exhausted. I still have no idea how long I'd been unconscious when you and Edwin found me on the kitchen floor. Edwin came to see me and told me my phone had been in my hand, the screen unlocked and mid-tweet, the words 'Gerard F. Kane' before a blinking cursor. How I got there, I don't know.

I left Del outside the museum. That I remember. I walked home past the castle. That I remember. I remember the light of the smartphone screen flickering, rotating through social networks, from

Facebook to Twitter to Instagram and back again and back again and back again, the blur of pixels biting away at my brain, edgy as an addict, the words, the pictures, the profiles losing meaning in the rush, the greatest connector in human history frying my connectors to a crisp. When I woke up in the white room, my first instinct was to reach for my phone to finish the tweet.

It wasn't there. In that moment, I thought, 'If I've died and heaven is a WiFi free zone, drag me to hell.'

I've not logged-on since.

I imagine in my absence my Facebook page has turned from hope to desperation to tribute. From 'Come home mate' to 'Just call us' to links to local news stories on the search effort, my twin sister Stephanie (you didn't meet her. Total legend.) looking determined but worn out. The latest posts would be from earnest types: my Auntie Bronwen, if they could escort her out of the online casino; a girl I sat next to in A-level English Literature. If my removal had been better planned, I'd have scheduled 12 months' worth of low-risk, non-time-sensitive posts, kidding my community into thinking I was fully engaging in twenty-first-century life, securing my legacy as a chilled out, good time guy/future auteur.

'Pizza then party time'

'Spent the last hour Airbnbing ranches for Sundance'

'Making money is the greatest work of art of all'.

But I've gone cold turkey. It was the only way.

'Hi, my name is Gerard and I've been an internet addict for about fifteen years now. It's been four months since my last log-in.' I'm in a support group of one. Even when I wasn't on the internet, the internet was in me. My brain became conditioned to think only in 140 characters, the documentation meaning so much more than the moment. I'd have missed the second plane hitting the tower. At some point, the exact moment unknown, the world around me ceased to be in widescreen and narrowed to the size of an Instagram frame. There's no truth or beauty in using the world as Like bait. I'm learning to find validation from within. It's surprised me how good that can feel.

If this letter ever goes viral, my message to the people is, 'leave the internet, reclaim your being, you will be astounded by the transformation.' And yes, I appreciate the irony of spreading this advice through the internet, but how else do you recommend reaching the mass market this sagacity deserves?

For the first time in my adult life it feels like my brain has the space to breathe. The shackles are off. Some days I'll even just think about thinking. Pretty meta, right? Have you ever done that? Of course you have. You're an artist with a regularly updated Wikipedia page. People look up to you. People look at the things you create and search for meaning. I think a niche but committed audience may have done that with my tweets for a little while there (I'm thinking my strong content years of 2009-2013 particularly here), but none of that lasts. It's all temporary.

I read that the internet is going to lose all of its data. They always told us to be careful what we posted. 'It'll be there forever'. All of that manufactured emotion, a human history of the early part of the twenty-first century permanently wiped out, future generations left with server farms as far as the eye can see, mausoleums of corrupted information. I envy you for becoming an artist in the pre-internet age. There's literally no reason not to be prolific under those circumstances.

I wanted to say, because I never got the chance, that I really dug your exhibition. Your photographs have the rare quality of capturing something about the human condition that transfers the feeling from subject to viewer. But not in a voyeuristic way, it's not reality TV. I experienced the pain, the pride, the hope, the wisdom, the vulnerability of those people, the Argentinian butcher, the Rotterdam rave heads, and yes, even of my stepdad Geoff. You gave me empathy.

Stood there in the marble hall of the museum, lost in your pictures, looking at the face of someone I knew or didn't yet, it hit me it was the first time I'd considered someone's else's feelings outside of my social feeds in a long, long time. Your work deserves to be seen by millions of people in the flesh, feeling what I felt that night. I am privileged you brought them to Wales and honoured that I might have played some small part in making you feel at home there. I've realised home isn't a place, or if it is, it isn't bricks and mortar or a mark on a map. I think I'm closer to it than I've ever been before.

The journey here – and I'm talking literally here, metaphor corner is closed for an hour – was a real trip. I checked myself out of the hospital, took a cab back to the cottage and left the meter running outside. Nothing personal, but I hoped you wouldn't be there. Someone listened.

It was the first time since the day I moved in that the first thing I did when I walked in wasn't hook up to the WiFi and check my profiles. I found my passport, put a few clothes in a bag and shut the door behind me. I don't remember much about the drive to Bristol Airport. I might have slept for the whole hour, I might have been awake. There was little difference right then. I was sleepwalking my way to sanity.

Like everyone, I suppose I'd always wanted to turn up to an airport and book a one-way ticket on the next flight out of town. The cliché belonged to all of us. I bet you've done it a load of times. An international artist like yourself. But when it happened to me, it wasn't through a sense of insatiable adventure. It was pure survival instinct.

I stood in front of the departure board in a daze, the page turning, the words blending into a blur. I lived the alternative realities. Barefoot on a Portuguese beach. High in a Berlin basement. Struggling for rent on the Lower East Side. Three letters stood out, bold against the backdrop.

CPN. Copenhagen.

I walked onto the plane drunk on caffeine, two double espressos down from the departure lounge. I got the distinct impression the rest of the passengers were eyeballing me like I was the terrorist. I understood. You'll never see into the depths of your soul like you do looking in the mirror in the yellow light of an aeroplane bathroom. I hadn't shaved since the day before your exhibition; the uneven stubble gave me the look of a heart-throb turned hobo from a straight-to-streaming character study. My pupils were like plates. I pushed down on the tap, a jet of water squirting my hands, and realised I was still wearing a wristband from the hospital.

Gerard Kane. No allergies.

I splashed some water on my face, squeezed two or three blackheads, wiped away the whiteness and opened the door. Back in my seat, the lady in the window wanted a friend. She'd already offered me a boiled sweet (I'd refused). It was a generational thing I guess, the gesture. It made me feel good.

We got back to it by comparing ticket prices. Hers had cost £90. She'd booked it the day before. A family emergency. I didn't know how much I'd paid for mine so I said something that I thought would make her happy. Three days ago, her son-in-law Anders had suffered a heart attack. He'd had the seizure at a teppanyaki restaurant. His assistant caught his head before it stuck to the hot plate. Anders was a cryptologist, forever crouched over his laptop, tapping away. I'd been imagining some Scandinavian Indiana Jones type, knee-deep in cursed treasures and mummified child kings, but it seemed, like the rest of us, cryptologists were just glorified computer programmers.

The skin on her face sagged and stretched as she talked, as if someone was playing the accordion over her jawbone. I guessed she was maybe sixty-five, but she dressed like a younger woman. I was sure I recognised her shirt from Del's Instagram. There was a strong possibility Del's picture was hashtagged #vintage and my travelling partner was still wearing it from the first time around.

She seemed to tell his story with a perverse happiness. Maybe she was just glad of human contact. Anders ate a lot of junk food, she said, her vegetarian daughter couldn't wean him off Big Macs. (Big Macs are called Big Macs in Denmark too.) They'd lived in Paris for three years and in Bergen for four before that. She had to catch a ferry to visit them there. 'I would take turbulence over sea sickness everyday,' she said. I had to agree. Her grandchildren were born in Norway to her English daughter and a Danish father. She didn't think this made them any more Norwegian than Rudyard Kipling was Indian, but the

Norwegian government gave her daughter three grand for each child.

She told her to have ten. I don't think she meant just for the money. She seemed to really love those kids, clutching the chance to be relevant by stepping in to provide low-risk, low-cost childcare in her family's time of crisis. She talked for what seemed like an hour just about how tidy the cupboards were in the house, how her daughter had picked up this stereotypical Scandinavian trait for order.

I drifted off. I was a rollmop herring in a jar in the cupboard. The water tasted like the end of a battery. My family floated next to me, cold and dead. The light shone in and then the dark came again.

I didn't get the tidy thing then, but I do now. My room here is bare apart from a small wardrobe, a clock and a portrait painting of a wizened old fisherman looking out to sea. The wardrobe contains just the right amount of appropriate clothing. I threw away the few clothes I brought with me. Wearing them felt like I'd been cast in the wrong period drama. It's minimalism by necessity perhaps, but I feel freer now, happier definitely. Reading that back it sounds a little like I've joined a cult. It reminds me of a song we'd sing in primary school (Follow me, follow me/leave your homes and family/leave your fishing nets and boats along the shore). Well, it's not like that.

'Nanny's cupboards were always so messy.'

My neighbour laughed, not a 'haha' but an old person's laugh, and drained her gin and tonic. The alcohol had been served in a plastic bag. She got her smartphone out to show me pictures of her grandchildren. I had to navigate to the gallery for her. The phone was new and she hadn't mastered it yet. The plastic felt cold and familiar in my hand. The WiFi status lines were blocked by a cross. This was not doctor's orders.

I found the pictures and handed it straight back. The children were unremarkable, maybe seven and five, red hair and rosy cheeks. Her kids were fifty now. When they were young, she and her husband, Terry, used to bring them to Wales. Terry liked Wales. She liked the way the ladies in Cardiff dressed as if for a visit from the Queen when they went shopping.

Terry had talked about a tsunami in Wales in the fourteenth century that had caused an earthquake in Lisbon, of all places. The whole city had perished. Terry had ordered a meal from a menu in Lisbon and the waiter had brought over a whole calf's head with the eyeballs still in. He'd asked the waiter for some bread and butter. He was like that.

She asked me if I lived in Denmark. I paused and told her yes, I did.

Anyway, I'd better go, there's a meeting soon and I need to mentally prepare. If you're still in the cottage, I hope Geoff is proving an accommodating landlord. Being a Yorkshireman, he's probably put the rent up now you've got the whole place and not just a room, but I doubt his mastery of the internet would allow him to change the rental settings.

Keep creating. You're a beautiful soul.

Yours, Gerard.

CHAPTER

Dear Stephanie,

If I had to rank the most traumatic incidents of my childhood in the listicle-style format that dominated discourse as I checked out of life back home, I wouldn't start with '5 ways Dad dying fucked me up', or '11 ways your stepdad is trying to poison you' but '7 reasons why you should never sing West Coast gangsta rap in an initiation ceremony'.

"Woodland Friends do not curse and cuss."

Mum was beyond upset, claiming the Folkmarshal blanked her in the petrol station the next day. That's hardly 'spanning the world with friendship', is it? I must have heard that motto a hundred times over my three Thursday evenings in that tin hut, the first of which will never leave me. As the only two newcomers that week, we were encouraged to end the hour with an impromptu performance to introduce ourselves to the other children.

In a reversal of our births, you went first, a gentle interpretation of 'Heal the World' drawing appreciative applause, some of the crowd even joining in on the chorus. My retrospect was rapid. NWA definitely wasn't the best choice of artist to ingratiate myself to a group of dippy hippies. While Mum had sent us to fill a hole in our schedules, most of the other kids were Woodland Friends in protest at the imperialist tyranny of the Cubs and Brownies. Just writing that down to you makes me think they should have loved my song, bum notes aside, that my choice was much more socially aware than Michael Jackson. It must have been the repeated swearing. My card was marked from then on in.

Sometimes you've got to know when you're fighting a losing battle. I'm still convinced they buddied me up with the slowest kids in south Wales to force me out. It took us the whole hour of the next meeting to get a tent out of the bag, but it was too late by then, some other new kid poised with a ukulele to strum her way into their hearts. I pretended I didn't care when you went camping to the Lake District, but I did. I could have done with learning those outdoor skills for here.

When I got off the plane, I didn't know what I was meant to do next. There was no pre-booked pick-up from an Airbnb host. No smartphone for an Uber XL. I walked past the baggage carousel, its conveyor belt tracing a figure of eight through the arrivals hall, through the sliding double doors of customs, (nothing to declare), a fist of terror rising from the pit of my gut. What next?

But then I saw her.

'Gerard Kane' was written on a whiteboard in three-inch high black marker bubble writing. Stina smiled, in her ice-blue eyes the promise of home.

She had a minivan waiting outside. I sat in the front, next to her. The scenery was urban at first, the usual things you get around an airport: Ikeas, storage warehouses, frozen food depots, before the blur out of the window turned greener. She drove like Geoff, slow, steady, with the occasional burst of road rage. I'd started to tell her about my journey, but she said I must be tired and told me there was lots of time for talking; that's what we did there, sometimes talking, sometimes without words.

I didn't ask exactly where there was. I didn't feel like it was necessary. The terror suddenly felt a long way away. So I drifted off. The seats were comfy, much comfier than the plane. It was the deepest sleep I'd had in months. You'd have definitely snored, Stepher. And then she broke it, banging on the brakes, my body jerking under the belt.

'Are you okay?'

'Yeah, I think so, what's happening?'

We got out of the van, down onto the road. The air smelt like the downstairs bathroom at Mum's house when she's got guests coming around. I imagined this was where the cleaning product companies sent teams to capture the scent. It was pitch black now, the headlights shining on a body, its fur ripped open. I couldn't tell what it was. A moose maybe, an elk? Where was my Shazam for animals? The blood gushing out of its side seemed so hyper-real, I swear it was ketchup.

'What do you think we should do?' Stina asked me.

I hesitated.

'I don't know. What is it?'

Was this part of the initiation?

'The safest thing to do would be to pass it on.' It took me a breath or two – I could count them out like little clouds in the air in front of me – to realise she meant to kill it. I know how this will sound to you. Pretty brutal back there. But this is the great outdoors. Real life and real death. The natural cycle of things.

The thing that struck me as most strange throughout the whole thing (as if that wasn't strange enough?) was she seemed to be whispering to somebody else, nodding, agreeing. Maybe it was a Danish death ritual, maybe it wasn't. I don't know.

Back in the minivan, she told me that I'd just had 'a real experience.' And I said, 'You know what? I suppose I have.'

She told me that a good thing to do would be to compose a haiku about it, that I could commemorate the animal that way. She continued driving, slow and steady again, and reached to the dashboard, handing me a pencil and a receipt to write on. I didn't have my phone to Google the structure so I just kind of riffed it out. This is what I wrote (I've tidied it up a bit since, the journey was dark, there were mistakes).

It appeared there
when we least expected it
that's life and death huh

An elk on the road
its blood so red it's unreal
maybe it was, is

The viewers love gore
What is that supposed to mean?
I'm unsure, unsure

The real initiation was a lot less bloody, but maybe just as disturbing. But I needed it. I know that now. You can't expect to disconnect just by switching the WiFi off. It went much deeper than that. My reliance had become almost metaphysical. I tweet, therefore I am.

It was late by the time we arrived. I wasn't sure how long we'd been driving for after I finished the haiku, but I was dog tired. I remember the shape of a tall, well-built man, dressed all in blue, opening the door of the minivan.

'Welcome.'

'This is the Gerard I've been telling you about,' Stina said, her hand on my shoulder.

'Yes, I can see that it is.'

I felt Stina's hand move away. She was gone. I haven't seen her since.

'Where am I?'

'You must be hungry?' I couldn't see his face by the car-light but he was right.

'You can eat in your room tonight and then you should rest. We've prepared you a simple meal; nourishing food. You can eat with the others tomorrow. You have a big day ahead.'

I was woken up in my room by the sound of a shrieking bell, the door opening and two women dressed in blue overalls entering just as my eyes focused on the fisherman's face hanging from the wall. One of them had the left half of her head shaved, the other was black. I don't remember her hairstyle.

'Who are you?'

They said nothing. I knew they wanted me to go with them. I pulled back the covers. I was sure I'd fallen asleep in the clothes I'd been wearing: black jeans and a New York Yankees sweater. I was wearing blue overalls now.

You'll be as confused as I was.

They led me outside. I discovered we were in a woodland. The sun hadn't risen properly yet. The air had teeth, not content it'd made its mind up about how it was going to play it today. I hadn't seen the sky like this after sleeping since...I don't know when, maybe never. The only early mornings I was awake for were the post-shift lock-in, the hazy stumble home to the cottage, the guests, Del, sometimes.

This day was different.

We walked across a clearing in the woods, no conversation, just the squelch of three pairs of shoes against the wet grass, until we reached a wooden door. The building it led to was covered with leaves.

'You're all set,' said the black lady. Her partner nodded her shaved head and looked towards the floor. I opened the door. Darkness dimmed the morning light. I made out the outline of a table and chair and walked towards it.

A voice like God, God from a Hollywood epic we used to watch on Easter Sunday, filled the air. He sounded Old Testament angry.

'Why are you here?'

Before I could answer, something whirred, like a computer booting up. The projections started. The walls lit up. It was an immersive 4D experience. It was like that time we went on the Back to the Future ride at Universal Studios and Nanna Judy came on but wished she'd stayed outside and held the bags. It took me a few seconds, it'd been a while, my eye was out. They were posts and tweets and posts and tweets. All over the walls.

'@G_FK is not okay.'

'Gerard Kane couldn't watch a good movie let alone make one'

'Gerard Kane is the world's biggest try-hard'

'Gerard Kane, so close, so far, ta-ta'

'Would luv to do a Lee Harvey on @G_FK'

'People on Facebook I'd most like to punch: 1. Gerard Kane'

'Gerard Kane, you are the highest bidder on lameness.'

'@G_FK sucks virtual monster cock.'

'@G_FK is gay for pay.'

'Gerard Kane is fucking insane.'

'Gerard Kane is fucking insane.'

'Gerard Kane is fucking insane.'

It made me sick, bile biting the back of my throat.

I was hazed.

I was mortified.

I was trolled.

They said sexist things. Racist things. Sick, inhumane things. An online holocaust denier. The worst trolling the internet could ever imagine. I didn't know then if they were real and I'm not sure now. I'm not sure it matters. What matters is the sentiment.

The flashes stopped. The darkness returned.

The voice of Hollywood God was back, louder this time, but kinder, more like the one who let the animals off the ark.

'Are you ready to know yourself?'

'I am,' the words stuck and squirmed.

'Are you ready for your inner-truth?'

'I am,' my throat cleared, the words clearer.

'Are you ready to connect and contribute?'

'I am,' louder, bolder.

'The old you is deleted.'

And then the door opened. A mass of bodies moved in. The room seemed to expand, the walls becoming malleable to let the humanity in. The lights stayed low. I couldn't make out the faces but I knew they were smiling. I knew they were warm. I knew they wanted to know me, the real me. They hadn't said a word.

I'd created a construct back at home. I'd kidded myself into thinking I was bored of people because I was bored of how they projected themselves online. Happiness was not hip. Disengagement was de rigour. But Steph, I was so wrong. Haha. I can just imagine you taking that in. 'Gerard admitted he was wrong?!' One for the record books, right? I'd write down the time and date for posterity but I've got no idea what it is.

People are wonderful.

My snap judgements on humans, whether they were worth my time, whether they were worth their breath, were based purely on their online output. How narrow-minded is that? Homo sapiens had communicated through sketches, sounds, words, wisdom for thousands of years and then the internet came along and I thought someone was a douche if they couldn't carry off a mix of cool-clever-couldn't care less in 140 characters. It's like basing someone's worth on their arm movements ten years after semaphore had been invented.

People couldn't help but be contrived online.

There's nothing new to say.

Goodbye medium, hello message.

I had a hundred online exchanges each day but I can't remember the last time I had a real conversation. Every time we'd chat on Messenger, I'd already half-typed out my response by the time your message had pinged into my inbox.

I was a beat poet.

When I think back over my chats, when I think of how historians will see them in the future (if any of them still exist, and by that I mean the messages and the historians), they'll see us as a generation of Macbeths in the mirror. Two lost souls soliloquising together, waiting for a reflection, afraid to be alone.

I'm not afraid anymore.

Yours, Gerard

CHAPTER

23

Dear Stephanie,

I used to get really freaked out by how alike we were. Okay, we weren't identical twins, but however we styled our hair or changed our wardrobes (I'm thinking your ill-fated three week Goth stage here. You'd given up before the black nail varnish had chipped off), we couldn't get away from the fact that that narrowing of the eyes I had, you had, and that dimple in the chin you had, I had too. Don't take it personally. If I had to share genes with anyone, I'm so glad it was you. It's just I wanted to be unique. A one-off. A 'Who To Follow' for anyone who ever existed.

I'd see them in restaurants, enjoying family occasions, fathers like sons, daughters like mothers, pattern baldness and double chins passed through generations and I'd think, is this it? Are we happy to be a photocopy of a fading original? Darwin had promised so much more.

It's obvious to everyone here that Jonas and Seth are related. (The human mass is becoming known to me now). Jonas looks like a human Bassett hound, his oversized jowls droop south and look like they've got room to store enough nuts for a long, cold winter. His hair is straggly, dark and pushed behind his ears. It escapes when he gets animated, a daily occurrence when discussing anything from existentialism to lentils. Seth looks the same, just thirty years younger. He's maybe twenty-five or twenty-six. Halcyon days. In fairness, his hair is pretty lustrous, so blond it's white almost. He's broken the mould on that count.

But there are no blood relations here. We're all soul relations. They've managed to simultaneously destroy and reimagine the notion of family.

I can see now the quest for uniqueness was a vanity project. I'm no snowflake. We all need to work together.

The living arrangements here bring us close, but also give us the space to breathe. There are around sixty or seventy of us, but the numbers fluctuate. My cabin is one of eight or nine spaced out equidistant among the woods. They converge around a meeting space, covered from the elements with the timber felled for our stools, fifty or sixty tree stumps arranged in concentric circles over a space of around half a football field. We call this the *Hygge*. Back where you are, this was a temporary trend. Two seasons at best. There's a permanence here. Hygge isn't so last autumn-winter. It's a place of warmth. Of camaraderie. It's where the meetings take place.

Unless he decides otherwise, these are led by Gustav. Gustav is a pretty inspirational man. Despite the climate, he has a deep, rich tan and a head the size of a lion, fringed by six inches of white hair and set off by the most magnificent handlebar moustache, its design defiantly pre-hipster. His skin looks like it belonged to a man twice his not inconsiderable size and his body like it was once used to excess, in a phase of his life that's now distant but still just under the surface. His voice is our dominant sound, yet it's at least two octaves higher than it looks like it should be and carries an exaggerated English accent that makes him sound like a Bond villain by way of a miscast Elizabethan period drama.

It's hard to say how old he is. Some people seem to think he's in his seventies, others are adamant he's in his early forties. It's as if he exists in a wormhole in the galaxy, a place where the ageing process has become malleable, immaterial. Our souls are thousands of years old, so does it matter how long this shell has been switched on?

That's something we learn in the sessions here. It feels like every time I close my eyes I can see us, see where we've been before. It made me think about Nanna Judy. Remember that Mum reckoned she always lied about her age? She must be the only woman in the western world who said she was five years older than she actually was.

Gustav's the spirit animal of the CEO of AlePunk (they share similar facial hair). When he talks, everyone listens. His vision is compelling.

The rules we agree to live by are simple enough.

1. We do not lie to each other. Here we do not have to pretend to be who we're not.

2. We are open with each other. Secrets sap the soul.

3. The only technology we need is our breath and our brains.

4. Platonic love is the only unselfish kind. Physical love corrupts.

5. Possessions possess us. Here we're free.

6. Each hut is for the residents of that hut and that hut only.

Some of these I can take. Some I can leave. I didn't bother with the small print. Did you ever read the Facebook Ts & Cs?

Do you remember when Mum caught you and Stacey Jones smoking outside the conservatory and tried to create a list of household rules? I think she thought that after Dad died we'd be like a communist propaganda poster power trio, all smiles and spades, pulling in the same direction for the greater good. But it didn't quite work out like that. What did she expect? We were teenagers with a sad story and dial-up internet access and she was a useless authoritarian. She made you smoke the rest of the pack of cigarettes in front of her and you asked if you could have a vodka and coke to wash them down. She was not amused. I had full television rights that night.

In the session today, Gustav explained that although language is the only thing that sets us apart from the animals, it can also be corrosive for our souls. He asked us to make our way around the Hygge but to use only our expressions to communicate how we feel about ourselves, each other and the universe. It's still hard to know how I feel about myself, the others and the universe. I decided to recreate the emoji alphabet with my face. I think the hopeful smile emoji would convey my current emotions. I walked slowly around the trees and the people, smiling progressively wider and then winking simultaneously, before straightening my mouth and making my eyes go as big and as round as the Hawaiian pizzas we used to burn the roofs of our mouths on after swimming lessons on Friday nights.

My next-door neighbour caught my eye. (It was hard not to. They were huge.) She's our resident doctor, although I've yet to see her training put to the test. Some say she's an ordinary nurse, others that she led a Médecins Sans Frontières crisis response team in the aftermath of the Haiti earthquake.

Her small, bird-like face started to redden with rage, she the wronged housewife, me, seemingly, the adulterous male caught out after sending a sext meant for my teenage lover to her number instead. I furrowed my brow to the anxious emoji (is that one next? It's been so long since I've used them), but my contrition seemed to make her madder.

I whispered her name, 'Francine', over and over to bring her to her senses, but Gustav turned around, seeming to hear. I returned to my non-verbal anxiety projection. I wanted to hold Francine, to tell her everything was going to be okay now, that I'd actually meant to send her the message, that I'd wanted to get caught, that now we could work through our issues, perhaps just the two of us, that we shouldn't be afraid to call upon a marriage counsellor if we hit a roadblock, that our relationship had that level of maturity. I wanted her to know that we could move forward together, that yes, we really could take the plunge and buy that share in the cottage by the coast, but I was unsure how to say all of this using only my face.

Francine's rage turned to laughter, long, hard, sad laughter, and I wondered if this was against the rules. Gustav didn't turn around so I guess laughter isn't language after all. I felt pleased for Francine's uneasy peace but worried for myself. I wish we could have resolved things in a more amicable way. I'll have to watch out how I behave around her in the cabin's communal areas now. I wouldn't want to upset her again.

Some nights I'll sit in the dark and leave her with the last candle. I'm getting to know where her pressure points are.

I moved through the bodies, trying to find a more relaxing scene. An older lady, perhaps in her seventies, pursed her lips in my direction. I was unsure if she'd tasted something sour or was mimicking a selfie, but realised that depending on how long she'd been here, she might not know what a selfie is. I pursed my lips in response and she seemed happy.

Jonas was stood on top of the next tree stump. His face seemed calm and commanding, his jowls strong and steady. His Adam's apple gave him away, shaking a little, a bead of sweat dripping down his left temple. I imagined him as a president trying to hold it together in his first televised response following a terrorist attack, his absolute confidence built by entitlement and the electorate finally cracking under the light and heat, if you looked hard enough. Seth was stood at his feet, his thin, twenty-something body stooped in compliance. As I got closer I saw his face was scheming, ambitious, like maybe he was an undercover mole for the terrorist cell, turned by his father's indifference and neo-con foreign policy. My chin dropped and my palms raised to my cheeks, my mouth opened wide but no sound came out.

Edvard Munch emoji.

It was all pretty emotional, Stepher, but Gustav warned us it would be. He said it's easier to be true to your real feelings without language in the way. I couldn't stop thinking about Carpet, our cat. Do you remember Mum tried to tell us cats couldn't commit suicide? But we both knew the real story. Her parental M.O. was to shield us from reality, which is all well and good when you're eleven, but by the time you reach thirty-one and you realise you've been kept from the truth your whole life, it doesn't half fuck you up.

Carpet was petrified of the road, but that day he was different. He just sat in the middle of the tarmac, purring patiently as the lorry approached, as still as the stone statues Nanna Judy had to scare off the birds in that crazy garden of hers. We watched the whole thing from your bedroom window, the net curtains pulled back, both frozen with the inevitability of it all. You held my hand and we cried silently, together.

That moment is the closest I've ever felt to another human being. I have a new hope I can capture that feeling again.

Yours, Gerard.

CHAPTER 24

Dear Stephanie,

It's funny (funny good) how perspective changes with space and time. You've learned that with your move, I'm sure. Everything looks different from far away. The big stuff seems to get smaller, become less significant, and the little things become the things that matter. Wales' patron saint, Saint David, was into them. Pethau Bychain. The little things. I hope wherever you are the universe is treating you with the love you deserve.

I'm kidding myself, clearly. A guilty conscience letting me off lightly. You'll have gone through pain. My leaving like that must have been a surprise, if not a shock. When I imagine what's going on back there, Mum's learning how to perfect puff pastry as grief therapy, breaking down in the dairy aisle, Geoff's lost in trivia, setting tools at right angles, making sure he's got a fully-loaded ballpoint in his top pocket poised to autograph anything for anyone who recognises him from his portrait. And then there's you, at the heart of it, holding everyone together. I think I'm finally developing that twinny sixth sense everyone always expected us to have.

Psychic abilities may have escaped us, but we did build a Chinese wall or six between me, you and the rest of the world. Do you remember our secret code for talking about people we didn't like to their faces? 'You're good in groups.' Such faint praise, damn, such a diss on the down-low to those people who loved being the centre of attention but had nothing killer to say (as if we did anyway...well, you did, often; me, not so much).

I'm learning that groups can be stronger than their constituent parts. One man didn't build the pyramids, the rocks didn't magic themselves to Stonehenge (I'm so glad I discovered the rocks were from Wales before I left. Go Wales). Individualism is over. Napoleon's dead, ditto Caesar, even ISIS has no leader. It's the monuments of the many we flock to, they're what we hold dear to our hearts.

It's been a busy time since I last wrote. I've discovered I can do things I never thought were possible. It started with Gustav, as things often do here. But he's a catalyst, not a dictator, that's what he tells us, that's what we know is true. He called a special meeting in the Hygge. The meeting was to take place on a Friday night and would be a reflection on our inner-selves and a celebration of our little community.

On the Wednesday morning, I received a note under my door with special instructions about how I was to contribute. It said I was to communicate my greatest creative achievement, but using a form of expression different from the previous output. Hmm. Geoff would have said, 'That problem's got more layers than an onion, son,' but when I said that in my head, it felt like I was beginning to forget what his accent sounded like. I think I might even be missing Geoff. Now that's a sentence I never thought I'd write (although, to be honest, I don't think I ever thought I'd write a sentence again. My handwriting is bordering on calligraphy now).

I'd run straight to Francine's room to see if she'd had a message, but she pushed her door ajar, the rope of a blue robe dangling down, and told me telling was against the rules and that they'd all know that I'd asked her and it'd be marked against me. I didn't know what she meant, still don't. I'm not sure Francine has quite adjusted to the vibe here yet. It must be difficult for her though, being French and being a doctor, living with the special blend of nonchalance and superiority that must bring.

The meeting was set for six o'clock in the evening. The sun was still illuminating the site then, the temperature dropping enough from the daytime to make a sweater the sensible wardrobe decision. Mum would be proud with my self-preservation. Fashion first is no longer the abiding rule. I walked the few minutes from my hut alone, my thoughts clear, my mind steady, ready for what was to come. I wasn't nervous. I hadn't prepared anything. No autocue. I was living in the moment, grabbing the now.

As I got closer, I could hear the hum from the Hygge. Some people were massed around a canopy, others sat cross-legged and conversational, eating something. The something smelled totally delicious. Yoko was behind a counter under the canvas, serving up from a giant pot I'd heard was saved for special occasions. She looked totally engrossed in her role, making the hungry happy. There were no customer service issues here, no serving under fear of a bad TripAdvisor review. She was content to provide and we were content to receive. This'll sound weird, Steph, but it felt as natural as breastfeeding. Totally virtuous. Pure devotion on both sides. I could have stood there and watched her all day, the greeting, the scooping of the soup, the giving with grace, but I was drawn into her. (Okay, maybe I was hungry too. Busted.)

When she saw me standing there, I'm sure she stuttered a little, that her body broke its practiced motion, giving away that the person she'd been thinking of was right there, that this could be a defining moment in her romantic life.

'Hey Yoko.'

'Hey...Gerard.'

'So, you can cook too?'

'Well...I can serve...I can most certainly scoop from a pot into a bowl, sometimes even without spilling.' She let out a nervous laugh.

'You know what they say?'

'Who's they?'

'Good question.' It was like we'd both learned the lines.

'How's the answer?'

'Umm...old fish wives? Academics? The Bilderberg Group?'

'I'm not sure I'd trust any of them...'

'True. Well, what they say, whoever they are, is that the way to a man's—'

'—it's a wild vegetable stew.'

'Okay, that's one way. But—'

She handed me a bowl and moved her attention towards the Korean man behind me. I walked over to a clearing among the bodies and sat down before my stomach somersaulted me over the trees. I made a pact not to look at her as I ate. Absence makes the heart grow fonder etc. I didn't want to be like that weirdo with the sweet tooth and carrier bags who used to come and watch you when you worked in Krispy Kreme. Although, unlike in that highly patrolled retail environment, there are no security guards here to move me on.

The food was great, Steph, so nourishing, it felt like it was doing my insides all kinds of good. It tasted like the stew Mum would make when we were young and we'd cry because all we wanted was French bread pizza and curly fries. The good stuff we didn't quite know was good for us then. But I couldn't help watching her. It feels like fate has thrown me here for a few reasons, and the biggest one was stood right in front of me.

'So, welcome, welcome everybody. I trust you have eaten well. You deserve it. You are all wonderful people.' Ripples of applause broke out across the Hygge. Gustav was speaking, we were listening.

'You've come here from all over the world, from the old world, for a new way of living, a life where you can live in the moment. And when moments can be as beautiful as this, just look around you...then that is a wonderful thing.' He's right, Stepher. I wish you could see it here. It's the best of nature and, I'm learning, the best of nurture.

'You all bring many talents to our little community. Some of you are dancers, some of you are doctors. You're very clever, very creative people. That's why we've been drawn to each other. And tonight we're going to celebrate that creativity. We're going to see how the creativity you had at home can be adapted here for the greater good. You've all received a message and now it's time for you to share with the group.' Some people laughed, I think a little apprehensively.

'You'll all know that we don't queue here, that is a very British thing, no? Haha – you'll come up and share when it feels right.'

Now I know what you'll be thinking, you'll be thinking that it sounds like Miss Winterbottom's English class. How many times did we sit there as she asked the room for volunteers to read from Shakespeare, silently cursing ourselves to an hour of her Elizabethan am dram? For a moment, I thought that was going to happen here. I looked around and wondered what was going through everyone else's minds, what other situations they were thinking of, when else they'd been asked to stand up and bear their souls in front of a group of other humans. Vulnerability might just be my new black.

Seth broke the stand-off, bounding off a tree stump to the front of the Hygge. Gustav greeted him at the front like his prodigal son, his leg of lamb arms drumming Seth's slender back. It made me miss Dad. Do you ever get that? But I don't think it was Dad I missed, more the idea of a dad.

'Welcome Seth, everyone.'

Everyone welcomed Seth, their first syllables a millisecond or more out of sync, making a chorus of sound in the round. Yoko had moved from behind the counter and joined the crowd. I shuffled across the grass, trying to get closer to her, wanting to share this experience, for it to be a thing we did together, a shared history milestone.

The setting sun shone on Seth's face, his blonde hair ringing his head like a halo. His face looked serene, like he'd swallowed down the nerves, but also a little like he was wearing make-up, his cheeks rouged to bring out the lustre. It's kind of hard to describe what Seth did next.

I suppose the best way of describing it, and trust me, I've sat here for at least a minute thinking about this, was like an unholy matrimony between Riverdance and avant-garde gymnastics. Just sit there (or stand. Where are you, Steph? What are you doing?) and picture that. All I can relate it to was when Angharad (remember her?) dragged me to some contemporary dance show in the Southbank Centre and all I could think was, how many drugs has this man taken? And, isn't exercise under the influence of narcotics dangerous?

Seth started by raising his left hand above his head and pointing his finger to the sky, getting darker now. He jumped off one foot, high, quickly, pirouetting around the Hygge, weaving like a drunk on New Year's Eve in and out of the tree stumps, missing them by luck more than judgement, the shrieks from the crowd just drowned out by his howls.

'Very good, Seth,' said Gustav, 'very expressive.' Seth collapsed on the floor in the middle of the Hygge, his flailing arm missing Francine, a little too close for her comfort. Gustav clapped the base of his palms against each other at a right angle, the acoustics created more like the

Albert Hall than the great outdoors. His voice sounded stereophonic, praising Seth's performance as an abstract that could be applied here, when the time and the situation was right, Seth's unsteady panting providing the beat. The group gave thanks. What the hell was that all about, you'll be wondering? I was. Seth later told me it was a manifestation of his three years studying Town and Regional Planning at the University in Johannesburg. His dance was a reflection on the chaos of the modern city. It reminded me a bit of Cardiff at midnight on a Saturday.

As the last applause faded, a sound like a songbird started up. The opening bars sounded like that tape Mum bought from the mariachi band on the street in Brittany. She played it so much she must have worn out the reel. Their Latin yodelling soundtracking our over-competitive games of Eye Spy are all I've been unable to block out from that road trip around France. It was one of those times (there were lots of them), when it felt like Mum was just trying too hard after Dad had died.

The singing was coming from Yoko. The Hygge fell silent, all eyes and ears on her. The arch of her back rose and fell with her breath. I moved around the edges of the space to see her from the front. The emotion on her face said everything I needed to hear. I swear I could see a tear rolling down her cheek. It was too much to take. I looked away to the floor, but I could feel her eyes looking at me, looking into me. I couldn't make out the words, I'm not sure there actually were any words, not any conventional ones at least. It was the sound of her soul.

I felt as if 101 cameras were trained on the two of us, like an audience of millions was watching our narrative unfold like a pay-per-view telenovela.

The song lasted seconds but it felt like a lifetime. After she'd finished, she lay back on the ground, her eyes closed, as Jonas juggled pine cones (badly), Francine primal screamed, and a red-haired man I hadn't seen before cartwheeled around the Hygge, humming show tunes as he went.

'Yes, yes, give yourselves a round of applause. You deserve it.'

Gustav had everyone eating out of his not inconsiderable hands. In my head, I'd planned to mime out key scenes from my film, to show Ren's journey in a series of hand movements choreographed to illustrate the complexity of origins in a future world not a million light years away from ours. But I didn't. It was too much for me. This day I was to be a reflector for the rest of the group, a sounding board for their sanity, or otherwise.

'You've shared your creativity with the group. Sharing is caring, as they say, haha. Through sharing you can see that humans are malleable beings. That the things you create don't want to be bound by the barriers the old world puts on them. Collaboration is king.'

'You're the king, Gustav!' someone shouted out.

'No, no, I am not the king. I am not great. Not alone anyway. Every human has the capacity for greatness but not every human is great, not every human is wonderful. You know this from your time back in the old world. The old world is broken. You know this too. That is why you are here, with others like you. We will achieve great things together.' Jonas starting clapping, but Gustav cut him off. Jonas turned around sheepishly, apologising with his eyes for interrupting the great Gustav's flow.

'Thank you, Jonas. Save your applause.' He laughed sharply, from the pit of his stomach, and continued.

'So, you may be wondering what my party piece is? Guess what? It's all of you. And this party is going to get bigger...'

From nowhere, two more men in blue overalls appeared, wheeling in a curtain on legs. Gustav asked for a drum roll. Those of us who were close by tapped our hands on the tops of the tree stumps. It sounded tribal, primal. Gustav pulled back the curtain.

'Others have heard of how we are living here. Others want what you are experiencing. They want to know what life can be like if they look up from their phones, not just for a moment, but forever. Come closer, gather round...'

A series of architect's plans were pinned to the whiteboard. The drawings showed the outline of a community like ours but bigger, much, much bigger, an emblem saying 'DK1' in the bottom right corner.

'Now we are sixty, maybe seventy people, with eight or nine huts. Think of us as being in the New Amsterdam phase. More settlers are coming to this brave new world and we need to be ready for them. And now your creativity needs to be channelled into building this new future.'

'Building the houses?' Seth asked.

'Yes, or helping at the very least. You can do it. You can do anything.' Now you know how useless I am around the house. Geoff always said I was more DIcry than DIY, which I thought was quite clever, for him. He did have a point. My botched attempt at reupholstering the leatherette booth in the kitchen made the back look like a Hells Angels jacket after a shoot-out, Del's strategically located throw minimising the damage, hiding the heinousness from the eyes of the guests.

I did learn some bits and pieces from a talk at an event back at home called Ignite. Speakers stood up in front of a slide-deck which charged forward every thirty seconds to talk about their passions (mainly their cats, sometimes their dead cats) to a progressively drunker audience. A red-haired man ('Did he dye it?' we asked. 'Red hair is the new black,' we decided) renovated his entire house using only YouTube as his mentor. I thought about how the trades were dying, how there was more money in the ads you could sell next to your 'how to bleed a radiator video' than there was for bleeding radiators. But I'm not sure if any of that stuck. Gustav continued to rally us.

'One of the greatest humans said, "Around here, we don't look backwards for very long. We keep moving forward, opening up new doors and doing new things, because we're curious…and curiosity keeps leading us down new paths." Does anybody know who it was?' A few murmurs started around the group.

'Don't be shy now, just because I shushed Jonas, haha.'

'Einstein,' Seth said.

'No, not the great Albert,' he replied, 'come on, next?'

'Andy Warhol?' I said, looking to Yoko for validation.

'Good try! But no...' He didn't say my name. I'm not sure he knew who I was.

'Michael Jackson?' a female voice called out, I think belonging to Francine.

'No, definitely not. It was Walt Disney. Walt Disney. Because, like him, I'm in the entertainment business. And he built a new world, a better world. And that's what we're doing here.'

'Does this mean we're going to get Space Mountain?' Seth said, half-joking, I think. It can be hard to tell with Seth, a bit like when Auntie Bronwen drops a bombshell and you're not sure if she's playing with you or just plain stupid.

'Who knows? Not yet, Seth, not now. But tomorrow is ours for the taking. Some of you have been here for months, others for weeks. Others like you will come when they know what we are building here. A world of wonder. A world free from negativity. A world where you can just be.' Spontaneous applause and whooping broke out across the Hygge.

'We're going to need to build more accommodation to house the newcomers. We'll need better services. More robust irrigation. But together, we can do anything.'

'We love you, Gustav!' someone shouted.

'And I love you. I truly do.' The cheering continued.

I couldn't help thinking if Gustav was mad, that he was also a genius, an unorthodox leader bringing a band of nomads together for the good of...I don't know...maybe the world.

My eye scanned across the Hygge, drinking the scene in: smiling faces, pure X-rated humanity. I felt happy, Steph, truly happy, but as it passed over Francine, over Seth, over Jonas, it reached Yoko, stood back behind her pot. She wasn't smiling.

Yours, Gerard

CHAPTER 25

Dear Mum,

I'm sorry. I understand by this juncture of your life you had expected to have had grandkids. And that it wouldn't even be a wish or dream, just an expectation that the twins you bore three decades ago would have fulfilled their role in the natural order of things and created new lives for you to love and nurture.

We haven't done this for you.

I can't speak for Stephanie – who knows, maybe as I write this letter she's sat in an antenatal class, breathing on request and squeezing Al's hand as he contemplates the realisation that his latest art project is the antithesis of digital – but on my behalf, please accept my apologies for jamming the spokes of the cycle.

I've begun to understand that somewhere in a parallel universe, I may well be a virile provider, the proud father to a collection of sturdy, earnest offspring who excel at team sports, wind instruments and computer coding, creating regular platforms for advice, inspiration and reward from their favourite grandmother. You'll be great at the job, maybe even better suited than you were to the maternal role. (This may not sound like it, but it's a compliment.)

I know we never spoke about our feelings when we were growing up and I think I know why now. There was a lot of emotional stuff going on back then. The image I carry of you from those days is with your hair curled up in that tight perm, your expression all red lipstick and courage under fire, like the defendant's wife on the court steps.

You're wearing that lime green jacket with the shoulder pads. It was like your fashion sense stopped still the day Dad died – God knows why, he was hardly Wales' answer to Yves Saint Laurent. The bigger kids used to call you 'Widow Spice', they talked about how they'd 'definitely fuck you' and how you 'definitely would'. The first one made me a little proud at least. You never let anything get to you, get to us. You protected us. It was almost animalistic.

It was pissing down that day, our football training was rained off because Mr Muñez believed that football was a fairweather sport and practicing in the wet conditions would only reinforce our inherent urge to play a long ball game. I got home earlier than expected and got the key from underneath the ceramic alligator Nanna Judy and Grampy Joe had brought us back from the Florida Keys. The house seemed empty but I didn't feel alone. I opened the fridge door, my usual routine. It slammed shut in the breeze, almost slicing the ends of my fingers clean off. The back door was open and the rain had soaked the lino floor. I followed a faint sound into the yard. Your car music was blasting from the shed.

'I'm every woman...'

I mouthed along with Whitney Houston.

I reached the shed and peered through the window. You couldn't hear me but I could see you, sat on top of the lawnmower handle, crying and crying, your face red. I went back into the house and mopped the rain off the floor with a tea towel, a cartoon map of the Canary Islands soaking up the wet.

I think now that you must have been listening to the tearjerker song from *The Bodyguard* but the CD had skipped on. You came in half an hour later and gave me a fiver to go to the chip shop. By the time I'd got back, I'd forgotten all about it.

We were in the Hygge yesterday. Jonas was leading the session. Gustav had been 'resting' since the previous day. He'd made a big announcement about how we were gearing up for growth. It must have taken it out of him. There were loud whispers that years ago he'd been caught up in a bar brawl and got knifed in the stomach over a point of principle (what it was changed depending on who you were talking to – Seth thinks it was some neo-Darwinism argument, he's got Gustav on a real pedestal, but Francine, she swears it was over a woman. Apparently, Gustav used to be quite the ladies' man, or so she reckons). I've heard whispers his rest periods were all down to these abdomen problems, but when I asked him about them last month he snapped at me. I don't think he wants to show any weakness. I only wanted to tell him that Grampy Joe swore by peppermint tea for tummy aches.

Jonas was a nervous front man. It was like he was hosting a dinner party under duress for his husband's new boss, confidence only skin deep, concern about the conversation, panic over the pastry bubbling under the surface.

He'd asked us to write down a story from our past life and handed some lined paper around the group, his yellowy hand shaking a little. It was to be the story that upset us most when we thought of things back there. The story that spurred us on to be where we are today. The session was called 'My Story of Why'. It was our first of the day. Gustav believed that the mind was at its most creative in the morning. I wondered what stories were in Jonas' head, what dark secrets and spindly skeletons hid in the corners of his closet.

Maybe there was nothing. Maybe he just wanted to save Seth. Maybe he was just impressionable. Maybe he just wanted a different way.

I watched Yoko as she wrote her story. She sat motionless at first, her hand poised, almost as if she was willing the words to come, for the things she felt to form some kind of narrative. In the first weeks, I'd struggled with the act of handwriting. It had felt nostalgic, as much of a throwback to the past as the smell of school custard or mouthing the words to the Hail Mary, never quite sure what they meant.

When her words came, they came quickly, furiously. Her face was sad, then happy, then sad again. She slowed to a stop. Her pen had run dry under the pressure. I moved towards her and offered my support, motioning for the biro. She passed it to me and I took it in my hands and rolled it back and forth, the heat loosening up the ink.

'Try it now.'

'Okay everybody, time is up,' said Jonas. People were sat cross-legged, or on stumps, all around the Hygge. Most had been or were still crying.

In the next part of the session, we read what had been written, alone and in silence. It's meant to give us an understanding of how our fellow residents had come to be here, to make us feel that we aren't alone, to strengthen our belief that the old way is broken.

I think a lot of us use it as tabloid gossip replacement. I wonder how much of what I read in these sessions has been made up but I needed to know what Yoko had written, why she was here. I wanted to believe every word and to hold her and tell her everything was going to better now, now that we were here, not alone, together.

After the session we were given free time. I went back to my room to write this letter to you, but I was restless. Francine seemed to be exercising close by. I could hear grunting. I started to write, but I needed to see Yoko. I walked across the Hygge towards her hut, a few people sat around on the stumps talking, laughing. I approached it from behind. We weren't meant to visit other people's huts. But I didn't care for the rules today.

I looked through her window, the blinds letting in the light. She was sat on the edge of her bed, her eyes closed, counting just above her breath. I watched her reach 100 and tapped lightly. She opened her eyes. She didn't seem startled. She was calm. It was as if she knew I would be there, like she'd read the script. She got up from the bed and joined me outside.

'Hi,' I said.

'Hey,' she said.

'I want to know—'

'I know you do. Walk with me.' I followed her around the back of the huts, trying to get close enough to feel her aura on my skin.

'You want to know why I'm here. I know that. It's a silly thing really. We were doing fine until—'

'Who's we?' I asked.

'Me and my husband.'

'Your husband?'

'My ex-husband, I suppose, although we're not technically divorced.' My heart sank and rose. I didn't know what to feel.

'But aren't we divorced from everything back in the old world, as Gustav calls it?'

'I suppose we are,' I answered. I wanted it to be true.

'I think I'd dampened everything down inside of me. But that's not healthy. Bad things can eat you up from the inside until there's nothing left. It started again at the vets.'

'The vets?' I couldn't help thinking about Carpet.

'Yes. An unlikely stage for a breakdown, admittedly. But I felt like we'd built up a camaraderie, me and the other people in the waiting room. There was the elderly man with the Scottie dog. He kept calling the dog Toby, but Toby was his other Scottie dog, the one he said went to sleep three years ago. This was Pedro. Pedro had belonged to an old man across the road from him. The old man had died. This old man told me he'd never have another dog after Toby, but he couldn't live with himself if Pedro went to the pound. All I could think about was how old the dead man across the road must have been to pass his dog on to this guy.'

'Okay, I don't get it.'

'Just listen, Gerard. We have time.' There was nearly an hour and a half until our next group, a contemplative session run by a mindfulness expert who'd arrived about a week before. I could roughly tell the time just from looking at the sun. You'd be proud of me, Mum.

'On the other side of the room was a middle-aged lesbian with a cat who looked just like our cat, its head popping out of the top of a Prawn Cocktail box.'

'Whose cat?'

'Mine and my husband's.' That's what I thought she was going to say.

'The receptionist called my name. Well, the cat's name, technically. Our cat was called Sushi.'

'Cute. I love Sushi,' I said.

'So did I.'

'Oh, I'm sorry.'

'It's okay. I carried her to the desk in the carry case which smelled of next door's dog. "It was nice of them to lend it to us," he said.'

'Your husband?'

'Yes.'

'The room was with me. We were all rooting for Sushi. We felt in control, breezy, together, just a group of pet owners taking the time out of our busy schedules to ensure our animals got the best in medical attention. And that's when they said it.'

'What did they say?' I asked.

"If we discover she's pregnant, should we just continue?"

'Oh.' I didn't know what to say, where this was going.

'I looked to the lesbian for an answer but she had her head buried in her cat's box, as if she was looking for a spare pack of crisps which might be buried between the cardboard flaps. Pedro's owner – I hadn't caught his name – he had his eyes closed.'

'Was she pregnant?' I asked. It seemed like the logical thing to do.

'I'm not sure. I didn't even know abortion was a thing for cats. I asked if they could just call me at work.'

'We had cats,' I said, in solidarity.

'Your wife and you?'

'Ha! No. No. No. Me and my sister. My twin. Stephanie. You'll have to meet her.'

'Is she coming here?'

'Umm...I don't know, I don't think I'd ever entertained the thought of any of my people from back there coming here. I'm not sure it feels right.'

'I understand,' said Yoko.

'We're convinced our cat Carpet committed suicide. He just sat in the road one day and let the lorry come full force towards him, not moving a whisker.'

'That sounds sad,' she said.

'It was. It still is.' Voices carried from the Hygge to our path. We kept on.

'What kind of cat was Sushi?' I asked.

'She was a half-Himalayan pedigree. This gave her enough class to lord it over the neighbourhood moggies, but not too much to make it look like we had nothing better to spend our money on than an inbred super-feline.'

I laughed.

'Carpet was a pure-bred moggie,' I said.

'The cat had the kind of effortless excellence we had planned for our children.'

She'd planned children. I'd never planned children. You'd planned children for me but I'd not delivered. Could she help me give you that, Mum?

'We got her from an ad on Gumtree. A lady we'd never met before came into our house with a box that moved and an attitude that let us know in no uncertain terms she was used to going into people's houses she didn't know and asking for money.'

'Pet breeders are pure pimps.' I was trying to lighten the mood, still taking the kid news in.

'We gave her thirty pounds. She waited while I went upstairs to my change jar to make up the last five pounds in coins. "Sometimes we spend that on a takeaway we don't even like," he said.'

'I'd kill Seth for a takeaway.' I thought about Del. About our nights on the sofa with a fourteen-inch pizza and a streaming service.

'Joke. I wouldn't kill Seth.'

'Someone else might,' she said.

'What?'

'Nothing. I was daydreaming.'

'About death?'

'You can't control what comes out, Gerard.'

'True.' It was true. The sessions here bring everything to the fore. Who knows what lies beneath.

'My favourite daydream back then centred on thinking about how our lives would be different if we'd messaged another lady about another cat. Would we have been happier with another cat, a cat with ginger tortoise shells called Skip that we could get an agent and star in TV ad work while we sat at home and watched nature documentaries on Netflix?'

'Maybe.' All this talk of her old life made me feel insignificant.

'Don't be jealous, Gerard. We were ridiculous. Not suited at all. Incapable of life together. We were a two Mont Blanc pen household but we didn't own a car. We told ourselves it was because we cared about the future of the planet but it felt pretty shitty when you needed to get to work and it was raining outside.

'"You can't get a lift on a pen," he said. We never even tried.'

'I think he was probably right, Yoko,' I said.

'Maybe he was. I'll never know.'

'What did you do back in the old world?' I asked, trying to move the conversation on.

'Apart from break down in veterinary practices? I'm joking, Gerard. Don't be so stony-faced. I was a low-level computer coder at a government agency.'

'Cool,' I said.

'Not cool. I hated my colleagues.'

'Hate's a strong word.'

'And I mean it.' I'd only seen her vulnerable side up to now, but I'm learning she is not a lady to be messed with, Mother. You'd like her.

'One day I was at work and I'd read the same line of code for the fourteenth time when I overheard my line manager Moira on the phone, bitching about how infantile "pet people" were.'

'What a douchebag.'

'She was. She made me so mad. I wanted to rush at her from behind, to use all of my yellow belt level Tae Kwon Do moves that I promised my Sa Bum Nim I'd never use unless provoked and crush her tiny little marsupial-like skull with my bare hands. But I thought about how wrong that was. My mum used to tell us, "count to ten, think again." Plus my 360-degree appraisal was the next week and the last guy who got violent in the office ended up working in a Chunky Chicken. Errol saw him there on lunch break one time. Errol said they just stood there in silence, Errol checking his phone without reception, the other guy wishing he could, the meal deal frying in the background. I've not been angry like that since I came here.'

I didn't ask who Errol was. It didn't seem important to the story.

'Thinking about it, I never used to get angry,' I said, 'I don't think I cared enough. I was so caught up in perception that I forgot to care too much about anything else.'

'I wish I was the same.'

I wondered where she was going with this. I bet you are too. Then it came out.

'We were all set to get the car when the baby was coming.' She looked at me for a split second and then to the grass, her eyes avoiding mine.

'He had created a spreadsheet ranking the appropriateness of different models based on factors such as cup holder size, clutch tightness and wipeability. The winning car was a German brand. He was reading *Beowulf* at the time, but convinced me this hadn't influenced the outcome. I didn't care so much anyway, German felt right for our first and last shared, self-driven car. I joked about how much easier it would be to breastfeed in a car driven by Google.'

'That's funny,' I said, not smiling.

'He really let his mind go wild with the possibilities. He could get like that. In his old company, he made a facilitator cry with his "blue-sky thinking". He swore she was smiling as the tears fell.' She made the speech marks in the air with her fingers. Usually I hated it when people did that, Geoff especially, but with her it seemed to ground her. To make me realise that she wasn't the coolest kid around. That she could love me. It's crazy, isn't it? The things we read into the most innocuous of actions.

'Weeks later I found a testimonial he'd written the facilitator for his website sat in his draft folder. When I asked him why he hadn't sent it, he said he hadn't known if the facilitator would find the contact passive-aggressive. He didn't need to ask me why I was in his draft folder. We were beyond that by then.'

'He came up with a wet room, a ping pong room and a virtual reality space. I vetoed all of them, sometimes with good reason, sometimes just because. When I think about it now, I know I just wasn't ready to accept the space back into the body of the house. I was like a farmer leaving the field fallow to give it some rest so the crops could grow extra tasty next season.'

'It was going to be the first time we'd seen Dave and Helen since everything had happened. We were a little nervous. He opened a bottle of wine. I got half-drunk off just the smell most times. I had written a list of conversation topics in lip liner on the back of a receipt. It was the first time we'd had alcohol in the house since his brother had brought the champagne. The broken flute was still on the worktop next to the recycling bin. We heard a squeal through the French doors. I ran out into garden. The first thing that hit me was the smell of shit. A big cat, much bigger than Sushi, was poised on the fence that divided our yard from the neighbour's. This cat was grey and its left eye was closed. It didn't move as I rushed toward it, screaming River, River, River.'

'Who's River?' I asked.

'River was going to be the name of our child. Sushi was crouched in the corner of next door's yard, shivering and scared. I vaulted the fence, snapping the lip off, and picked her up under my arm. The bigger cat looked at us and sauntered off for dessert.'

'Carpet used to get bullied by next door's cat too. That cat always used to pee against our patio doors. Stephanie caught him at it one time, chased after him with a washing up bottle filled with warm water.' That thought made me smile.

Yoko was lost in her own story.

'It wasn't until the waiter brought the limoncello that I noticed I had cat shit on my dress.'

'That's pretty awkward. To think I've never knowingly worn shit in an Italian restaurant before. I feel like I haven't lived now,' I said.

'None of us have,' she replied.

'The counsellor told us that we needed to imagine a future for ourselves without a child. I told him I found that difficult, that all of my thoughts of the 2020s had involved a son with ringlets and a no-bullshit attitude. I would think about our life without the baby and wonder what I was going to talk to my mum about when we visited. Our small talk had been building up to the distraction and focus another living thing could bring.'

I feel like I identify with that, Mum. I'm sure you can too. But the next time I see you, wherever that is, I'll talk to you, truly talk to you, like I'm doing here. But face to face, so you can see my eyes and really get to know me again.

'River was going to have a brother called Ty. We'd have liked a girl too, of course, but sometimes it just works out like that. We'd live in a powder-blue house called 'Zanzibar' with a brook running through the garden and a hedgerow that hadn't been cut for two years because that's how we wanted it to be. The boys would have made a rope swing from this big old tree that dominated the back of the garden, the seat a tyre from the car I didn't drive anymore now we lived in the nice neighbourhood with the shops and the school just a few steps outside the front door. That was how we decided it would be on our second date at the Thai restaurant. I couldn't yet tell him I didn't like spicy food but we'd planned our whole lives out. That was eight years ago. It feels like I've lived a century since then.'

She'd finished. She was exhausted, I could tell.

'Yoko, I don't know what to say. I'm sorry.'

'You don't have to be sorry.'

'But I'm also not sorry. I'm glad that happened. I'm glad those bad things happened to you and now you're here.'

'You know what, Gerard? So am I.'

As soon as she'd finished telling her story, I felt a calmness. The light shone through the trees over the huts, breaking through the canopy like it had all of the answers. The rays hit her hair as if they radiated out and not the other way around.

It was her hair I'd noticed first. She'd been sat with her back to me, her hair knee-length and black, concertinaed on the grass around her. We were in the middle of a Freedom session (I'll explain the details another time) and I was finding the whole concept challenging. It was only my second day.

When Gustav was finished, she'd stood up and turned around. I'd been unsure until then if she'd been female or male, half-expecting her to be some Maharishi type, George Harrison only a sitar-beat away. Now I was sure. Her skin was so pale. Her eyebrows were wide.

She was authentic. She is authentic. I knew I had to talk to her. I was nervous. I don't think I'd ever spoken to a girl in real life who I hadn't softened up on the internet first. Not a girl like that, at least.

'Hi, I'm Gerard.'

'Hi, I'm Yoko.'

'Did you break up the band?'

'You know what, I guess I sort of did...'

They were the first words we ever spoke to each other. I don't know why I said that. I guess I was nervous. I hadn't convinced her of my winning personality via instant message. I hadn't searched all of her photos to find the imperfections, the spots she couldn't cover up, the off-centre nose, the haircut that she hadn't worn well, the little things that let me know that she was fallible, that she would be insecure too, that we could be together. She was older, thirty-five, thirty-six maybe. She was beautiful. All I had on her was exactly what I saw stood in front of me.

It turns out that she's not Japanese. But she could be, she looks as if she could be. She grew up in a market town in the East Midlands called Dunchurch, infamous for hosting a meeting of Guy Fawkes and the rest of the gunpowder plot conspirators in 1605. Not much had happened since then, but she was protective of its legacy.

'Without Dunchurch, the guy in the Anonymous hacker YouTube clips would have had to show you his face, and where the world be then?'

Her name came from her mum, not that she was Japanese either. Her dad had been working away when she was born. He had worked away a lot. He was the area manager for the top-performing region in a moderately successful kitchen appliances store. All her mum had been left with was her morning sickness and his Beatles back catalogue in mono.

She'd found out about the affair on the due date. She'd been having contractions and had telephoned the Leamington Spa store to ask to speak to her husband. The deputy manager had told her he was on holiday with his wife. He'd banked on the first one always being late.

If you're going to gamble, bank on the exception, that's what Grampy Joe told me.

'That hairy Jap has broken up the best band that ever was and ever will be.' Her dad had never forgiven her for taking John away. The name on the birth certificate had been a dish served cold.

When I heard this story, I thought for the first time in my life that actually, we were pretty lucky. We were rolling along to middle-class mediocrity for a while. I suppose at least when he was alive, you and Dad didn't actively hate each other. You just kind of existed next to each other, bound by some kind of sadistic pact to raise two children while holding down fair-to-middling jobs and displaying mild-to-medium levels of happiness against the backdrop of some pretty seismic geo-political, socio-economic paradigm shifts. That's something. Not everyone can say that.

One in two marriages break down. The family unit is dead, long live the internet. That's why the way we have of living here seems more highly evolved. What we have here is more relevant for the changing needs of an always-on society. I've pressed the off switch. You can too, Mum.

It must have been tough for you when Dad broke the pact. I may not have ever said it, but I know you tried your best. It's only when you get older that you realise superheroes aren't in comic books, they're in real life, battling on past death and debt, trying to raise the next generation of human beings.

It must have been hell for you when we stopped speaking...or who knows, maybe you were glad of the rest. I don't want to sound like I'm still twelve years old, but Steph started it. She always started things – at least that's my side of the story. I think I felt that if she didn't speak then I wouldn't speak. It was a solidarity move. She was sick of people asking how she was feeling. I knew what she meant. We were twelve years old. We felt hungry or we felt sleepy or we felt bored, but that wasn't good enough for most people. Most people wanted to know more, to know how we felt 'in ourselves', as if we should be glad they wanted to probe our innermost emotions, like they had the softest tissue shoulders around.

We weren't the clichéd twins with a psychic connection, but I know we had you all pretty freaked out back there. It wasn't like we were total mutes. We were still speaking to each other, more than we ever had done. We quickly realised that sooner or later, people stop asking questions, bring you food and move onto the next shitty situation they have to deal with.

Despite getting off to a bad start, Dr Hanslip seemed to get where we were coming from, eventually. The first time you took us to his office, we'd been sat opposite him on his sofa in silence for about ten minutes when he went across to his desk and came back with a sock puppet on his hand. He tried to use it to ask Steph a question about Dad. She gave him a look that would have raised a saint from his grave and bludgeoned him halfway to hell. He cut the kiddie crap with us from then on in.

It feels pretty luxurious that we live in a country where the state will pay a man with a PhD large sums per hour to sit and listen to two twelve-year-olds talk among themselves in elaborate code, but they're the rights we fight for. Keep on rocking, free world.

By the third session, he let us play with our Game Boys. I'd love to see the thesis: 'Tetris as a grief enabler in young teenagers'. It must be something to do with the game's ambition for order. It was the doctor who had suggested that you bought Steph a Tamagotchi for Christmas that year. Nanna Judy was beyond confused with the concept. What will be the equivalent evolution to feeding a computerized pocket-sized pet with the push of a button that will blow my mind when I'm grey and old? If I live here forever it may just be a text message.

Steph had killed it by New Year's Day. Overfeeding. As if she hadn't had enough loss to deal with.

I've never told you this (a theme of this letter!), but I'm glad you met Geoff. He's a good man. He'd fit in pretty well around here. When you cut yourself out of mainstream society, you quickly realise that it's no good having a population full of computer coders or psychology graduates or baristas. You need fixers. People who can make things with their bare hands. People who can work their way laterally around a problem. The YouTube tutorial in human form. Geoff is that man. His aptitude for engineering the big and small is frankly astonishing. I'd never realised I'd be envious of these skills until now.

It won't surprise you at all that I've been close to useless on the practical side of things here. I'm not the kind of man you want to rely on if you're hoping to build an outhouse from scratch or to woodchip a nature area or to devise a system to carry more berries back from the forest. My skillset is more suited to the equivalent of the prison library job.

I think Gustav has a plan for me. Everything will become clearer soon.

Before I was here I would have freaked if I'd have thought I could see myself with a divorcee, but I'm learning to accept that people have other lives, before and after my juncture in their story. I mean, I don't really know too much about Yoko's ex-husband, but I thought he seemed like a cool enough guy from her story. I'm with him on the creativity side of things. I think a ping pong room would be a neat use of space.

Apparently there used to be a ping pong table here, but Gustav had it burned because it was causing too much tension. There had been an unofficial inter-hut league and my hut, well, my hut before it was my hut, got caught up in some kind of beef about a net call. Yoko's right, we're not here for trivialities.

If you'd have lost a baby before we were born, do you think we'd have turned out differently? Would my soul have been destined for that body? Was I just sat there waiting in your insides, Steph just behind me in the queue, checking her phone or her nails or her nails in the reflection of her phone (I don't know why she does this)? Would you have treated me differently if I was born then to how you did when I was born?

Yoko and her husband lost a baby and replaced it with a cat. She says that she got to feeling like the baby was living inside of the cat, that she would look into the eyes of the cat and the cat would look back and she could sense a sorrow, a deep, bottomless sorrow.

'The problem was, I couldn't tell if it was the cat or a reflection. That's when I knew I had to leave,' she said.

You did it, Mum. You made a family. You pulled us together when things got tough. Something binds us Kanes and people who used to be Kanes and people who are married to people who used to be Kanes together. That's down to you. There's a network of invisible pulleys between us, each cog that turns impacting on the cog next door. Only you know how the levers work.

After the session we walked back to the huts together, not hand-in-hand but close enough to feel the heat from her forearm on the hairs of my body.

We were talking about the person who was reading my story. I'd never seen him before. He was a large man, thickset, his skin almost purple, his hair soft to the eyes. He was laughing manically. Yoko had asked me what my story was, if I was embarrassed. I'd told her no, that I'd just written an anecdote from the footballer George Best. He'd been staying in the hotel of a casino when a bellboy brought room service champagne to his bed. George was draped over Miss World and hundreds of pounds in winnings. 'Where did it all go wrong?' he asked him. For the purposes of the exercise, I'd pretended I was George Best. The new guy had clearly liked it. Yoko not as much.

Yoko's hut was one along from mine. There's so much I want to tell her. But there's no rush, no enforced boundaries, no three-day rule. What will be will be. She says she has something to tell me, that she'll tell me when we can find a quiet moment together. I'm waiting.

Yours, Gerard.

CHAPTER

Dear Del,

Hello stranger...

How's things in your world? It's hard to know how long it is since we last spoke to each other. I'm hoping any post-break up awkwardness is over. I'm hoping I can be frank.

And don't worry. This isn't a:

I'm gay letter

Or a:

I've got HIV letter

Or a:

Suicide note

Far from it. Things are good.

You're probably wondering where I am. Or at least, my ego hopes you're wondering where I am.

I'm in the middle of nowhere and I love it. I'm not sure you'd cope without the chain coffee shops. I'm joking. Yes, that infamous Gerard F. Kane humour you knew and tolerated is still alive and well. You would cope just fine. You'd give yourself over to what we have here and you would be just fine.

It should be no shock to you to hear that I now know my life was going round and round like a tourist on the Circle line. I'd sometimes check my junk folder for hours at a time, reading every word, hoping and praying for a sign.

That's not down to you. I know you felt it too.

I finally feel like I'm on the right track.

It was Stina who first mentioned it to me. She said there was a place in Denmark without internet. It's a place where people like me, people like us, live new lives, relying on each other, relying on our surroundings, relying on the spirit that lives inside of each and every one of us. And I don't mean spirit in a religious sense. I haven't joined a cult. I mean it in the inherent being sense, like the thing they talked about on your mindfulness app. I used to overhear it through your headphones at night.

It's probably worth pointing out here that another thing this isn't is a recruitment letter, although there are others joining us soon. Our little community is expanding, new people are arriving every day, but there's no recommend a friend bonus, as far as I'm aware.

I didn't get it then, your search for calm.

I didn't really understand what you were trying to achieve. I'd turn over and scroll through Twitter, going faster and faster until the profile pictures blurred and the words lost all meaning.

Superbowl

Muslim

Outrageous

Robots

Putin

Trump

Goal

Hashtag

Hashtag

Hashtag

I found it comforting.

I've since discovered that human beings are incredibly resourceful creatures when we're unhooked from the grid.

The genesis of our relationship probably set the tone for what was to come. We were thrown together by a computer algorithm.

Modern romance.

When you realised I wasn't as close to my first million/Academy Award as I'd maybe made out, you threw the dice of the algorithm again. I hope they dropped for you. I really do.

Despite these conceits, I think we made a pretty good fist of things. We did the best we could under the circumstances. We shared some good times.

There was that meal at the Mexican cantina. That was nice. And that gig. You liked that. The nights on the sofa. Fun times.

When I think of all of us now, when I see us in my mind's eye, we're sat there, or we're stood there, perfectly content, paying the other person absolutely no attention, each of us with our heads buried in our phones.

Our love was like a pull on an electric cigarette. It didn't taste like the real thing.

You don't need a weather app to know which way the wind blows. You can tell from the trees that it's autumn. Wrapping up is essential here if you're going into the outdoors. I know that it's your favourite time of year. It brought out the best in your wardrobe. You'd love my new look. I guess I'm what you would call normcore now, although here, it's less normcore and more just normal. People here wouldn't get it that our functional clothes fitted the narrative of a reactionary fashion craze. We're just a regular fit kind of community.

The clothes are provided to us:

two shirts

two pairs of trousers

two sweaters

one hat

one scarf

one pair of gloves

two pairs of thermal underclothes

three pairs of underpants

three pairs of thick socks

one pair of wellington boots

one pair of training shoes.

Everything is royal blue, including the training shoes. You always liked my photos when I wore blue. Only Gustav, our de facto leader, is permitted a different dress code.

This is probably the thing you'd hate the most, the dress code. The man you've got in your arms now almost certainly has a beard and almost definitely tattoos up and down his arms. I've come to realise that history will look back on this look just like it does the curly perm and the bell bottom.

Unfavourably.

Some people say Gustav is the son of a workwear magnate, that he turned away from his family's millions after a disagreement with his fascist father, something to do with discovering the company supplied the Nazis during occupation. They say he still has moles within the company and they send a regular shipment of clothing to the settlement for wear and tear and the slow trickle of newcomers.

The label on the clothes has been cut out but I think it used to say Fruit of the Loom.

I forgive you for the cheating. I'm assuming there was cheating. It's fine. I get it. Life's too short. You can't cage a butterfly. Any hole's a goal. Party on.

I remember the day we took Stina on the tour, when we walked across the barrage and rode the carousel and I had the phone call from Stephanie telling me Nanna Judy was dead. That day I was unsure if my love, if that's what it was, could cover all the variables. The same thoughts would come to me at the bar; halfway through pouring a craft ale, my mind would drift to us. Sometimes I'd clean the same spot of the same fridge for up to an hour. Did I love you?

I tested myself further. Would I love you with a broken nose? A cleft palete? Third-degree facial burns? I couldn't answer the questions. All I could think of was how any positive engagement our selfies got would be in sympathy, while a thousand private inbox conversations began.

I'm sure you have found another man. Maybe someone from Tinder. Sorry, I couldn't resist. I hope you find real love. Our love didn't stand a chance offline. We deserved better. (Or maybe we didn't, but I'm working on that.) Next time, I'd love her if she had dinosaur shit on her face. I'd love her if she had a sink hole for a mouth. I'd love her if she blew smoke from her nostrils every time she thought of cheese. I'd take our picture and I'd paste it on the largest billboard on the highest hill in the most densely populated area of the universe. Give that the thumbs up.

There was a terrible accident here yesterday. One of the guys who lived in my hut is dead. That's partly why I'm writing to you. When someone close to you, at least in proximity, passes on unexpectedly, it makes you think about the loose ends you've left untied, dangling dangerously out there in the world. I wanted to tell you it was alright. I wanted to tell you that everything was going to be alright.

Gustav called an extraordinary meeting in the Hygge, our meeting place, to talk to us before breakfast. He'd told us there had been an explosion just after dawn. We already knew this. We'd all heard it. It had sounded like gunfire and fireworks all at once. I'd sat up with a start, the first time anything other than natural sunlight had woken me since I'd arrived here.

Seth had been working in the kitchen when it had happened. Francine, our resident doctor, had been the first on the scene. He was dead on arrival. They were blaming it on a faulty pipe. There had been a gas leak but it was now under control. Gustav delivered the words clearly, loudly, seeming to relish the control.

He said that we had to deal with the consequences of the teething problems in establishing and providing the parts of our old lives we couldn't give up just yet. I don't know if he was talking about breakfast as a concept or blueberry pancakes specifically. Seth made really excellent blueberry pancakes. That's how I'll remember him, as a man who knew how to use the best in organic produce to create a hearty, inspiring breakfast. And that's more than enough.

Gustav said if we had any questions about what had happened we should ask them now. He reassured us that the accident had nothing to do with our expansion, that all health and safety protocols would be met in the building work that would take place. Francine raised her hand and everybody looked around towards her. She shuffled on the stump a little nervously, stood up and cleared her throat.

'I'd like to give my sincere condolences to Jonas.'

Spontaneous applause broke out across the Hygge. It stopped respectfully after six or seven rotations. Gustav told us that Jonas was resting. He told us that breakfast would be served an hour later today as they came to terms with the tragedy from a kitchen workflow perspective. He announced that blueberry pancakes would be off the menu indefinitely until a new solution could be found.

He said that in the meanwhile, we could stay in the Hygge and talk among ourselves about how we were feeling. And then he left.

An excited buzz of conversation rose across the Hygge. This was the first time I'd seen our new society gossip in a way which needed a collective noun. There were a range of emotions; some people were inconsolable, others were angry, some were scared, a small few vindictive.

'I thought we'd eradicated death. I really did. I thought we would live forever.'

'We have to get to the bottom of this. Something smells fishy.'

'I didn't even know Seth worked in the kitchen. He had pretty bad allergies.'

'Who's next?'

'He deserved it.'

The hum might have carried to Jonas' room, but he was too far away to hear the details of what was being said. If you put a group of people anywhere on earth, you can bet that by the time they've erected their first tent, they'll be gossiping. It's what makes us human, our desire to make up stories around the nonlinear, unexplainable events that happen in our lives, trying to string together some kind of narrative around our lives, some kind of cause and effect morality tale. If only life was as simple as a storybook.

I made those people stop talking. You'd have been proud of me. I stood on one of the tree stumps at first, but nobody seemed to notice. I started slowly and got louder and louder as the noise fell in inverse proportion. The group gradually stopped their conversations and turned to me, surprised at first, and began to listen.

'Friends, friends, friends. The last time I spoke in public was at my sixth form assembly. I was nervous then and I'm nervous now. But right now I'm not going to talk about the films of Ken Woo.' One or two laughs broke out in the Hygge. Grampy Joe told me the key to public speaking was getting a laugh in early doors. I had their attention.

'I'm standing up here because we need to be united. We mustn't talk like this. Seth was a good man. He liked blueberries and he liked pancakes and he brought his two loves together for all of us to enjoy.

Also, one time he told me he had a real craving for blue cheese, so who knows what innovations were to come from him. This isn't just a time for reflection but a time for action. I give you my word that I'll get to the bottom of what happened this morning. But for now, we need unity. We need to remember why we are here. We need to realise that we have found a better way of living and grasp that opportunity with both hands, starting again now. We are stronger together.'

Yoko started to clap before I finished the last word, as if she'd read the script. The rest of the group joined in enthusiastically. It seemed to have no end. They were clapping me, Del. They were clapping our society.

I matter here. It feels good to be able to tell you that.

I will get to the bottom of this.

Yours, Gerard

CHAPTER 27

Dear Nanna Judy,

I'm sorry you died. It's hard to know how to say that, so I thought it was best to just come right out with it. In a way, we're both in an afterlife.

The last few years of your life must have confused the hell out of you. Your time on earth took in evolution from the plough to the poke. What did you think of us all? Our eyes constantly drawn to the light in our hands, half-listening, half-there. Before the recordings, hand on heart, I don't think I had a conversation with you in the last fifteen years of your life when I wasn't looking at my phone at the same time. What was I looking for? A better conversation? Who could say something more interesting to me than a blood relation who was brought up by blood relations who lived two centuries ago.

It was my third visit. We'd gone through the chronology. Born, married, gave birth, brought them up, about to die. I'd quizzed you around key dates and events, playing at being the reporter; relishing being in control and pushing for a performance.

It came out of nowhere really. It hadn't felt like what you'd said had been a response to my amateur hour attempts at documentary, but from here, with the distance of space and time, I've realised that maybe it was your way of giving me what you thought I wanted.

You'd just made a pot of tea (I'd offered, you'd refused) and started to pour into the cups on the table between us.

'They must be as old me, Nan, these cups,' I said.

'What?'

'The cups. Old. As me, I reckon.' Looking around the room, the only thing younger than me was the new TV.

I remember thinking of the box set I was halfway through and wondering if the night would have been more productive spent in its easy company. I can tell you that now. But then you spoke. Every word of that interaction is vivid to me.

'You want to know what it's all about then, do you? That's it, I imagine.'

'What's that, Nan?'

'Tea?' I got up to pour my own but you didn't give me a chance.

'Number one, if you want to do something, don't spend your life dreaming about it. After my father died, we went through his personal effects and found a memoir he'd written about his time in the Australian army.'

'Oh wow, Nan, that's incredible.'

'He'd finished it years before, bound up right and proper, it was. Douglas found his diary too, full of wistful passages about how he never had the confidence to show anybody.'

This was his Xanadu.

'It was terrible, really turgid prose, but that's by the by. If you've got a dream, do it. Don't let it die.'

'There's a lot to be said—'

'Where was I?' You poured the tea again, even though you'd not drunk a drop since filling it minutes earlier.

'Number two, I guess, Nan,' I said.

'Yes. You've got two ears and one mouth. Use them in that order. That voice in your head is talking all day long. When you've been around for as long as I have, you'll have heard it say an awful lot. Not all of it you're going to like. Give some other bugger a chance and you might just learn something.' It was the first time I'd ever heard you swear. You were on a roll now, reeling off the lines.

'Number three, don't spend your life worrying 'til the early hours about what other folk think of you. If it makes you happy, do it.'

'I like this one.' I did. I do.

'If I'd have followed my own advice, I'd have left Joe six months after we were married. Never should have let him walk me down the aisle. Malcolm Jones had my heart. Always had, always will. Looked like Clark Gable. He lived four doors up from us. I only married Joe because he asked me and then I couldn't take the shame of walking away.'

'But Nan, Mum would never have been born then.'

'I don't know what you're talking about.' We sat in silence, me taking in the magnitude of what you'd told me, you drinking tea, muttering something under your breath.

'And apart from that I've got no more bloody clue than you.'

When I went to stop recording, the camera had switched itself off. I was inconsolable at the time, unsure it happened even. But now, from here, it feels perfect that way.

I'm so happy that we got to spend that time together. I honestly think recording your stories – or trying to – was the best thing I ever did back in the old world. It gave me a perspective nothing else could have. I have a lot of that now. Perspective. It's 20/20.

I hope that back there, something's being done to help the older generation with their online profiles. I'm confident your films would have gone viral. People really lap up that history stuff online, and you're the guys with the golden gun. Or at least you were, when you were alive. What stories will my generation have to pass down?

'I remember the time when I used slightly slower technology than you.'

'I remember the time when your grandmother sent me her first sext.'

'I remember the time when people used to leave their lifestyle complexes for entertainment.'

Try and make a six-part documentary series about that (although, granted, streaming services are content hungry beasts).

The internet can be a force for good. I'm not denying that. Viva la revolution. But look at our family. It enabled Uncle Derek. It was a family decision that Grampy Joe was too ill to understand what was going on. The feeling was that he'd be terribly confused, that he had enough to deal with making peace with a world he understood.

The leaps of faith you must have needed to take to comprehend just how Uncle Derek was doing what he was doing amaze me. Maybe you never really knew. Maybe that's for the best.

And then there's Auntie Bronwen. She could do with coming here. There's nothing more desperate than waking up to a Candy Crush notification from your auntie, sent to her whole friend list as she sat at the kitchen table of her one-bedroomed flat trying to eliminate coloured fruits at a quarter to four in the morning. Maybe it was a cry for help. Maybe she just wanted to communicate to another human being.

I hate myself for it, but I don't even know how old you were when you died. Mum would have told me. I'm sure she would have told me. But I can't remember now.

I could still tell you the ages of some of my Facebook friends – Mari Davies (thirty-five next birthday), Steffan Gomez (twenty-nine next birthday), Carey Smith (it's Carey's twenty-sixth birthday today – wish her happy birthday).

I don't even know who those people are.

What will the world look like when I reach your age? (I'm going with mid-eighties here, not that you looked that old.) Faster, stronger, more streamlined, more productive? I've found a place where I'm hopeful it'll be the same as it is today. It's called the Hygge. I like to think you've found it too.

There was an explosion here recently. At first, I thought it was fireworks. One of my most vivid childhood memories is when you took us to Sparks in the Park and I'm loving the colours and the crowds and the noise and Stephanie is hating the colours and the crowds and the noise and you're holding our hands, squeezing the black and white mittens Nanna Gwen had knitted for us tight against our skin so we wouldn't get lost or feel cold. I remember Grampy Joe was there, saying we looked like Dalmatians, then smoking with disinterest somewhere on the periphery, thinking maybe about some other explosions on some other field a long way from home.

You lived through a war. You were used to explosions. How did you react? People here have reacted in different ways. As much as history tries to simplify by short-handing a society's reaction under a broad theme, the reality is that on the ground people feel all sorts of things. I'm trying to lead the people. It feels like something I'm meant to do.

My neighbour died in the explosion. His name is Seth Van Der Beek and he is twenty-six years old and he comes from Cape Town in South Africa. Say hi from me. Perhaps one day, I'll see you both again. We can eat blueberry pancakes, undo our belt buckles and sit back

and watch the fireworks light up the world we once knew and loved.
    Yours, Gerard

CHAPTER

28

Dear Edwin,

If you're reading this (if you ever read this) stood behind the bar at AlePunk, my key message to you is this:

Get the hell out of there.

Just walk out.

Leave.

Hang up your barman's friend.

Do not serve another three-quarter pint of their overpriced craft ale.

Do not upsell another artisan burger stack.

Wipe your chalk caricature from the wall.

Delete their social media accounts from your phone.

Remove all push notifications.

Write a new bio.

Your first question probably is: where the fuck are you? That's valid. That's a valid line of questioning. You'll no doubt have seen I've not been online for a long time. Actually, you've probably unfollowed me. You were always about ratios. A worthy tribute to my legacy. When is too soon to remove the flag of solidarity you added to your profile picture following the terrorist atrocities? In the attacks against Gerard F. Kane, that time has most definitely passed.

I'm in a place where I feel like I'm needed. It's a first.

What did you want to be when you were a child? It feels hard for the juvenile brain to think in terms of the abstract feelings I've now accepted. What seven year old tells you they just want to be happy? That they just want to make a difference? That they want to lie on their deathbed knowing they did everything they could to make the world a better, safer, more opportunity-laden place for the next generation?

They wanted to be train drivers, astronauts, track and field stars, and, more lately, app developers, internet entrepreneurs. I thought my life could be about making money just from home rentals and generation-defining cinema. That the flux could be productised. But I was wrong.

I haven't thought about our daydream schemes for a long time.

I'm sure among the countless plans we had to get a million followers and a billion pounds, there was an idea that would have achieved that for us. We were lacking the application. We needed a Geoff. (He's my stepdad. A real doer.)

In no particular order, my favourite ideas were:

#1: Meme Gaga.

Do you remember the one where we were going to monetise a status generator that gave you randomly selected supportive posts for commenting on a friend's photo of their new baby on Facebook?

'Halloween's meant to be scary, not CUTE ☺'

'I know they say all babies look misshapen potatoes, but he looks just like you!'

'Could literally eat her all up with a side of slaw.'

'Future heartbreaker.'

'Who needs a paternity test?'

That one could have been a contender.

#2: And then there was our organic lifestyle label, Quinoa Scars. The pitch: 'Bringing a little bit of Sid and Nancy to sustainable lifestyles'. Our marketing strategy was based around converting your (Facebook) friend in the electronic indie band into a brand ambassador. The key creative moment was incentivising him to carry one of our tote bags over his shoulder on a shopping date with his on-off reality TV star girlfriend in return for some points in the business. Online gossip sites here we come. Our projections showed that we'd have shipped a half a million worldwide by Q3. 'The internet has democratised global trade,' you said.

#3: Our label, Mummy's Boy Records. While this idea stemmed from a doodled logo on an AlePunk bar napkin, I think we may have finally cracked how to make money from music in the digital age.

Mummy's Boy's Records existed at the intersection of music, art and commerce like nothing else since Warhol before it. The baby in the logo even looked a little bit like him, but I think we'd both admit that was purely coincidental, the happy accident that all billionaires cite in the formative chapters of their ghost-written best-selling autobiography.

The revenue generation model was based around the creation of a next-level streaming channel (working name: NuTube). The structure involved a high security compound populated by Scandinavian starlets, a superfast broadband connection, lifestyle brand partnerships and a state-sponsored subscription model.

The centrepiece would be the annual release of a highly limited-edition compilation vinyl made from meme-friendly materials like cat's milk, human placenta and kale. The vinyl would retail for the price of a minor Van Gogh and hang on the walls in the summer homes of oligarchs and sit in the private collections of the most discerning too-rich art punks. It would contain no music.

For all I know, you've already done this.

Finally, I'm happy with the abstract.

This is the bit you've been waiting for. Settle in. Reach for the savoury popcorn. Yes, there's a girl. For the first time, she's actually a woman. She's thirty-six years old, last time she checked. She was married. She lost a baby. Her name is Yoko, but she is not Japanese. She is from an unhip town. It doesn't matter. All that matters is that she is here now.

Before you choke on your snack, I am cool with all of this. Yes, I know. We'd have swiped left on someone with baggage like this before. But now I'm ready for this. If we were cavemen we'd have been grandfathers by now, Edwin.

You'll notice I haven't even mentioned how attractive she is yet. Or how cool she is. I know these are going to be your primary questions? Is she hot? Is she cool? I know what you'll be thinking. I know how your mind works because my mind worked the same. It was hard for me to train my brain to think differently but when you live in a society where validation takes a different form, beauty can be a malleable concept.

But relax. She is hot and cool. And I don't mean just like the girls you'd go for (no offence – I went for them too). The filter-fit girls. You know only too well the all too familiar disappointment of casting your eyes on a girl's face in real life after stalking her online for months. Why didn't that tell you that way of meeting people was broken?

Yoko is beautiful. Truly beautiful. It's a beauty from the inside, the kind Jesus must have seen. And no, I've not turned into a religious nutter. The new religions are just as bad as the old ones.

Remember all the time we'd spend thinking up first dates, trying to outdo each other?

Adventure golf.

Dog walking.

Laser Quest.

Experiential theatre.

The petting zoo.

Zorbing.

Pony trekking.

A speedboat ride.

It's like our lives were defined by our competitive 'Blind Date' situation, the distraction of the sub-stag do activity intended to viralise her posts, to skip past the silences and straight into bed.

One of the last things I remember seeing on the internet was that they were going to replace the killer whales at SeaWorld with an informative orca experience. Looks like they finally freed Willy.

One time I remember you took a girl out for dinner and drinks.

'Retro,' I said.

'I know,' you said, 'she thought it was some kind of set-up.'

Yoko and I just went for a walk. The entertainment options are a bit more limited here. This is not Europe's fastest growing capital city. I'd met her on my second day. We'd talked (not messaged – actually talked!). There was a connection. I could feel it. Then just last week in a session, I'd read her story of why. This is the story of why she's here. Why she skipped existence 2.0. It was the stuff I mentioned earlier – the husband (ex), the baby (ex). It didn't scare me. It told me about who she'd been, who she wanted to be. It made me think about the answers to those questions myself.

I was meant to be writing my story of why, about the way my life was balanced perilously on this thin web of virtual reality, about how it had led to a break-up, a break-down, but I'd been transfixed by her, watching her express her emotions on the page. I imagined me and her in the future, our own hut, our own cat, our own baby. Our own pact to make the world a better place for the next generation.

Jonas (he was leading the session – he's a nice man, but he seems sad – not sad like he's having a bad day but sad like he's grieving for something or someone. And this was before he actually was. Maybe he was just settling in to the role) called time. I looked down at my page. I'd stolen one of George Best's anecdotes and filled the rest of the page with a drawing of a sun, smiling and in wraparound sunglasses, its rays braided into plaits, a cloud hovering just over its head like a beanie hat. As Yoko and I walked back to our huts, I looked back towards the meeting place (it's called the Hygge – it means...ah, Google it) and saw Jonas looking at my paper, holding it up to the light. I think he was trying to trace the shape of the sun behind the sketch to work out which was real.

Jonas' son Seth died in an explosion recently. People are anxious that others are coming. That the dynamic will change. But we'll move on. Life always moves on.

The message had been delivered at breakfast that morning. The daylight had shone through my window early, waking me before you'd probably even got home. After some mild meditation, I'd washed (think the communal shower at a festival but with less drugs casualties) and dressed for the day. Meals are served in the only brick building in the settlement. It's about the size of a football pitch and has the very particular smell of a thousand school assemblies.

Queuing isn't a thing here. We just congregate in the middle of the hall and approach the kitchen staff when we feel like it's our turn to do so. People have been more reticent to do so after what happened. It's like they're waiting for the next challenge. I hadn't been paying much attention – I wasn't really that hungry and was still feeling mainly chilled from my exercises earlier – but then I saw Yoko. She was behind the counter, wearing a royal blue tabard. Against her pale skin it made her look like a child's drawing of winter.

It was my turn.

Francine, our resident doctor, had started to walk to the counter too but I strode ahead of her, my training shoes connecting with the wooden floor like a county level squash player on his way to the national finals. Yoko handed me a tray and avoided my eyes. I walked away and found myself a seat alone in the corner of the room.

AlePunk was at the epicentre of the artisan trick. Everything we eat here is locally sourced. It's not just spin. We grow it ourselves. There is a team that predicts demand, a team that prepares the land, a team that plants the seeds, a team that irrigates the crops, a team that harvests the produce. Back at home there was too much choice, too many trends. Foods I was previously trying to like included olives, avocados and wasabi. Why? Have you ever asked yourself why? Here I eat a plant-based diet and it's all grown in my garden. I eat better, I feel better, I look better.

She had hidden a note in my spinach:

'Meet me at noon at the back of my hut.
Y.'

I was unsure then why she was being so secretive about things, but it has become clear.

We walked away from the huts, into the grounds of the settlement. She seemed flustered, like she wanted to get me away from the others. However much I wanted to, I didn't reach out to hold her hand.

The tall grasses bowed to the ground under the pressure of my wellington boots. I followed her footsteps further and further away from the clearing. She'd look around every now and then to check I was still on her tail. I tried to say something to break the tension, but she shushed me.

'Where are we going?'

'Just follow me.'

I'd been out walking plenty of times but had always stuck to the footpaths. A trail had been cut around the settlement in a figure of eight about two or three miles wide, the pathway pebble dashed between the trees. One day I'd even fallen asleep and been woken up by a deer. (A real deer! I bet the closest you've come to one is eating venison at a street food festival.) But Yoko was taking me much further than that. The grasses had turned to trees.

'We've only got two hours free time. Will we make it back?'

'We will. It's not much further.'

And then we came to it. The clearing was much smaller than the one where we live. You could have fitted five or six of these in our clearing, yet it seemed more open, perhaps because there were no huts, no humans, no Hygge. A small wooden building the size of the average garden shed stood in the centre of the space. The sign outside had been chopped from its post. The windows were too dirty to see in. I looked through the door. It was an old café. It didn't look like it had served a drink this side of Starbucks. It looked like it came straight from the pages of the Brothers Grimm.

We sat on a bench outside, our bodies close enough but not touching. I thought about playing with magnets in science class, about that exact spot where the force fields fought against each other, cancelled each other out, how a move just a millimetre either way would repel or attract.

'I come here to think sometimes.'

'Can't you think where we are?'

'Not always. It's difficult for me. I was here before you. Everything changes. Familiarity breeds contempt.'

I tried to understand.

I told her about my life. I told her how everything I had, everything I did was supported through the internet. My relationships, my conversations, my motivations. I needed more. I needed to be part of more than a trending topic. I needed to get real.

She understood. She had felt the same. She had met her husband through the internet. She had arranged a date with another man that night, but her husband had sent her a link to a DVD rip of every X Files season ever made and she felt like this was someone she needed in her life. He'd seemed like a good guy but his profile hadn't listed his lack of direction and general untidiness. They'd been co-habiting for a solid but unspectacular four years when she found out she was pregnant. They married pretty much immediately without fuss or ceremony. Family and friends found out through a photo they'd posted online.

They'd talked about kids but she'd figured that was part of the game, a pre-requisite for the covenant of living together, as hypothetical as wishing away lottery winnings on spiral staircases or airstream caravans.

She had been determined to be the best mum she could be. The internet was not helping but she just couldn't log off.

She had read blogs which said that caffeine was bad for the baby.

She had read blogs which said that caffeine was good for the baby.

She had worried herself sick self-diagnosing. Hiccups, fevers, trapped wind, all became fatal to the living thing growing inside of her.

This had gone on for ten weeks.

They had just posted their first picture online.

It had received 247 likes and congratulatory comments from at least seven people that neither of them claimed to know.

'The medical term is a spontaneous abortion. I always thought that sounded like a death metal band. The doctors said it was a chromosomal abnormality and I just nodded.'

After that, she spiralled worse than I had. It made me feel like a fake that I hadn't been through all of this but had ended up in the same place. But I suppose it's about where you're going, not where you've come from. A trimester later, she found herself here. It had been Moira, her former colleague, who had made the intervention.

That was over a year ago now.

'Do you know why you're here, Gerard?'

'I've told you all of that.'

'But why here? Specifically?'

'Maybe not...I suppose I don't.'

'You're in a place called The Offline Project. Some people say

Gustav is a disgruntled former Facebook employee. Others say he's still working for them. I'm not so sure either way. Their big idea is to restart a society in the internet age, just without the internet. And to populate that society with—'

'—with internet addicts?'

'—correct. With the worst kind of internet addicts. You and I are at the gentler end of the spectrum, but there are people here who have waged acts of war through the internet. People who have shared the most odious of files through the internet.' I thought of my Uncle Derek.

'Like who?'

'I don't know. Nobody knows except Gustav. We're all people who became defined by the internet. We're all people who weren't people anymore without the internet.'

'What's he trying to achieve?'

'Whoever's behind it, they want to see if our consciousness has been irrevocably damaged. They're trying to find out if we can create a new society without the biggest crutch the world's ever had. They're trying to find out if our brains still work. They're trying to find out if we're still human.'

'Why did you have to bring me all the way out here to tell me?'

'They're listening to us. They're listening to everything that goes on. We're not meant to know what they're doing here. Self-awareness might be a plus point in the internet age, but here, they think it'll foul up the experiment.'

'So how do you know?'

'Others have found out, others who were here before you were. They've disappeared them.'

'But I thought we came here to disappear?'

'Temporarily so, yes. Like a fat camp for the constantly online. But it's bigger than that. This isn't just a retreat. The exercises we do, yes, they're part of a digital detox, but it's just preparation for the next step. Seth's accident wasn't an accident. They planned it. They want to see how we'll react. It's just the beginning of what's next. I can feel it.'

'Why did you tell me this?'

'Because I like you, Gerard. You can find out what's coming next. I know it.'

I leaned in to kiss her. She kissed me back, for a half a second, but then pushed me away.

'Remember rule number four. All relationships should be platonic. Their rules are bullshit but there's no point in arousing suspicion. We have work to do.'

I wanted to say thank you for taking me to the hospital. You are a true friend. The first thing I remember is waking up on a plastic covered bed to a male nurse filling out a form he held up with a clipboard. The room was white and his teeth were yellow. He wished me good morning and left the room. I had a sharp pain in my temples, the kind you get from a pin prick. The next thing I remember is another man, this one a doctor, I think, an Asian man, being sat next to my bed asking me a list of questions.

The questions were simple mainly:

'What year is this?'

'Who's the Prime Minister?'

'What is the capital of England?'

'Who founded Facebook?'

But every now and then he would throw in a non-sequitur:

'How many times a day do you get an erection?'

'When is a friend not a friend?'

'When was the last time you told your mother you loved her?'

'What is more powerful: an orgasm or a retweet?'

I told him I was tired and needed to rest and he nodded like he understood. I'm not sure how long I was in that place. It can be difficult to keep a track of the days when you're sleeping through them.

My dreams were rich and vivid.

You were in one. We were working behind the bar at AlePunk, except it wasn't the AlePunk in Cardiff. You could tell from the customers that AlePunk had gone intergalactic. The clientele had changed. Think the Star Wars bar. Think scaly space cowboys with hipster beards, two-headed beings with John Lennon glasses. We weren't serving craft ale. When they came to the bar, they'd pay us via some highly evolved contactless system and in return we'd look in their eyes and tell them an irrefutable truth. Things like:

'God didn't build the world in seven days.'

'Hitler was a monster.'

'The iPhone is the greatest human triumph since the wheel.'

But the dream I had most frequently wasn't that one. I was dressed for a Western, denim waistcoat and leather holster, battered boots walking across a great plain. The kind of vast expanse you associate with pioneer day America. I was leaving something behind. I felt hope and hunger in my stomach, the shape of a pregnant woman next to me, her face covered by her hair blowing in the wind. I never got to see her face. I never got to see where we were going.

The letter was on the bed when I woke up. I opened the envelope and cleared the sleep out of my eyes. It was from Stina. Stina was one of my house guests, but you probably wouldn't remember me mentioning her because she wasn't Italian and nineteen. Stina works for Gustav. This much I know now.

She told me to fly to Copenhagen. She'd picked out the flight. I was to leave the hospital without telling anybody. If I needed to return home to pick up some things I should do it quickly and quietly. She would meet me at the airport. She would take me to somewhere I would be safe, to somewhere I could be happy, to somewhere where I could work out who Gerard F. Kane really was.

They wanted me here. I always knew my online profile would propel me to greatness and now it has, but I don't know what they want from me.

I really hope things are working out with you and Lenka. If not, don't sweat it. You'll find your Yoko.

Yours, Gerard.

CHAPTER

Dear Mum,

I've been thinking a lot recently about happiness.

We don't always admit it, but isn't everything we do in search of it? Every time we give, every time we receive, every time we flirt, every time we cheat, every time we eat, every time we get up in the morning to go to work, every time we post a selfie, every time we have sex, every time we drink wine, all of these things, they're all a vain attempt at validation, a shot in the dark to feel better about ourselves when we lie alone, awake at night.

Happiness as a management tool.

Happiness as the ultimate human achievement.

When we were seven, you and Dad took me and Steph on holiday to that campsite in France. Do you remember? We drove down in Dad's big saloon car with the wooden doors like we were an American family and you tried to sleep the whole way to Portsmouth and the rest of us sang the Henry VIII song until you snapped at us. And on the ferry over Dad gave us £20 each to get some Francs and we spent all of Steph's playing on the arcade games.

When we got to the campsite you and Dad argued about which pole went in which hole as you were putting the tent up and me and Steph moaned because we were tired and it was cold and dark and wet. Then every day we'd wake up and Dad would be cooking bacon and eggs on the stove and he'd always burn the toast and you'd scrape the burnt bits off using your keys because Dad had left the cutlery in the garage.

We made friends with a German brother and sister and spent the days running around the camp in no direction in particular, chasing after balls or the breeze. Then on the last morning you said that playtime was over and we were going on a family expedition to the beach. We rolled our eyes but playtime had really just begun. We walked along the cliffs and onto the shore, crabbing in the rock pools, writing our names in the sand, eating the fish paste sandwiches Dad had wrapped in yesterday's newspaper.

That's the happiest I've ever been. It seemed so much simpler when we were younger. Adults have a very special way of overcomplicating life. I think I came home from London to try and reverse this process, to try and strip back to basics, to get back to the safe place and take stock.

I think about you and the others all the time.

Geoff makes you happy. I can see that. Don't underestimate it.

Yours, Gerard

CHAPTER 30

Dear Stephanie,

Since I last wrote to you I've found out a few things about where I am and why I might be here.

Our community is populated entirely by internet addicts. It may or may not be called The Offline Project. People may or may not be dying.

You're probably thinking: get the hell out of there, brother!

Escaping's not such an easy option. Yoko thinks we're at least a hundred miles away from civilisation, in the middle of a forest somewhere in Denmark. We'd need to steal a lot of blueberry pancakes to survive that long. And anyway, even if we were in a suburb of Copenhagen, I wouldn't leave. Not now. Not like this.

I was happy to be in a new place with new people and a new way of living. But ever since I knew something was happening here, I've needed to get to Gustav.

Yoko came up with a plan.

A lot of people didn't know how to act around Jonas now. He had always seemed sad, so it had been hard for people to appreciate how something might have changed in him. Everyone here had a reason to be melancholic, but those reasons were meant to be left behind in the old world. Jonas was reminded of his constantly. He had come here with Seth to make a new life and now he was alone. We needed to make him feel like he was part of something bigger.

Yoko had taken her blue tabard off and hid it under her arm as she walked away from her shift in the kitchen. I watched out my window for her and opened the door to my hut, ushering her in. It was against the rules to enter a hut you weren't resident in.

It was early afternoon. The two-hour free period had just started. People had their own routines; some would sit in the Hygge and talk, others would meditate in their rooms, a group of four regularly played mahjong. Seth had been in this group. His room has been taken by a new settler. The new settler's name is Moses and, from what I can work out, he's from West Africa originally. He's a big guy, the biggest here, six foot six maybe, and built like an MMA fighter. The royal blue shirt looks like a child's size on his frame, his stomach showing like a homoerotic belly dancer, his sleeves at 3/4 length, but he doesn't seem to mind. He's got a constant grin and is permanently high-fiving. I haven't seen him in a session yet.

We knocked on Jonas's door and could hear him shuffling around inside. When he answered he was surprised and a little nervous.

'She shouldn't be in here.'

'Let me in, Jonas. We've got something for you.'

He didn't have much choice. His room was about half as big again as mine but the layout was the same:

Bed (single)

Chair

Desk

Lamp

Rug (worn)

Clock

Calming artwork.

Jonas pulled the chair out for Yoko and motioned her to sit down. He looked around for a place for me and resignedly pointed to the corner of the bed. I tried to stand but a minute or so later gave in and perched on the edge. Jonas sat at the other end, half-turned against the headboard. His body seemed considerably older than it had a week ago. I revised my earlier guesses on his age. He reminded me of Grampy Joe in the last days.

'We brought you this, to cheer you up.'

Yoko uncovered a big stack of blueberry pancakes and handed out three forks.

'If you don't mind, we'll help you dig in.'

Jonas' eyes grew wider. He looked at Yoko, then to me. The green of his iris got darker, his eyes starting to fill with tears.

'It's my birthday today.'

As we passed the plate around, Jonas told us his story. His wife had died when Seth was three years old and Jonas had given up his job to look after him. He ran the region's largest construction firm and had made enough money by then for five lifetimes. He'd home-schooled Seth, partly for selfish reasons, he admitted; he didn't know what he'd do with his time if Seth was gone all day. He created what he still feels is the most sophisticated curriculum in the western world, combining academic rigour with emerging languages, DIY skills, computer coding and community service. He wrote a series of letters to the National Council of Provinces but never received a reply.

When Seth reached the age of eighteen, he accepted a place to study at university in Johannesburg. Jonas hadn't even known he'd applied. He'd realised he couldn't keep him confined from the outside world forever, but it hit him hard. He needed something to fill the void in his life. The internet stepped in.

He signed up for as many dating sites as he could find. Jonas's wife had been twenty-three when she'd died. He'd adored her. While he'd aged, his view of what was beautiful hadn't moved on. He hadn't allowed himself to have other women, even to entertain the thought of them. He had been fully committed to Seth's education.

His days took on a familiar shape. He'd wake at seven and log on immediately. He'd check his message boxes first and attend to any overnight correspondence, before trawling the recently logged in members and starting new lines of enquiry with them. Sometimes he'd be keeping up conversations with forty or fifty women at once.

He'd construct a series of different characters for his responses, Googling pop culture references and job descriptions to weave a string of perfectly believable narratives. His evenings were reserved for meeting his new friends. His searches extended for hundreds of miles, so it was not uncommon for him to leave his home at 2 or 3 p.m. and to travel back throughout the night. The meetings followed a pattern. He'd arrive to the pre-arranged venue ten or fifteen minutes late, generally to be greeted with his date nervously nursing a glass of wine or checking her phone.

He'd arrive at her table, sit down and introduce himself, telling her about his journey, apologising for being ever so slightly late. The girl would become more nervous now. This guy was in his fifties. The guy she had been speaking to was in his early twenties. She had his picture on her phone. This was not him.

He'd used Seth's picture on his profiles.

Some left immediately, others stayed for a drink, one even offered him to go back to her place. On numerous occasions a male friend seated in another part of the restaurant came over to confront him, but in those days, Jonas could handle himself. Almost all of them reported him to the dating site. He was an old guy. Tall, wiry, with grey hair and a square jaw. He wore black glasses. He had a moustache. He'd change his appearance, but it was a losing battle. He spent half his days masking his IP address.

One girl jumped off a transport bridge on the way home from a particularly awkward meeting. One bad date too many, the papers said. The dating sites informed the police. He was arrested and his computer confiscated. A high-profile legal case was brought against him. The South African media called him the 'Silver Tongued Surfer'. His defence was that he meant no harm, that he had always used an accurate likeness, that there must have been gremlins at the server farm. He received a short custodial sentence. Seth visited him every day.

It was his lawyer who suggested he come here. Seth suspended his studies to join him. He felt like he still owed him that much.

Jonas finished talking and dropped his eyes to the pancakes on the plate in his lap. I wondered how many degrees of separation there were from swiping right to what Jonas had done. It was Yoko who broke the silence.

'Thank you for sharing that with us, Jonas. Everybody has a story that's brought them to this place. I've read some difficult stories in the sessions. I've read some sad stories in the sessions. But all of that is behind us now. We don't judge you. We're here to focus on the future.'

'Seth would want you to contribute to the new world. We need people like you. Let it be your tribute to him,' I said.

He was quiet for a while, taking it all in.

'You've made my birthday bearable,' he said. 'The memory of my best-ever birthday is so vivid I feel like I could step out of the door and I'd walk right into it. Seth was only fifteen, but he'd arranged this big surprise for me. He'd been on edge, certain all month that I'd find out. He'd get like that, he always wanted things to be just so, he was a good kid.

'He'd made a breakfast for me, my favourite, smoked salmon and scrambled eggs, I couldn't eat it every day, too rich, but it reminded me of the first breakfast me and his mother shared as man and wife, all those years before. After I'd finished eating, he asked me to wear a blindfold. A blindfold, of all things!

"Hang on, mate," I said to him.

"'Come on, Dad, I'm not a burglar who's bust through your security system."

'So I did it, I played his game. I got in the back of a car and we must have driven for about half an hour before it pulled to a stop. I thought about peeking out, about pulling the blindfold down, but the kid had put so much work into it, I didn't want to seem like a spoilsport. He took my hand and guided me out of the car and walked me through a crowd of people. I could hear them pointing me out, turning their heads towards me and laughing. "What's that silly old duffer doing?"

'I stepped up again and he guided me into a seat. I heard a door close and we started to move. I started to feel a little uneasy now. Come on, kid, what's the big surprise? But then the radio came on. It was the test match. South Africa v England. I bloody loved cricket, still would if I had the chance. Allan Donald, he was our bowler, must have got the cue – he was ferocious back then, the way he'd launch it down the green. The first bloke fell leg before wicket and we'd cheered, the sound reverberating around us. Then he did it again, this time delivering the ball in just the right place, so it started to drift away from the batsman just as he was tempted to smash it. But the batsman only managed to nick it with the edge of his bat. You could hear the South Africans in the crowd cheering before the commentator came in:

"'Oh and the wicket keeper's got it in his glove. That's two in two for Donald."

'We sat in silence for the third ball – that would have been his hat-trick – that's a very rare thing in cricket – but he bowled it wide.

"'Dad, take your blindfold off."

'And when I did we were halfway up to Table Mountain in a cable car, the bay sweeping below us like a landscape painting, the views 360 across the skyscrapers of the city over to Robben Island and the Atlantic seaboard.

"'Bloody hell, Seth!"

'I sat back down. I bloody hated heights.

"'Here, Dad," he said, handing me a bottle of Castle milk stout, "I had to get you up here somehow before you kicked the bucket. Happy birthday, you old bastard."'

Jonas's door pushed open.

'Gerard Kane, Yoko O'Neal, come with us.'

I'd never seen these two men before. The first thing that stood out was that they weren't wearing royal blue. Even the people in my memories and dreams had started to wear our uniform. (You look pretty good in it, Steph, you've customised it, of course.) The man who spoke was, I'd guess, in his late twenties, his hair closely clipped to his skull, the necessity haircut of an early victim to male pattern baldness taking on a more sinister air in the circumstances. He seemed serious, in taking care of business mode. His partner seemed suspicious, like an identikit sketch drawn in the dark, a bad ponytail and adult acne. He looked like he'd be a computer hacker for the bad guys, a cyber-terrorist saying fuck you to a lifetime of bullies and hand jobs.

They led us through the clearing in silence.

'Where are you taking us?'

Despite it being free time, nobody was about, even the usually busy Hygge was empty. We walked past the huts, through the grass to a cut off the pathway I'd never noticed before. I tried to reach out for Yoko's hand but the man with the ponytail had cut between us. I dropped the pace to hang back but he did the same.

We walked across some trampled down grass, across the figure of eight pathway and came to a building in the trees. It wasn't a clearing as such, it seemed to just appear out of nowhere, like a treehouse on the flat. It was wooden, the same colour as its surrounding, and about the size of our primary school.

This was where Gustav lived. We'd always wondered.

The men split in two, directing us to opposite ends of the building. I turned and tried to run after her, but the ponytail grabbed my arm.

'Get your hands off me!'

Yoko was already too far away. She looked back over her shoulder and I think I caught her eye. I shouted out, 'I love you.'

'That won't help you,' the ponytail told me.

'Fuck you.'

I was ushered into a room and told to sit down and wait. The room was tastefully decorated. Compared to the Scandinavian minimalism of the huts, it had the feel of an Aspen ski lodge belonging to a hedge fund manager, ruby red Chesterfield sofas, investment artwork from acclaimed living painters. I wanted to take my training shoes off and run my toes through the deep shag pile rug, but they were watching me. That much was clear.

The ponytail remembered his manners and served me sparkling water from a glass bottle and some kind of Bombay mix snack. It was delicious, the first synthetic food I'd eaten in longer than I could remember. I don't think it was grown on the settlement. A dark mahogany coffee table carried a selection of reading material. The surroundings were easing my nerves, but I was anxious about what came next and where Yoko was.

I lost an hour or two in an article about the destruction of the Great Barrier Reef. In the last thirty years, it had lost half its coral. I daydreamed I was underwater, swimming on the back of a green sea turtle, Yoko's arms around my waist. I remembered that Sunday afternoon we took Nanna Judy on a virtual tour of the Reef, hooking the street view up to the flat screen TV, Nanna shrieking and stooping down as a humpbacked dolphin swam towards the sofa.

'He'll see you now.'

The room was similar, smaller, a moose's head looking out from a plinth, the eyes dead. I assumed it was real. I assumed Gustav had killed it himself. He was stood with his back to me, looking out of a window into the woodland. His shoulders were covered by some kind of ceremonial kaftan, red and green satin flecked with gold. He looked ridiculous compared to the dress code to which I've become accustomed.

'If that was the Taj Mahal, people would step up and take notice. There'd be an international outcry, a million online petitions...'

'Sorry?'

'The Reef. It's a perfect storm...rising temperatures, increases in cyclonic activity, manmade ports shipping coal to China.' He turned towards me. His face was fringed with white hair, like a lion that had been left out in the snow. 'Have you ever been?'

'All the time,' I answered. And I didn't need Google to visit. I could close my eyes and be anywhere now. I had that power.

'Of course. Of course.' He moved from the window to the desk which separated the two of us. It looked like it had been moved from an industrialist's office at the turn of the century before last.

'Gerard. It's good to finally see you. Sit down, sit down, sit down. You'll make a man nervous.'

'I could say the same.'

'Come, my boy, I've been meaning to talk to you for a while now. Mano a mano, as they say. That's it, isn't it? My Spanish is terrible. Do excuse the pronunciation.'

His accent was more pronounced indoors, the affectations bouncing between the wooden walls.

'Yes, I believe that's the term. I'm hoping we're not going to grapple, but just so you know, I watched a lot of wrestling as a kid. I'm prepared for whichever way this goes.'

A laugh came from deep in his insides.

'Relax, relax...'

I sat down. The chair was the most comfortable thing I'd put next to my body for a long time. My cheeks sank into the cushions.

'That's the spunk that drew us to you, Gerard. You really have been a star attraction. I can reassure you, you won't have to wrestle me today, not physically anyway. I've got a hundred pounds on you at least. It's one of the only pursuits where the fat man has a natural advantage.'

'Then what the hell is going on here?' I asked.

'Don't you like it here? We've tried our very best to make you feel at home.'

I paused for a second to think about my answer. I studied his eyes. He was teasing me.

'I liked it here. Now I want to know what the fuck is going on.'

'Use the swearwords, Gerard,' he said, his tone rising like a teenage boy. 'How does it feel in your throat? Does it make you feel powerful or powerless? You'll have noticed it's a long time since you heard language like that. It tends to be one of the first things that goes, which is very useful for us on a whole host of levels.'

'Fuck you.'

'On queue. Very good.' A shrill noise hung in the air and then left. It did nothing for my nerves. He could tell.

'Oh, don't worry. Just a call for refreshments. I trust Cliff treated you well? You know, when we found him, he was living like Howard Hughes in a bedsit in Cambridge, hair down to his waist, a long scraggly beard, fingernails like Shylock. Absolutely filthy pyjamas. He'd dropped out of his studies to focus on creating a programme to revolutionise the way the world learns a second language. A genius, a real diamond in the rough. Just the kind of fella we need here.'

'And he makes your tea?'

That deep laugh again.

'Not usually, no, no, no. My other man is otherwise disposed. Cliff's not proud. He's very versatile.'

'Good for Cliff, but are you going to answer my question?'

'Soon enough, Gerard, soon enough.'

I needed to know now.

'It's like we're all Adam and you've shown us the Garden of Eden and then slammed the gates shut.'

He considered me and drew in a breath.

'A strong biblical reference, Gerard. Learned from Wikipedia, no doubt. Ah, I forget. Excuse me. You had a church education. We know all about that.'

'Of course you do.'

'But wasn't it better for Adam to be protected from the serpent? Don't you think this is a better place than back there in the old world? The people are friendlier. They hold actual conversations, meaningful conversations which aren't distracted by the beep or buzz of a telephone. They don't make assumptions based on the other person's online footprint. They don't have preconceptions based on their recent search history.'

'But people here don't have any information. Information is power. We need to know what's going on,' I said.

'The opposite of what you say is true. Too much information is tiring. Life here has more spontaneity. When was the last time you ate at a restaurant without checking out its online reviews? The last time you saw a film and skipped the crowd-sourced score? Discovery is dead back in the old world.'

His voice was exaggerated, his accent slipping in and out of plausibility.

'That's all very good, but why am I here?' The door behind me opened. I twitched, turning to see who it was. It was Cliff. He carried a tray over to the desk and arranged some sparkling waters in front of the two of us.

'Most people think they've been brought here to cure them of their addiction, to find a simpler way of living. And that is part of it. Of course it is. Haven't you noticed your brain has started to go back to being, well, your brain? That you have the capacity for much deeper thought?'

He was right.

'Okay, I'll give you that one, Gustav. That's a fair assessment. Back then I'd have been sat here writing and rewriting the 140 characters in my head I thought had the most potential to go viral.'

'Exactly, you would. You'd have been living for the likes, not experiencing the moment. What do we have if we don't have the moment? We have nothing, Gerard. Nothing of real consequence. Do you think our forefathers would have made such giant strides if they'd have been blunting their brains on the internet all day? What we're doing here is phase two. You can think of it as a petri dish for the second Renaissance. What comes next is anyone's guess, but at least it'll be real. What happens here could be all important. It could help save the human race.' He sat back in his chair like he'd delivered the killer blow in a courtroom drama.

'That sounds pretty dramatic.'

'It could be the most engrossing drama in human history.'

'Who the fuck are you to do this?'

'Ah, with the language again. Hahaha, he didn't mean it.'

'Enough of that. Who are you?'

'I'm Gustav. You know this, Gerard. I'm just the figurehead, really. A lot of people, a lot of very powerful organisations are invested in what happens here.'

'Like who?'

'Social media companies. Media conglomerates. Governments. Energy companies. Hedge funds. Many people have a very real interest in how the world might reboot itself after an apocalypse-style scenario. The situation the world has got itself into, my soundbite for the launch was, 'It might not be apocalypse now, but it's certainly apocalypse when'. It doesn't really matter if it's global jihad or an asteroid, climate change or a super-flu. Simultaneously, I always find that word hard to say in English, sim-ull-tay-nee-us-lee. There's a very real chance the internet will lose all of the data we're storing in it. The collective memory of the last few generations lost forever. A perfect storm is brewing.'

I searched the lines of his face for a crack in the mask.

'I can see you need some time to take this in, sit back, have a drink, we can talk more later if you like.'

'Thank you. I don't want to rest. I want some answers.' I looked at the glass, motioned to drink, but carried on.

'Why here?'

'A good question. We could have been anywhere. The location was not specifically important. If you follow international business news, you'll have known that the Danish forestry industry has been in dire straits for decades now. Just like the rest of that world, cheap imports from the east of Asia undercut the market. Even Ikea uses Asian wood in its furniture. The only loyalty back in the old world is to the profit margin. We picked up the land pretty cheaply.' He lifted his glass and took a sip of the water, seemingly all too aware of the irony.

'What happened to Seth?'

'Ah, Seth. Seth Van Der Beek from Cape Town, South Africa.' He leaned in over the desk, his upper body a walrus disguised as a Mediterranean folk singer.

'People died in the old society, people die in the new society. Death and taxes,' he laughed again, 'but who knows when you'll come up with those?'

'Very good, but you made that happen. You killed a man.' I was projecting.

'Did Seth really die? Is Seth really Seth? Who are we, anyway?'

'You're babbling, Gustav,' I shouted.

He returned the volume.

'Do you not think your government made deaths happen, Gerard? Don't be so naïve.' He pulled back in his chair and stood up. I mirrored his movement.

'But people came here for something different and you've scared the shit out of them.'

'Fear is an aphrodisiac. Tragedy is an inevitability in life. We didn't want to take that away. We couldn't just switch the WiFi off. We needed to put people in situations of peril. We want to see how you'd react, without the modern crutch, without the tribute pages, without the hashtags, without the how to organise a protest march video tutorial. This isn't a utopia unless you build it that way.'

Yoko was right. Of course, Yoko was right.

'How long until we invent the internet here?'

'It took the old lot the best part of two millennia. It'll happen, I'm sure, but other things are needed first. New civilisations rarely learn from history. Do you think the pilgrims hopped off the Mayflower and thought their descendants would wage holy wars? The caution is lost after a generation or two.'

'You sound like a dictator. I think you might actually be crazy.'

'Maybe I am. I was elected by the organisations who fund the project, but I haven't been elected by the people. For now, the people are congregated around me, but who knows what's next? People rise up and overthrow dictators. That's where the real drama will come.'

'Why are you telling me all of this?'

'You'll work it out. Maybe that's why you're here. It could have been you who overthrew me. You could have finally come into your own. Maybe that's why you were chosen.'

'By Stina?'

'By us, Gerard. Who do you think was liking your posts all along? It wasn't only people you knew in real life. We saw the trailer you made for Xanadu. We've watched that a lot. You are a visionary, Gerard.'

'How the fuck did you see that? Nobody knows about that.' It was on a private YouTube link. It wasn't ready. Nobody was meant to see that. Ever. Or at least not yet.

He laughed again, deeper and longer than I'd ever heard before. Nobody knew about that video. It wasn't ready for the trolls. I'd thought about sharing it with Del but she would have seen how bad it was, what a fraud I was.

'I want to see Yoko.'

'You can't, not now.'

'I need to know she's okay.'

'Oh, she can handle herself, don't you worry.'

'I love her.'

'I truly believe that you do. So does the rest of the world. It's been a huge positive, your relationship, for all of us.'

'Well, I'm glad you think so. You know what the worst thing is? It's that this is all manufactured. You managed to take something which felt pure and real and make it the same as everything else.'

'I can see you're tired now, Gerard. Too much talking. A lot to take in. You should rest now.'

I love you Steph.

Gerard xoxo

CHAPTER
31

I woke up from the deepest sleep. The bed was the most comfortable I'd been in since the old world. My room was unfamiliar but well-appointed, the air was warm, the eiderdown thick, the pillows forgiving. I leaned over and pulled back the curtain. I fell back down and stretched out like a starfish. My mind was blank. I felt like I didn't have a care in the world, bathing in the half light.

Time passed, a knock at the door. It opened before I had the chance to say anything about it. It was a tall, thin man with a ponytail. Cliff. His eyes looked to the ground.

'There's someone here to see you.'

'Can't you see I'm not quite ready for receiving visitors today?'

Cliff moved out of the doorway and a girl walked in, wrapped up tight in a scarf and gloves, a familiar pea coat.

'Steph!'

'Gerard...'

'What the hell are you doing here? I mean, it's great to see you. Let me get dressed. Cliff will get you some tea.'

'Gerard, it's over. This is not a game...'

CHAPTER

32

We left the settlement through a thick wire security fence about twenty feet high. I'd never seen it before. We were ushered into a building through a fire exit, a pair of muscular guards shielding our faces from flashing lights.

They walked us through a room the size of a football field. It was busy with bodies; an air of electric tension. People seemed nervous, excited, like something really iconic was happening. Men rushed by with lights, clipboards carrying a DK1 emblem. I'd seen it before. A lady handed me a craft ale. Another came over and tried to take me to a chair in front of a mirror. I refused. She spoke into her radio and said, 'Perhaps it's better, perhaps it's more authentic this way.'

I took a sip of the beer and let the bubbles fizzle and die on my tongue. The beer was one of AlePunk's. I looked for Stephanie but she was over the other side of the room, her back towards me. She was talking to a man in a Hawaiian shirt, big boned and junk food for breakfast fat. He was gesticulating wildly, in the midst of telling the funniest story he'd ever heard. A man in an expensive suit walked by and high-fived him, their synchronicity effortless, like they'd been practicing for weeks just for this moment.

'Five, four, three, you're on.' The security guard from earlier pushed out through a doorway.

'Ladies and gentlemen, DK1 viewers, give a warm welcome to Gerard F. Kane!'

I was at the edge of a stage. I could hear the sounds of an appreciative crowd. The noise twanged, as if it was being played through a television speaker. It became louder and louder. There were whoops. A handclap started up and then broke into spontaneous cheers.

A lady with a big microphone and long legs winked at me. She motioned me towards her. I froze to the spot. She walked over and took my hand and dragged me out into the spotlight. The cheers became louder, too loud now, deafening almost. I put my index fingers into the holes of my ears but it made little difference.

'How does it feel to be out of there? This could just be the best reception we've ever had.' She spoke English with a foreigner's accent.

She sounded alluring, interested, like she'd learned the language just for me.

In front of the stage was the biggest television screen I'd ever seen. The camera was positioned in the sky and swept over a crowd like a bird, hundreds and hundreds of people congregated in the dark night, wrapped up warm and holding signs.

Go Gerard!

Gerard + Yoko 4EVA.

Gerard for leader.

Their faces were red and happy. The camera focused on one man who cheersed a beer to the screen. His eyes were full of tears. In the corner of the screen it said 'Live: Rådhuspladsen, København'.

'You had us all hooked there for a while. The freedom therapy sessions, the secrets you shared with Yoko, Jonas' birthday...'

Some people in the crowd were wearing masks of Gustav's face. One old lady wore a sweater emblazoned with a picture of Jonas. He was in a superman outfit with royal blue pants on the outside, the S replaced by a J.

'Tell us about your final scene with Gustav. That was award-winning stuff.'

'I don't know what you mean. I don't know what any of this means. What have you done with Yoko?'

I started to cry. She backed away slightly.

'Ladies and gentlemen, Gerard F. Kane!'

The guard came again and walked me from the stage. The noise was louder than ever.

Despite the crowd, I spotted him, stood on the side of the stage but looking different, more handsome, his hair styled and slicked back, his royal blue work-wear replaced by a sports jacket and smart jeans. Seth, as real or unreal as he'd ever been.

*

I looked out of the window. The sun was coming up from behind the clouds, turning the sky an orange-red. I could feel its warmth through the aluminium frame. The clouds floated like giant pieces of candy floss, a flick of the artist's wrist across a legacy-defining canvas.

I reached into my pocket for my phone, an urge to take a photograph through the reinforced glass, trying not to catch my reflection in the image. There were no tourists in the way, no passing traffic to spoil this perfect moment. Why do people always wait until they're off the plane to take their photographs?

My pocket was empty. I looked through the window again, the clouds moving across the sky to form her face.

CHAPTER

33

If I was being really pedantic, the house is more of a cobalt blue, but she loves it all the same. I like the way it looks against the sky on a sunny day from the field, as if the roof is just floating there like an umlaut.

It's small, I suppose, but big enough for us. We don't have many things this time around. The building dates back to the fourteenth century and sometimes it feels like it hasn't been updated since. One winter, the walls got so damp we spent what felt like a whole week scraping the wallpaper off. We didn't have the right tools so resorted to butter knives and fingernails. We left it for a day or so, but got back to work in case we had a visitor and they wondered why we were living like this. We laughed a lot at that, at every word.

In the bedroom, our scraping uncovered a whole load of messages written on the walls by previous owners. Sometimes we call each other by the names; she's Diane and I'm Patrick. Sometimes the other way around.

We decided against getting a cat. We joke that we'd both had enough bad luck with them in the past, but it's not that funny. A dog seemed a better choice. She chose it before she'd even seen it, a miniature chocolate brown dachshund. 'Her name is Audrey.' We're both fine with the unconditional love she gives us. It doesn't feel unearned.

I talk about making a rope swing from the tree at the end of the field every summer. She reminds me of this frequently, generally after her second gin and tonic, usually when she's beating me at Scrabble.

'Every time I think "I'll make that rope swing today," there just never seems to be any rope about,' I tell her, and she laughs and she gets it because there isn't and because it's better as an idea anyway.

We've got too much to do to spend our time swinging on ropes.

Dan Tyte

Dan Tyte was born and raised in Cardiff before studying English Literature at the University of Liverpool.

His debut novel, *Half Plus Seven* (Parthian, 2014), was very well received.

His short story 'Onwards' featured in the short story collection *Rarebit* (Parthian, 2014) and is frequently taught at the American University of Paris.

The *Western Mail* newspaper selected him as their 'Writer to Watch' for 2014.

Dan has performed at the Hay Festival, Southbank Centre, and Edinburgh Fringe, and is a regular commentator on BBC Radio Wales. He's on Twitter @dantyte. www.dantyte.com

Praise for *Half Plus Seven:*

'A lethal cocktail of Bukowski and Mad Men' NME

'A coming-of-age novel snorting with energy' THE DAILY MAIL

'Dan Tyte should take a well earned bow for his raw and impressive debut' NEW WELSH REVIEW

'Sharp, spiky satire, a masculine and propulsive romantic comedy' WALES ARTS REVIEW

Graffeg Fiction

Down The Road and Round The Bend by Roy Noble

In this collection of 20 short tales, Roy Noble celebrates the fascinating histories and traditional stories rooted in Wales, some canonical, and others less well-known today but equally deserving of attention. Seamlessly blending anecdote and personal insight with historical detail, Roy has compiled a selection of humorous and engrosing explorations of traditional Wales spanning the length and breadth of the country.

Praise for Roy Noble:

'...he seems unerringly to know every yard on every road in Wales. He presses mental buttons and comes up with a story, a memory or a reflection about every community he has ever called in or driven through.' MICHAEL BOON, WESTERN MAIL

'Many uplifting tales that had me laughing out loud' DENNIS GETHIN, PRESIDENT OF THE WELSH RUGBY UNION

Publication May 2018 £8.99 ISBN 9781912050178

Mostyn Thomas and The Big Rave by Richard Williams

An electrifying debut thriller from author Richard Williams. A brilliant evocation of place and people during a pioneering period, capturing voice and character with a journalistic eye for detail.

'A terrific debut, warm and emotive without being sentimental, the story skips along with some hilarious dialogue.' DAREN KING, AUTHOR OF BOXY AN STAR AND BOOKER PRIZE FINALIST

'Richard Williams perfectly captures the brooding landscapes and complex characters of Pembrokeshire. A treat from cover to cover.' JAMIE OWEN, JOURNALIST AND BROADCASTER

Publication October 2018 £8.99 ISBN 9781912654161

Graffeg Books

The Most Glorious Prospect:
Garden Visiting In Wales 1639-1900 by Bettina Harden
Hardback, 250 x 250mm, 256 pages, £30.00
ISBN: 9781910862629

The Owl Book by Jane Russ
Hardback, 150 x 150mm, 160 pages, £9.99
ISBN: 9781912050420

Lost Lines of Wales: Bangor to Afon Wen
by Paul Lawton and David Southern
Hardback 150 x 200mm, 64 pages, £8.99
ISBN: 9781912213115

Lost Lines of Wales: Rhyl To Corwen
by Paul Lawton and David Southern
Hardback, 150 x 200mm, 64 pages, £8.99
ISBN: 9781912213108

Lost Tramways of Wales: Cardiff by Peter Waller
(Publication June 2018)
Hardback, 150 x 200mm, 64 pages, £8.99
ISBN: 9781912213122

A Year In Pembrokeshire
by Jamie Owen and David Wilson
(Publication June 2018) Hardback, 200 x 200mm
192 pages, £20.00 ISBN: 9781912213658

For a full list of Graffeg titles and to place an order, please
visit our website: www.graffeg.com.